Hearts Unbound

Book 5 of the *Moving Mountains* series

One

On their last day in Hawaii, Hannah awoke to the crashing of waves on the beach, the sound of kids frolicking down by the pool, and a monstrous hangover. She pulled the duvet over her eyes and turned away from the window, but it made little difference: their room opened directly onto the hotel's courtyard, mere steps away from the outdoor patio where families indulged in a breakfast of hot coffee, fresh fruit, and the traditional American fare of bacon and eggs. A short stroll in the opposite direction took guests to a wooden boardwalk that snaked along the beach, where the warm, salty air reminded her that they were thousands of miles away from home and the white-capped mountains that enclosed their ranch.

Ray came out of the bathroom and took a seat on the edge of the bed. He'd already showered and gotten dressed, and Hannah could smell the freshness of him through the thick, white comforter.

She scrunched her nose as he gently pulled back the duvet, causing a flood of light to pierce her eyes.

"What time is it?" Hannah groaned.

"It's just after 9:30. I got up a little while ago."

She caught a glimpse of his maroon button-down shirt, brown belt, and the jeans he'd bought specifically for their trip before bringing her hands up to cover her eyes once more. "You're going to get too warm in that shirt," Hannah mumbled.

Ray shrugged. "I'll take my chances. How are you feeling?"

"Terrible."

"Are you going to be sick this morning?"

"I don't think so."

Hannah sat up, reached for the bottle of water on the nightstand, and took a series of small sips until she was certain she wouldn't have to run to the bathroom. Her head was still pounding, but on the bright side, at least she remembered every detail from their vacation.

Last night, she and Ray had been one of a handful of couples to stumble across a small, but lively restaurant on the outskirts of town, far away from the busy tourist traps and well-known American franchises. The food had been heavenly, the atmosphere an eclectic combination of rustic steakhouse and tropical paradise. The music defied categorization, although after a couple glasses of wine, Hannah had found herself swaying to the beat, wondering why she found the sight of a longhorn draped in colourful leis so amusing. They'd taken their time, ordering appetizers, then entrées, then splitting a wedge of dark chocolate cake before walking back to their hotel around 11PM, buzzing from the wine and the humid air that rustled the fronds of the palm trees. For Hannah, there'd been another layer of intoxication, and that was the simple joy she felt at spending time with Ray and laughing at the unintentionally hilarious comments he made about the other tourists.

Ray had gone back into the bathroom. When he returned, he was holding a bottle of ibuprofen, which he opened and poured into her hand.

"Why didn't I take these last night?" she wondered before placing two of the tablets in her mouth and washing them down with the leftover water.

"I suggested it, but you said you were too tired."

"Next time, just force feed me, okay?"

He chuckled, resting a hand on her leg. "Deal." Twisting around to look out the sliding door that led to their balcony, Ray said, "I can't believe it's our last day. I almost don't want to go home."

"Me neither."

"Maybe we can come back next year. Or we can go somewhere else, as long as it's warm and sunny."

Hannah knew as well as he did that another trip wasn't in the cards any time soon. After the wedding, they'd opted to postpone their honeymoon until things settled down on the ranch. But a few months had turned into three years, until one day Hannah decided she'd had enough of frosty mornings, stinking piles of manure, and only seeing Ray for a few minutes at the beginning and end of each day. On a whim, she'd booked a pair of roundtrip tickets to Hawaii, saying they deserved a vacation after everything they'd been through. While they were away, Victor had agreed to turn out and feed the horses, clean the stalls, and plow the snow off the driveway.

"So, what do you say?" Ray was asking now. "Should we head down and get some coffee, try and sober up before our flight?"

"Yes, please. And next time, we are not ordering a bottle for the table." Hannah paused, the colour draining from her face. As her memories of the previous evening returned in flashes of candlelight and twinkles of moonlight on the water, an uncomfortable feeling of fullness rose in her throat, prompting her to cover her mouth with her hand.

She threw back the covers, swung her legs out of bed, and stumbled into the bathroom to be sick.

*

As soon as they landed in Aspen, Hannah changed out of her shorts and tank top and traded her running shoes for the all-purpose paddock boots she normally wore around the ranch. The most Ray had to do was put on a light jacket, and he was ready to face the crisp chill that awaited them outside.

"And you were worried I'd get too warm," he reminded her, his smile the same dazzling white as the mountain peaks jutting into the cloudless blue sky. He scanned the parking lot as they stepped through the doors and out onto the sidewalk, dragging one checked bag and a slightly smaller carry-on behind them. "Are you cold?"

"I was born in Canada. I'm used to cold." Hannah adjusted her grip on the carry-on's handle. She waited until they'd passed a young family struggling to cram their suitcases into a cab before saying, "I kind of miss it, you know? Travelling, seeing new places, meeting new people. Not that I don't love Colorado, but now that I'm living here…"

Ray looked up from the dark blob of his shadow on the pavement and smiled. "I know—it's not the same."

"I do love it here," she added, in case there were any doubts surrounding the matter, "and for the record, I used to get this feeling when I lived in Canada too. I'd come home after being in the States for a few weeks and everything felt overwhelming and underwhelming at the same time."

"That's life on a working ranch for you: every day is more or less the same." Ray nodded toward one of the cars in the parking lot. "There he is."

As the couple approached the vehicle, Victor stepped out from behind the wheel. Truth be told, he hadn't really minded looking after the ranch while Ray and Hannah were away: now that he and Adrianna had a baby at home, it had provided him with a few hours of much-needed peace and quiet each day.

"I hope you haven't been waiting long," Ray said, standing the suitcase on its base.

"Only about five minutes." Victor opened the SUV's hatchback and loaded the largest bag first. "How was the trip?"

"Beautiful. You and Addy should definitely go to Hawaii, if you get the chance," Hannah told him.

Victor smiled indulgently. "Maybe when the baby gets a bit older."

Ray picked up the carry-on and loaded it into the car. When he was satisfied with its fit, he lowered the door, made his way around to the passenger side, and climbed inside. At last, they were going home—back to early mornings and long, gruelling days. Ray cracked his window, enjoying the cool air on his face as they drove toward the mountains.

"So, did we miss anything exciting while we were gone?" he asked.

"Exciting? Not really. Mainly just the usual family drama," Victor replied.

"We picked up a few things in Hawaii for you guys. Hannah insisted on souvenirs for everyone, including Jim and Laney. I think they're in the carry-on," Ray said.

"They are," she confirmed.

Ray twisted around to face his brother once more. "Speaking of Jim and Laney, how are they?"

"They're all right, too. Everyone is fine—I was just kidding about the family drama."

They fell into silence, and Ray thought about all the work that awaited him back home. The ranch didn't feel quite the same with Marcus gone, but they were managing. For the past few years, Ray had focused on growing his horse training business: what had started out as a favour for Laney quickly turned into a lucrative side hustle. Now, thanks to her endorsement, Ray was getting requests from horse owners all over the state to work with their animals, doing everything from starting colts, to helping horses bond with their riders after injury. Abused and neglected horses often came to the ranch by way of concerned citizens and animal welfare organizations, and Ray did his best to rehabilitate them. When he wasn't "performing miracles" (according to Laney), he was breeding and selling his family's Black Angus cattle. The work never stopped, but the money had never been better, so Ray hardly had cause to complain.

Ray glanced at his brother. "The spring cattle drive is coming up. I'm going to need to start getting a team together."

"Hmm," Victor replied.

"Last year, Russ said Micah might be retiring. Hard to imagine anyone replacing him—he knows the backcountry like no one else."

"You know the backcountry pretty well yourself. Just need to use those instincts you were born with."

Ray nodded dubiously. "Yeah. I guess I shouldn't expect your participation then?"

Victor looked surprised. "In the cattle drive? Of course not. I gave that life up a long time ago."

"Must be nice," Ray muttered with a hint of playfulness. Victor merely shook his head, wondering how Marcus had put up with Ray for so long without wanting to deck him.

They soon arrived at the ranch, where a large, white sign had been affixed to the fence out by the road. Even though it had been installed last summer, Ray still wasn't used to seeing his name in bold, black typeface, the words *Quality Ranch Horses & Equine Rehabilitation* centred beneath it.

"Good to see the house is still standing." Ray stepped out of the passenger seat to find that spring had arrived virtually overnight, covering the ground and trees with a refreshing burst of green.

"I brought in your mail and put it in the kitchen," Victor told him. "I also took out the trash and did a walkthrough to make sure nothing was broken or leaking. I always worry, with a house this old."

Ray circled around to the back of the SUV and lifted the door to retrieve their luggage. After removing the larger suitcase, he laid the carry-on flat and unzipped its main compartment to reveal a couple days' worth of clothes (most of them hopelessly wrinkled from the heat and rigors of travel) and a series of packages wrapped in shiny plastic bags. He reached for one and handed it to Victor. "Consider this our way of saying thank you. There's a little something in there for Emily, too."

"We felt guilty about being away on vacation while you were stuck plowing the driveway. You know, since taking vacations is forbidden on a working ranch," Hannah added with a knowing look at her husband.

Victor smirked. "No need to feel guilty, but thank you."

"I guess we should go inside. That mail won't open itself," Ray said.

After saying their goodbyes, the couple each collected a bag and headed into the house. It was funny how, after being away for a certain length of time, one could almost forget how their home usually smelled. The subtle musk of leather and the resinous fragrance of pine hit Hannah with the suddenness of a Colorado thunderstorm as she set down the carry-on and took off her shoes. The mail Victor had collected sat in a neat pile in the middle of the kitchen table, along with a handwritten note on a sheet of robin's egg-blue paper. Since the work never stopped even when Ray was away from the ranch, he'd asked Victor to check their answering machine once a day. *Of course a house this old would still have a landline and an old-fashioned voicemail recorder,* Hannah mused.

Ray came up behind her. "Who called?"

"The hay guy, the sign guy, someone named Darrel, and Laney."

He sighed and shuffled the stack of bills. "I don't understand why Laney can't just call me on my cell. She knows I'm almost never at the house."

"I'm sure she has her reasons."

"You said Darrel called too?"

"Yeah. Who's Darrel?"

Ray set down the envelopes and walked over to the sink for a glass of water. "Darrel Reid. He's one of our neighbours. Well, kind of. Neighbour implies he lives close by, but he actually lives just outside of town."

"Okay, and what exactly does he want?"

"Probably to discuss the cattle drive. He doesn't own a ranch, but he's got a small fleet of ATVs he rents out to local ranchers around this time of year to make moving their herds a bit easier."

"I don't know—ATVs don't seem to be 'the cowboy way.'"

Ray shrugged and brought the glass to his lips.

Upon recovering his breath, he explained, "The cowboy way is whatever way gets the job done. I prefer to do the work on horseback, but only because ATVs trample the grass and pollute the natural environment."

"Oh, so it's about reducing your carbon footprint then." Hannah laughed and wrapped her arms around his waist. "I had no idea you were so conscientious."

"Well, there was that one time I took pity on a poor little Canadian girl and asked her to be my wife," he said rather sanctimoniously. His free arm encircled her, bringing Hannah deeper into the chiseled warmth of his body. "What can I say? I'm a swell guy… and a bit of a troublemaker."

"You're my troublemaker though, so that makes it okay."

He grinned, his expression softening as he held her gaze. "I love you."

"I love you, too."

Glimpsing the window behind him, Ray set his glass in the sink and turned his mind to the long list of tasks that awaited him down at the barn. He could hear Hannah unzipping the carry-on in the hallway and extracting the gifts for Marcus, Jim, and Laney before wheeling the suitcase over the knotted floorboards toward the laundry room.

"Do you need any help?" Ray called from the kitchen.

She opened the top of the washing machine and replied, "Not right now. Besides, I know you're dying to get outside and be around your horses."

"I'll be back before it gets dark," he promised. He placed the larger suitcase outside the laundry room, where his plaid shirts from last week were so caked with mud they looked like they were being modeled by invisible mannequins. "Are you sure you can handle all this? I know how to operate a washing machine, you know."

"I know. I don't mind—it beats answering work emails." Hannah tossed a couple of shirts into the washer and shooed him away.

Ray made for the front door, lifted his cowboy hat off the peg, and placed it on his head. His vacation had ended the moment they pulled into the driveway, and now it was time to get back to work.

Two

"Do you really think Laney will like the gift?" Hannah asked on the drive over to Fitzgerald Farms the following day.

Ray reached into the bag containing the gift for Jim and Laney and inspected the chocolate-covered Macadamia nuts more closely.

"There's nothing in here she can't have," he said as he skimmed the ingredients list. "Don't let it stress you out so much. She'll appreciate the gesture, if nothing else."

Hannah took the treats from him and tucked them back into the bag. "Eyes on the road, please."

"I *am* watching the road. Anyway, since when do you worry about what she thinks?"

She flashed him an incredulous look. "I've always worried about that—ever since we started dating. I wanted to make a good impression on her, not just because she's your godmother, but because she's practically the glue holding this town together."

Ray smiled inscrutably and made his final turn into Jim and Laney's driveway. In her younger days, Laney had sealed her fate in the world of pro rodeo by riding the roughest, toughest broncs on the circuit. From there, she'd pivoted into barrel racing, and after a few years of record-breaking runs she'd signed the papers for Fitzgerald Farms, with plans to host speed events of her own. Since then, the name Laney Fitzgerald had become synonymous with pedigree rodeo horses, award-winning entertainment, and good, old-fashioned western hospitality.

He parked under the trees as Hannah lifted the bag onto her shoulder. Both of them tried to ignore the unweeded garden and bone-dry birdbath, which only confirmed their unspoken fears about Laney's declining health.

"Shall we go in?" Ray asked, breaking the silence at last.

"I'm waiting for *you*," Hannah returned.

His smile evened out. "I worry about her."

Hannah reached for his hand.

"I worry too," she admitted, "but look on the bright side: she's outlived her stroke prognosis by several years. Maybe the damage wasn't as bad as the doctors feared."

"I tend not to trust doctors. My mom saw several before she died. They all told her she was fine—right before they threw another prescription for Prozac at her."

Hannah rolled her eyes and let go of Ray's hand. "For a guy who can't seem to stay out of the hospital, you seem to have a very low opinion of the people who provide care."

She stepped out of the truck, feeling a warm burst of sun on her face as she crossed the parking area with Ray following a pace or two behind her. Cowboys and modern medicine mixed like oil and water most days: just getting Ray to stay in bed when he had the flu was nigh impossible, but Hannah was grateful for his stubbornness when it mattered. Laney was the exact same way, which was why, as Hannah opened the front door, she couldn't have been less surprised to find her godmother-in-law in the kitchen, bouncing a baby on her hip while a pot of stew bubbled on the stove.

"Hi, Laney," Hannah called from the foyer.

Laney turned toward the door. "Hi, hon!" She picked up one of the baby's pudgy pink fists and waved it in Hannah's direction.

Ray stepped through the front door and scowled. "Where's your cane?"

"Don't use that tone of voice on me. And it's in the living room," Laney replied tartly. She let go of Emily's hand and explained, "I need both arms to hold the little one. Now that she's sitting up, I want her to be involved in what I'm doing."

"She's supposed to be in her playpen," Ray said in the middle of hunting for the cane.

"Babies need interaction, Raymond. It's how their brains develop."

"Maybe I can hold her for a while—give you a break," Hannah added, already extending her arms to receive the wriggly nine-month-old infant whose fist clutched the ruffled collar of Laney's shirt.

Laney sighed and relinquished the baby to Hannah's care before grudgingly accepting her cane from Ray.

"I know what I'm doing," Laney said as Hannah dipped toward the dining room with Emily and took a seat at the table, "for God's sake, I'm not a child."

"I never said you were. I just want you to be careful," he replied.

"I've wanted a grandbaby for years, and now I have one. I'm also aware of the fact that I'm not getting any younger, so if you don't mind, I'd like to devote whatever time I have left to reveling in the simple joy of watching a child grow up. When you have one of your own, you'll understand."

Ray stepped toward the stove and picked up the wooden spoon to stir the contents of the pot. He was quiet for a minute, Laney's talk of time making him queasy with dread.

"I can't tell who's doing a better job of stewing—you or the beef cubes," Laney mused.

He slanted her a look. "Keep this up, and I won't bring you any more beef."

The tinkle of Laney's laughter echoed throughout the kitchen. "Oh, enough about me. How was Hawaii?"

Hannah replied, "It was beautiful. I'd forgotten how much I missed the ocean until we were surrounded by it."

"I used to travel a lot when I was younger. Granted, I never left the mainland, but America is a glorious country—a good mix of everything. But the mountains are my home, and always will be." Laney's face crumpled in pain, prompting her to hobble toward the dining room. "Perhaps I should sit down for a minute."

"Good. I'll make coffee," Ray offered.

"We picked up a few small things for you and Jim," Hannah said as Laney sat down across from her and hooked her cane on the back of her chair. Emily, who was dressed in cotton-candy-pink pants and a pink polka dot dress, had taken to putting anything she could grab in her mouth, including her aunt's necklace. Hannah freed the chain from Emily's toothless maw and said, "We didn't see his truck when we pulled in."

"He's at the chiropractor's. His back has been putting up an awful fight lately—his doctor's talking about a back brace. As if Jim would ever agree to that!" Laney scoffed and raised her hands in a gesture that perfectly captured Hannah's feelings toward Ray's aversion to any kind of medical advice. "Lord help me if that man doesn't die from sheer stubbornness. I mean, he almost died of appendicitis because he didn't want to take time off work to go to the hospital."

"So, what changed his mind?" Hannah asked.

"The answer to that question is right in front of you." Ray spooned coffee grounds into the filter, added the water, and set the machine to brew. "I remember that day. Marc took me over to the hospital so I could see Jim, but I was too freaked out to go inside."

Laney nodded, instantly sober. "I remember that day, too. I left the hospital early and we got ice cream instead."

"And Marc got a banana split, I think."

Hannah's gaze flicked between them. "Where was Victor?"

"He was away at college. Marc insisted he go," Ray told her.

Hannah glanced down at her brother-in-law's daughter, her cheeks covered in the peach fuzz of babyhood and tiny bubbles of spit shimmering on her adorably puckered lips. She'd inherited her father's pale blue eyes and her mother's lovely blonde hair to form the picture-perfect, all-American girl. As if Hannah should have expected anything less from two college-educated, former high school sweethearts who'd rekindled their spark at a Fourth of July barbecue.

"Oh, I almost forgot," Laney said abruptly. "I called you a few days ago, while you were in Hawaii."

"I know. You said you had a business lead I might be interested in."

"Yes. Her name is Dolores Hooper. She called me because someone told her I was in the business of equine rehabilitation, and she has a horse in need of a little help. And I told her, well, I'm not really in a position to be of service, with my cane and all, but I know someone who's very capable. A true horse whisperer."

"Let me guess: that someone is me," Ray drawled.

"Of course that someone is you. Anyway, I told her you were away on vacation, but that you'd follow up with her as soon as you got home."

Ray furrowed his brows. "Did she happen to say what was wrong with the horse?"

"Not specifically. But it sounded quite urgent."

Ray had been leaning on the counter up to this point, but straightened in order to retrieve three mugs from the cupboard above the sink. These he lined up next to the coffee maker, buying himself time to articulate a reply that wouldn't make him sound ungrateful for Laney's support.

"Just because something sounds urgent doesn't mean it is," he said, pouring coffee into each of the mugs. "Did she at least leave a number for me to call back?"

"Better yet—she gave me her address. I'm sure she won't mind if you pop over. She's only a few minutes east of here."

"Laney, the last time I 'popped over' to see someone about a lead, I ended up getting shot." No sense beating around the bush, Ray figured. He delivered the coffees and sat down next to Hannah, in the exact same seat he'd occupied the first time he met Wilbur. Laney's expression hadn't changed, but he sensed a shift in her demeanor as her guilt returned. "I need a way to screen people. I appreciate that you want to help, but everything about that call sounds like a red flag to me."

"I understand. But I've been in this industry far longer than you have, and I've developed my own intuition about these things." Laney leaned forward and embraced her mug with both hands. "If you're not interested, that's fine. I know you're bringing in steady work with your

YouTube channel and your sign, but if you change your mind, Dolores's address is on the notepad by the microwave."

Right as Ray was about to decline her offer, Emily began to cry.

Laney tilted her head. "Looks like someone's ready to go down for a nap."

"I'll go put her in her playpen." Hannah rose from the table and carted the wailing infant into the living room, where a Pack 'n Play had been set up in the corner. Forgetting Dolores Hooper for a moment, Ray watched as she laid Emily down and arranged the blankets around her, the task coming to her hands as naturally as training young horses came to his. True, they'd had a daughter of their own once, but that was years ago: they'd been young and inexperienced, too afraid to face the consequences of their actions. He left Hannah to her instincts, and turned his attention back to Laney.

"You know," his godmother began, speaking softly, "if I had known what Wilbur's true intentions were, I would have never, *ever* suggested you work with him."

"I know. I'm not blaming you." Ray took a sip of his coffee and winced. "Things are different now. I have Hannah to think about, plus bills and other responsibilities. It's even harder because Marc's not around. If I get hurt..."

"I understand, hon." Laney studied him for a beat, then reached across the table to pat his arm. "Whatever you decide, I know you'll do the right thing, for the right reasons."

Hannah rejoined them and placed both hands on Ray's shoulders. His muscles hadn't been this tense since before they'd left for Hawaii, when the farmer who provided their hay had tried to sell them moldy bales. They'd sorted the situation out eventually, but it had taken two whole days of island sun and umbrella drinks for Ray to resemble a human being and not a marble sculpture.

Hannah paused mid-massage and sniffed the air. "Is something burning?"

Laney's eyes widened. "The bread!" Ray was already out of his seat by the time she noticed the palls of black smoke belching from the oven.

Reaching for the oven mitts, he lowered the door and waved the scorch clouds away from his face. He bent down to pull a charred brick of homemade sourdough from the middle rack and set it on the stove, right next to the stew it had been meant to accompany that evening.

"Oh, it's ruined, isn't it?" Laney lamented, trying to peer over the counter that separated the kitchen and dining room. "I knew I'd forgotten something!"

Ray tossed the oven mitts off to the side and tried to paint a more optimistic picture. "It's not totally ruined, I don't think. If you just shave off the burnt part of the crust, it might be okay."

Laney turned back to Hannah, who was poised to spring toward Emily or any one of the many windows if necessary. As Laney raised her hands to cover her eyes, Hannah moved to sit beside her, her heart settling into a normal rhythm once again as Ray handled matters in the kitchen.

"I'm fine—really," Laney insisted, "it's not the end of the world. I just wanted to make a nice meal for Jim. His back's been bothering him lately. Did you know his doctor wants him to consider wearing a back brace?" She snorted, her melancholy replaced by a sudden flush of disbelief. "As if he'd ever agree to that!"

Hannah exchanged a look with Ray, saying nothing as the smoke thinned in the air between them.

"Maybe we should open a window," Hannah suggested as she stood up. "All this smoke can't be good for us or the baby."

"Good idea, hon. I'd do it myself, but my right knee has been going out all day. One minute it's fine and then—pop!" Laney laughed and lifted her cane from the chairback, wrapping her hands around the metal shaft. "Good thing I have this, or I'd be on the floor."

As Hannah cracked the windows in the living room, Ray glanced toward the microwave. Sure enough, there was the notepad with Dolores Hooper's address, waiting to be torn off and tucked in his pocket. He could pop over there tomorrow, scope the place out, and decide if this lead was worth pursuing.

He ripped off the address just as Hannah returned from opening windows in the bedrooms and guest bathroom.

"I think we should head home," she told him, glancing at the dining room to find Laney inspecting the padding on the cane's handle. "Can you help her get back to her armchair?"

"I'll try."

To their surprise, Laney went willingly to the comfort of her armchair. On her assurances that Jim would be home soon, Hannah and Ray left the gifts on the coffee table and took their leave, the mood in the air made heavier by the lingering smell of smoke.

Hannah reached for the front door. As they stepped out onto the porch, she paused to take a breath. Laney's vegetable garden had seen better days, but at least the flowers in her window planters were determined to bloom, displaying their spectacular colours to passing pollinators. As she admired their blushing pinks and royal purples, a bee landed on a Dahlia, making a temporary home for itself amidst the profusion of frilly tubules.

"That was hard to watch," Ray sighed. The bee, startled by his voice, took wing and disappeared into the overgrown grass with an urgent drone.

"I'm debating whether we should tell Victor and Addy. What if we hadn't been here? Would Laney have burned the house down?"

Not wanting to entertain such grim thoughts, Ray led the way to the truck and unlocked the doors.

"I'd tell Jim first. He's her husband. He deserves to know if she requires more care," he said.

"Are you going to call him when we get home?"

Ray started the engine. "I guess I have to."

They were nearly halfway home before he told Hannah about his plan to pay Dolores a visit, despite the troubling lack of details surrounding her horse's condition.

"I'd come with you if I didn't have to work," Hannah said. "Just listen to your gut. If something feels off, you can always cut the conversation short."

"I don't know if you've noticed, but I tend to do the opposite of what my common sense tells me." Ray quickly changed the subject. "You were really good with Emily, you know. I was watching you when I was talking to Laney."

"It was nice to hold her. Now I see why Laney can't put her down. She's got that sweet baby smell." Hannah glanced at the driver's seat, but Ray didn't take his focus off the road. Probably still thinking about Dolores, or trying not to think about Wilbur. "Makes me wish we were parents. Imagine Laney's reaction to finding out she's having another grandchild."

Ray met her gaze. "You want to have a baby?"

"Well, not right now, of course. But maybe we can start talking about it."

His eyes bounced between her face and the road a couple of times and ultimately settled on the strip of asphalt winding through the trees.

"You don't want to?" Hannah asked when he hadn't replied after several seconds.

"It's not that I don't want to. Of course I do."

She nodded, feeling that faint spark of hope from a minute ago grow just a little dimmer thanks to Ray's lack of enthusiasm. "Are you still thinking about Dolores?"

"Actually, I was thinking of Laney: how she kept repeating herself, how she forgot about the bread…" Ray swallowed. "I know she's getting older, and that comes with its own challenges. I just didn't think I'd have to face them all so soon."

Now it was Hannah's turn to be silent, lost in the maze of her own thoughts. It felt like just last week she was sitting in a church pew, staring at Cameron's picture at the front of the room. That horrible, helpless moment that felt like it would never end was already ten years old, a middle-schooler compared to the toddler that was the memory of her wedding.

Ray felt for her hand, his rough skin colliding with the Nivea softness of her own.

"So, let's do it," he said, meeting her gaze, "let's have a baby."

Three

Hannah had already left for work by the time Ray set out to visit Dolores Hooper. Between Laney's troubling behaviour and Hannah's talk of wanting kids, he needed time to think, and a visit to a potential client provided the perfect opportunity to do so. He drove east, leaving the ski hills and heavy traffic in his rearview until he was surrounded by nothing but pine trees and blue skies. His truck's GPS guided him around the multitude of bends in the road, taking him deep into some of the best hiking country the state had to offer.

It had been Hannah's idea to get a new truck. They'd opted for a 2017 Chevy Silverado, which came equipped with all the towing capacity Ray needed to haul horses, move hay and firewood, and keep the ranch running during the harsh winter months. A phone holder enabled him to conduct business on the road—something he did often, usually while stuck in traffic. Today, he had a more personal call to make, and as much as he wasn't looking forward to delivering bad news, he was grateful to see a familiar face.

"What are you saying? Do you want me to come home?" Marcus asked after Ray had told him about their trip to Fitzgerald Farms the day before.

"I just want you to be aware of what's going on. I know Laney's had some problems since her stroke, but not like this." Ray glanced down at his phone. FaceTime was no match for seeing each other in person, but under the circumstances, it was better than nothing. "And on top of all that, Hannah wants to have a baby."

"That's a big step."

"I know. When we were talking about it last night, she said she's okay with waiting a couple more years so we can save up a bit of money, but then she said that if we wait too long, it might make things more difficult. Whatever that means."

"I don't think there's a perfect time to have kids. Better times, certainly, but at some point you guys are just going to have to jump in. You know, kind of like you did the first time."

Ray smirked. "Thanks for the pep talk."

"Always happy to be of service. So, where are you headed today?"

"I'm going to see a woman about a horse. Laney couldn't tell me anything about it other than the fact that it's urgent." Ray leaned forward in the driver's seat. "Wait, I think this is the place."

The driveway led him to a parking area covered in a layer of golden pine needles. As Ray stopped the truck, he sized up the small, blue, clapboard house on his left, which appeared to be in remarkably good shape despite its archaic construction style. The white trim around the picture frame windows was dull and peeling, but at least the front door, painted lemon-yellow, made up for the lack of sunlight. A rocking chair swayed on the porch, set in motion by the invisible hands of a cool breeze.

"I guess this is it," Ray said, removing his seatbelt. "There's a clearing behind the house. I'm assuming that's where the horse is."

"Okay. Just, you know, be careful."

"I will." Ray hung up the call, took a deep breath, and opened the door. The ineluctable buzz of wildlife was soothing out here—proof that he wasn't alone after all, and certainly not in any real danger. Ray made his way up the porch steps and knocked on the door. Dolores Hooper may have been a recluse, but wasn't he also a little isolated, living on his family's ranch in the middle of nowhere?

When there was no answer, Ray knocked again. Still nothing. He furrowed his brows and trotted down the steps, making his way around the side of the house toward the patch of sunlight he'd spotted earlier. Here, the trees opened up to reveal a flat area fringed by tall grasses. A two-stall barn sat on one side of the clearing, and directly to the left of it was a small paddock with just enough room for a single horse. Ray stepped into the barn and gazed around at the collection of water buckets, the coil of hose on the floor, and the stiff, leather bridles that hung neatly on the wall.

"Hello?" Ray looked left and right, but there was no answer. The stalls sat empty, their doors unbolted. He breathed in the smell of wood and pine shavings and released it in an irritated sigh. "Well, this was a productive trip."

He turned to leave, stopping suddenly when he noticed the property owner standing behind him. She wore a beaded blue top and shapeless white pants, and although her feet appeared bare at first glance, Ray could see now that they were separated from the ground by a pair of thin, wooden sandals. Her hair hung loose around her shoulders like a veil, but without the fragile quality one might expect from a woman long divorced from her youth. Ray hoped she hadn't heard his sarcastic remark as he walked toward her and extended his hand.

"I tried knocking at the house, but there was no answer. I'm Ray."

"I'm Dolores." As their hands met, her face lit up in wonderment. "Oh, my," she gasped.

"I'm sorry?"

"Your aura," she said wistfully, waving a hand around in illustration, "it's magnificent. So... powerful."

"Um. Thank you."

She smiled placidly. "I've been waiting a very long time to meet you, Ray," Dolores said. She indicated the woods behind the paddock. "I was taking a walk when I heard your truck pull in. Even then I had this feeling that you're searching for something."

"The horse," Ray specified. "I thought he might've been in the barn."

"No. You're searching for something else. Your soul yearns for peace. Your aura tells me you've suffered greatly, but you've also loved deeply, and that is why you're here." She raised her right hand and placed it ever so gently against his left shoulder, indicating the years-old bullet scar no one outside of his family and Wilbur knew existed.

She removed her hand. Ray stood motionless before her, his thoughts in a jumble that resembled the bees' erratic course. It was clear what *they* were searching for, but his needs were more complex, more elusive, and too intimate to be public knowledge.

Before Ray could dismiss Dolores's theories as nothing more than senile ramblings, she turned and started along an obscure path that vanished behind the barn. "Do you care to take a walk with me?"

"Actually, I should be getting home. I came out here because I thought you had a horse you wanted me to look at. I'm sorry to have wasted your time."

"Your presence here is a gift. Please, let me show you around."

He hesitated. That gut feeling Hannah had told him to listen to was ringing loud and clear throughout his body, but another part of him could think only of what she'd said on the way home yesterday. She wanted a family. A baby she could keep.

What he wouldn't give to make her happy.

"You're a skeptic," Ray heard Dolores say as they walked the path that edged the meadow. "You don't believe in auras."

He replied sheepishly, "I was always taught to question everything I hear."

"But people are drawn to you." Dolores looked at him. "Be it friends or enemies, your spirit has an unmistakable warmth to it, like a fire."

Their wandering took them around the side of the barn. Standing in the shade of it was a pale grey gelding approximately fifteen hands high, nibbling on a pile of hay Dolores had sprinkled on the ground. As Ray leaned on the fence, the horse lifted its head and twitched its ears toward the trees. Sensing no threat from the direction of the forest, it resumed its dissection of the hay pile, using its muzzle to seek out the more tender clumps of grass near the bottom.

"This is Lucky," Dolores said. "He looks calm now, but lately he's developed an odd habit of jumping the fence. He normally doesn't get very far, but last week, I found him in the woods."

"Was he hurt?"

"No, thank goodness. It makes you wonder though, doesn't it?"

Dolores turned to Ray, clearly expecting him to offer up an explanation for Lucky's behaviour. Unfortunately, he didn't have one. For one thing, there was nothing in the gelding's physical conformation to suggest he had any genetic predisposition for jumping fences. He might've jumped a fence if he were determined to flee a predator, but those were exceptional circumstances that typically resulted in some form of injury to the horse, and as far as Ray could tell, the animal had barely a nick on its body bigger than an insect bite.

"I just want you to know: Lucky is well cared for. I've had him for seven years, and I've always made sure he has everything he needs... in case you were thinking he had good reason for running away," Dolores added.

"That possibility never crossed my mind," Ray stated sincerely. He turned toward Lucky's owner and said, "I'll be honest with you, Dolores: I can't tell what's wrong with a horse just by looking at it. I wish I could, but their emotions are a lot more complex than we realize."

"So, what are you suggesting?"

"I'd like to work with him at my ranch. I'll start with groundwork, get him used to seeing and hearing me every day. From there, I'll look for clues that might explain the behaviour. If he's jumping because he's bored, he'll need more stimulation—possibly a herd mate or even a more vigorous exercise routine." Ray faltered, not wanting to make assumptions about Dolores based on her age. "How often do you ride him?"

She laughed cheerfully. "Ride him? Only in my dreams, dear."

"Do you get any other animals around here?"

"Oh, lots. Deer and turkeys, mainly."

"No bears or lions?"

"Gosh, I hope not. I'm not exactly in my prime, bear-hunting years anymore." She squinted at him. "Do you mean to take Lucky home with you? Is this what people who seek our your expertise usually do?"

"It's just easier that way. I'm in a familiar environment that I can tune out. Most people don't mind it, but if you're concerned the trip will be too upsetting for Lucky, maybe I can bring my skills here. Like a pop-up clinic."

"Do you charge extra to use your own facilities?"

"No. I only charge for time spent with the horse." Ray ventured, "I know we just met, but I can tell Lucky means a lot to you. I'd be willing to work out some kind of payment plan if needed."

"He used to belong to my husband, Felix. After he died, Lucky started standing by the fence at the same time every day—he'd stare at the woods for hours, waiting for Felix to come back from one of his daily walks."

"I'm sorry for your loss." At least the behaviour had an explanation now, if not a clear-cut solution.

She composed herself before turning to Ray with a smile, the sun poised above her like a spotlight. "I'm willing to take a chance on you, Ray. Laney said you have a gift. And I can see it's true—there's a presence that surrounds you like a light. The colours are rare. Very rare indeed."

Dolores's eyes roved over him, causing Ray to shift uncomfortably. Ever since Laney had latched onto this idea that he possessed some extraordinary ability to communicate with horses, everyone who agreed to work with him expected some kind of miracle. With great expectations came great disappointment—not that Ray had ever had an unhappy customer. But how was he supposed to tune the world out and concentrate on Lucky when he was surrounded by some invisible force he couldn't control?

"I'm glad we had a chance to meet. I'll arrange to have Lucky trailered to my ranch sometime in the next couple of days so I can start working with him."

"My, my, you really do have it all figured out. My Felix was the same way: a man who knew how to get things done."

They walked back to Ray's truck. As he opened the driver's door, he turned to Dolores and said, "We'll be in touch."

"I hope so. And Ray?" He glanced up from the ignition. "Forgiveness is the highest form of peace. Just because you've been hurt doesn't mean you have to carry that pain forever."

He arranged his face into a smile, closed the door, and put the truck in gear. When he was halfway down the driveway, he glimpsed his rearview to find Dolores standing right where he'd left her, glowing ethereally among the trees.

Four

"What are you looking at?" Ray asked when he found Hannah in the kitchen a few days later.

She replied, "An ovulation app I downloaded last night. It's supposed to help me keep track of my cycles so I'll know the best time to try and conceive."

Ray shook his head and went back to filling his coffee cup. "They really do have an app for everything these days, don't they?"

Hannah laid the phone down on the counter and watched him drop a spoonful of sugar into the mug. "You still want to do this, right? Because it's a huge decision and we both need to be fully on board."

"Of course I do. But if you ask me, it shouldn't be this complicated. It's not like our parents had apps when they were our age."

"I'm sure my mom had something. My obsessive planner genes had to have come from somewhere." Hannah went back to consulting the app, her forehead creasing in concentration. "Do we have a thermometer?"

"We should. Why?"

"I'll need to keep track of my temperature. It'll rise slightly if I'm fertile—it's not a foolproof method, but the more I know about what's going on inside my body, the better our odds of getting pregnant." She met his gaze, which waffled somewhere between confusion and disinterest. Clearly, she had to put this whole conversation into words he actually understood. "You wouldn't breed your cows unless you knew they were in heat, would you?"

"Of course not. That would be a waste of everyone's time."

"Exactly. So, it's better to have all the facts up front."

"Yes, but it's not like they have bovine ovulation apps. I wait until they start showing signs of being in heat, then I let the bull do its thing.

Besides, you and I have already had a baby. My boys know what they're doing."

"Every time you use 'my boys' to refer to your sperm, I can physically feel myself getting more turned off," Hannah warned. "You know what? Just forget it. We have enough on our plates at the moment."

Ray kept a smile fixed on his face. As if she was going to give up that easily.

He took a sip of his coffee, then said, "It's getting a bit warm in here, don't you think?" He pulled the green sweater over his head and draped it over the back of one of the chairs. As Hannah turned away from the counter, Ray flexed his left arm a couple of times and pointed to his bicep, saying, "You know, I think I got a tan when we were in Hawaii."

Hannah shook her head. "You're ridiculous."

"If I'm so ridiculous, why did you blush?"

She brought a hand up to cover her face, but it was impossible to hide the pink in her cheeks. "Why are you undressing in the kitchen?" she shot back.

He took a few steps toward her. As her gaze drank him in, he felt a sudden urge to ignore all his responsibilities and spend the whole day in bed with her—to strike while the iron was hot, so to speak.

"Because I live here," Ray said slowly, "and I'll undress wherever I want."

Hannah had to force herself to stay focused on the conversation. She felt the warmth of his breath on her face and shivered with anticipation.

Eventually, she said, "We can't just jump in. There has to be some kind of plan."

"Of course we can jump in. You want a baby, I want a baby. So, let's make one."

"When we talked about this the other night, you didn't seem so eager," Hannah reminded him. "In fact, every time we talk about it, you're lukewarm on the matter. Now you're all 'let's make a baby right here in the kitchen.' What gives?"

Ray took a step back. Everything about her face had returned to its normal state as if she hadn't been silently begging him to remove the rest of his clothes a mere thirty seconds earlier.

"You're the one who brought up the whole baby-making business with your little app," he said, indicating her phone. "I was just trying to prove we don't need that."

"I know we don't. It's just that ever since Victor and Addy had Emily, all I can think about is when it's going to be our turn."

"So it's about Victor and Addy now," Ray said. A wrinkle of irritation formed between his brows. "Look, I'm not trying to start an argument, but maybe this isn't something you can plan out like a budget."

"I like planning things. It makes me feel like I'm in control."

As Ray wrapped his arms around her, he said, "Crazy idea, but what if we stopped trying to control everything?"

"We have to control some things, or our life is quickly going to become unmanageable," Hannah replied matter-of-factly.

"Okay, so we control some things. The rest, we leave up to the universe." He pulled back to gauge her reaction to this compromise. "Deal?"

"Deal," she said, smiling, and rose up to kiss him at last.

In that moment, a truck Ray didn't recognize pulled into the driveway. Hannah twisted around as the sound of tires on gravel filled her ears, but her eyes couldn't make sense of what she was seeing.

"Who's that?" she asked.

Ray was already making his way to the door, an uneasy feeling building in his chest as Hannah followed him. He hadn't liked the look of that plywood contraption mounted in the bed of their visitor's truck, and he definitely didn't trust anyone who drove that fast around horses. "I don't know, but I'm guessing it isn't Dolores." He sat down on the bench and pulled on his boots.

Hannah peered out the living room window. "What's that wooden box behind the truck?"

"Looks like one of those homemade horse trailers." In answer to Hannah's flabbergasted expression, Ray explained, "If you saw where this woman lives, you wouldn't be surprised."

"She's crazy hauling him around in that… coffin. A strong wind could blow that thing down!"

"I know." Ray opened the front door and made his way down to the sand ring. Red flags were popping up everywhere now, and if he was nervous, then the horse was bound to be nervous too. He tried to control his breathing as the driver of the truck opened the door, only it wasn't Dolores's small, wispy presence that greeted him at the end of the laneway.

"Can I help you?" Ray asked as a burly man in a stained white t-shirt and dusty overalls lumbered around to the backend of the trailer.

"Name's Curtis," he huffed, offering a grimy hand for Ray to shake. "Curtis Hooper. I'm Dolores's youngest son."

Ray had to remind himself to act professional, despite feeling repulsed by Curtis's lack of basic hygiene and shoddy driving skills. "Ray Fisher. Is Dolores with you?"

Curtis laughed, all three of his chins jiggling. "Does it look like she's with me?"

"I'm just trying to understand what's going on here," Ray replied impatiently.

"I was told you're the guy who performs miracles." Pushing past Ray, Curtis continued on his current trajectory. He slapped a big, beefy hand against the wall of the so-called trailer, and Lucky responded with a frightened whinny that put every cell in Ray's body on high alert. "You ask me, that animal should've gotten a bullet to the brain years ago."

Hannah shot Ray a horrified look. From everything he'd told her, Dolores was a sweet, if slightly eccentric, old lady who enjoyed a special connection with nature. But maybe Curtis was adopted.

Ray said evenly, "I won't tolerate that kind of talk on my ranch. We rehabilitate horses here, we don't dispose of them at the first sign of trouble." He indicated the sand ring and said, "You're going to have to line your truck up with the gate. I'll open it and we'll—"

Curtis ignored him and opened the back door of the trailer. Startled, Lucky leapt out of the stuffy wooden container before making a run for the drive shed, his white tail flying out behind him in a panic.

Total chaos ensued. Between Curtis shouting like a madman, the horses in the paddock fleeing from his voice, and Lucky encountering the minefield of hazards in the old shed, Ray felt dangerously close to unleashing every curse word he knew. Some people understood horses, some gave them a wide berth, and a very small percentage succeeded in doing everything they weren't supposed to do, resulting in an animal that was a danger not only to itself, but to every human being in its path.

Ray followed Lucky into the darkness of the shed. To his right, an orange tractor loomed in the shadows. Various tools and equipment occupied the remaining floorspace, which was really just a patch of dirt protected from the elements by a tin roof and four wooden walls. Somehow, Lucky had managed to navigate this obstacle course to reach the back corner of the shed, only to become ensnared in a piece of scrap metal Ray had been meaning to throw out for months.

His heart was beating twice as fast as he picked his way over to the gelding, his eyes straining to make out the dangers scattered in his path.

"Easy," Ray murmured. Panicked, Lucky pulled back hard on his lead rope, but couldn't free himself from the jagged trap. He danced in place, knocking over a stack of empty flower pots in his efforts to escape.

Hannah followed Ray into the shed. As her eyes adjusted and Lucky came into view, a feeling of dread washed over her. "Is he okay?"

"I can't tell, but it looks like he's stuck on something." Ray patted his pockets. "I don't have my phone."

Hannah pulled hers out and activated the flashlight. Lucky's eyes flashed in the darkness, his nostrils round and pink and his back hollow. He stamped his front hoof and snorted a warning at Ray, who was slowly making his way through the disarray, pausing now and then to move something else.

Ray shifted a box containing old truck parts a few feet to his left, then made an earnest attempt to grab Lucky's rope. The gelding scuttled sideways, dodging Ray's hand and crashing against the side of the shed with a sharp racket.

"Ray, please be careful," Hannah blurted.

He nodded absently. Hannah wasn't sure if she felt relieved that Curtis had chosen to stay out of the way, or infuriated that he'd caused this situation in the first place. She inched forward, trying to shine the light only on the rope and not on the horse, while Ray continued to speak to his charge in a soothing voice.

"It's okay," he half-whispered. Very slowly, Ray bent down and extricated the rope from the rusty hunk of debris, then proceeded to lead Lucky back into the light of day. "I've got you. You're okay."

Hannah gasped. "Oh, my God."

Ray followed her gaze to Lucky's front right leg, which was swollen and covered in blood.

"Ah, shit." Ray glanced at Hannah. "There are some old towels in the storage room," he told her. As she went to retrieve them, he crouched down to inspect the wound. A more unscrupulous horse trainer might've blamed Lucky's leg injury on the animal's temperament, especially if it had a history of jumping the fence. But Ray knew the fault lay firmly with him: he should've ensured Lucky had safe transport to the ranch, and he should've cleaned this place up before any horses had a chance to tangle with his trash. Once again, he was paying for his lack of foresight in the worst way.

Hannah reappeared and passed him a wad of towels, which Ray pressed against the gash on Lucky's knee. She held the lead rope and stroked Lucky's muzzle as he hopped on three legs, still agitated but not quite so blind with terror.

"Where's Curtis?" Ray asked.

"Sitting in his truck. Obviously he doesn't care that his horse might've gotten hurt."

31

"Technically, Lucky's not his horse. People usually don't care about things that aren't theirs." Ray removed the towels for a moment to check the wound, then reapplied pressure. "He doesn't seem to be leaking synovial fluid, but the cut's deep."

As the sound of squealing tires filled the air, Ray and Hannah both turned to see Curtis racing for the exit. Hannah returned Lucky's lead rope to Ray and started running after him, but Curtis had already disappeared in a cloud of dust by the time she acknowledged the futility of her endeavor.

She spread her arms and shouted, "Are you kidding me?" She turned back to Ray, leading Lucky out of the shed one limping step at a time. "Now what?"

As he stared after Curtis, he wondered what he'd gotten himself into. He'd had to contend with people trying to steal his horses in the past; they didn't typically abandon them at his doorstep. But as long as Lucky was here, Ray was determined to help him as best he could.

"We'll deal with that scumbag later. I'll take Lucky to the barn while you call Dr. Bardwell. Tell her it's an emergency."

Five

Dr. Therese Bardwell showed up within minutes of Hannah's phone call. Ever since taking over her father's veterinary practice, she'd become a regular face around the ranch, though her professional relationship with Ray went all the way back to high school. They'd been lab partners in junior year, when the class had been assigned to dissect a fetal pig. The idea of cutting anything open had made Ray squeamish, but Therese had been more than prepared for the task, having shadowed her dad during visits to his clients' farms. Her attention to detail and level-headedness had come in handy then just as it did now, when Ray was too upset about Curtis's carelessness to think straight.

"Look on the bright side: now Lucky can't jump out," Therese said.

"At least one of us is optimistic," Ray replied. Therese had already examined and bandaged the horse's right knee—which had suffered no internal damage, thankfully—but the wound had set Ray's plans to start groundwork back by a week, if not more.

She popped the stethoscope in her ears and listened to Lucky's heart. "So, the guy just took off, eh?"

"I wouldn't have believed it if I hadn't seen it for myself. And of course, I can't even call Dolores to explain the situation." In hindsight, Ray wasn't sure why the thought of asking for her number had never crossed his mind. "I should've known as soon as I saw the trailer that something was off."

Therese removed the earpieces and draped the stethoscope around her shoulders. Like her father, she knew how to remain calm around a skittish horse, but that was where the similarities ended. Whereas Dr. Harry Bardwell was a short, stocky man with unevenly grey hair and an aversion to small talk, Therese was tall and lean, with springy coils of auburn hair framing her fine-boned face. Her eyes reminded Ray of summertime in the high country, when the last dregs of snow finally melted and revealed a world teeming with life. How could anyone not be willing to put their horse's care in Therese's hands?

"There has to be someone you can report this guy to," she said. "We're talking about animal abandonment here. If it were up to me, I'd have called the cops."

"I thought about it. And perhaps I will, but right now, I need to focus on helping Lucky."

"Well, the good news is, the joint should be fine, once the swelling comes down. I'll give him a tetanus shot just to be on the safe side." Walking around to Lucky's head, Therese gently pried apart the gelding's lips to reveal a mouth filled with yellow and brown teeth. "And he'll need his teeth floated. I can come back in a few days for that."

"How old do you think he is?"

"Sixteen, maybe? He's definitely no spring chicken." She released Lucky's lips and smiled. "You always go for the horses with the most obscure back stories, don't you?"

"To be fair, this was Laney's idea. And Dolores doesn't seem like a bad person—nowhere near as bad as her son, anyway."

"Do you have security cameras set up around here?"

"Sure. I've got one down by the main gate, one at the front door, and another right outside the barn here, looking down at the driveway. Marc insisted on beefing up our security after Wilbur tried to ruin us."

"That's the kind of world we live in now—you always have to be looking over your shoulder, especially if you're a business owner. Assuming your cameras captured Curtis's plates, tracking him down shouldn't be too difficult."

Ray felt queasy, as if he were back in that high school science lab watching their teacher explain the proper technique for incising the pig's belly. He didn't like this new world he lived in, where people like Wilbur and Curtis forced him to take additional precautions to protect his family. When he was a kid, everyone simply looked out for each other: if someone died, neighbours dropped by with homemade casserole and offered to do the grocery shopping. Now, Ray was on his own.

Hannah came around the corner and stepped into the barn. She looked at Lucky and asked, "How is he?"

"All things considered, he's not too bad," Ray replied. "Unfortunately, I won't be able to start working with him today. If I shift my schedule around a bit, I can probably make some headway with Tiger, though."

"I wouldn't go making any plans quite yet."

"Why not?"

"I've been trying to call Laney for an hour. I know she's got Emily today, but she always picks up eventually."

"She might be napping. Jim said she's been more tired than usual lately."

"She shouldn't be napping if she's babysitting," Hannah pointed out. Her brows pulled together in a show of unease. "Can you go and check on her? I'm supposed to be on a call for work in five minutes."

"Honey, I'm sure Laney's fine—probably just, you know, cooking something."

"She has a phone in the kitchen. Ray, please, I'm starting to worry."

He shot a glance at Therese, who offered, "I can finish up here and put Lucky in a stall. I'll check on a few of your other horses while I'm at it—I've been meaning to see how that bite on Poppy's neck is healing."

"Thanks," Ray replied. He fell into step with Hannah as they walked back to the house. If Ray hadn't already been on edge about having Lucky dumped on him like an unwanted litter of puppies, he might've chalked Laney's unreachability up to any number of passion projects around Fitzgerald Farms. But even when she was occupied with one of her hobbies, she always made sure she was near a phone.

Hannah said, "I know it might not be anything, but it doesn't hurt to be sure."

"She's too independent some days. Or too stubborn." He pulled his keys out of his pocket and unlocked his truck. Slipping into the stuffy cabin, he reached for the door and told her, "I'll give you a call as soon as I can."

She nodded, watching as Ray shifted gears and tore off in a cloud of dust toward his godparents' house.

*

Jim's truck wasn't in the driveway when Ray arrived at Fitzgerald Farms. Parking in his godfather's usual spot, Ray got out of his truck and made his way to the front door. With the weather warming up, Laney had seen to it that her porch was sufficiently populated by flowering plants, although how she intended to keep up with watering them in her condition was anyone's guess.

Ray knocked on the door. As a bee made a precarious landing on a purple coneflower, he thought about his last visit to Fitzgerald Farms, when he and Hannah had stood outside contemplating worst-case scenarios. Surely, Victor and Addy wouldn't have left their nine-month-old daughter in Laney's care if they had any reservations about her mental status, would they?

When there was no answer, Ray reached for the knob and turned it, but the door remained firmly shut.

He knocked again, louder this time. "Laney?" It had been years since she'd stopped driving, so she couldn't have gone out. Maybe she was down at the barn?

Ray began hunting for the spare key, peeking under the welcome mat and some of the heavier stone vases as several bees hovered around his face, outraged that he'd interrupted their meal. At last, he turned over a planter brimming with violet irises and scooped up the lone key, slotting it into the lock above the doorknob. The smell of laundry detergent and fresh bread surrounded him as he stepped inside the house, surprised Laney hadn't called out to ask who was there.

"Laney?" he said again, a prickle of apprehension bristling the hairs on the back of his neck. He left the key on the credenza and headed toward the living room, where Emily's playpen was set up in the corner. She was holding onto the mesh wall and sucking on the fingers of her left hand when Ray approached her.

"Hey, Em." He bent down to pick her up. Emily removed her hand from her mouth as Ray settled her in the crook of his arm and continued his search for Laney.

"Laney?" As Ray came around the corner, his eyes went to the master bedroom, the door to which stood open. And just beyond it, partially hidden by the queen-size bed, he saw a slippered foot.

He rushed into the bedroom and knelt next to his godmother, placing a hand on her shoulder in an effort to wake her. "Laney?"

Her eyes fluttered. When she'd fallen, she'd landed on the rug at the foot of the bed with her left arm pinned beneath her body. For something that was supposed to feel so nice under her bare feet, the rug made a rather awful pillow for her face.

"Laney, can you hear me?" Ray persisted.

She moaned and tried unsuccessfully to turn onto her back. It was as if all the strength in her right arm had suddenly evaporated.

His heart pounding, Ray reached into his back pocket and pulled out his phone. Emily was making a fuss in his arms, but putting her down would mean having to walk away from Laney, and he couldn't do that when she was so obviously disoriented. Even if it was only for a few seconds, he wasn't about to leave her alone.

"9-1-1, what's your emergency?"

"Hi, I need an ambulance," Ray said quickly, "it's for my godmother. She fell in her bedroom and I'm worried she might've hit her head."

He relayed the Fitzgeralds' address to the dispatcher as Laney attempted to lift her cheek from the carpet's itchy fibres. There was a throbbing pain in her arm, and when she tried to wriggle her fingers she felt only pins and needles above her wrist. Once again, her body had betrayed her, only now she didn't have the energy to pretend she didn't need help getting back on her feet.

"Do you think you can sit up, if I help you?" he asked a minute later, once the 9-1-1 operator had given him an ETA on the ambulance.

"I... I think so. I just need to get my arm free, you see."

This was going to be nearly impossible with Emily clinging to him, but he had to try. Setting his phone on the floor, Ray wrapped his left arm around Laney's body and pulled her toward him. She'd always been petite—a whopping 4'10"—but he couldn't remember her ever feeling this light. She was lean and bony like a kitten, but without the claws designed to shred the fur off a mouse's belly.

He pivoted her toward the footboard and placed one of the pillows behind her back as the dispatcher said, "The ambulance is two minutes away."

"Thank you," Ray replied, turning his attention back to Laney. He studied her for a moment before saying, "I noticed you don't have your cane." It occurred to him that perhaps the reason she didn't have it was because she'd forgotten where it was, and not because she was being stubborn.

"I wanted to show Emily some pictures," Laney explained, "the next thing I knew, I was lying on the floor."

She winced and cradled her right arm.

"I suppose this is how a child sees the world," she added, tipping her head back to gaze up at the armoire. The room had been designed with rustic comfort in mind, from the simple wooden furniture to the quilted pillow shams on the bed, but all Ray could see from down here was a colony of dust bunnies lurking under the bed—further proof that the sun was setting on Laney's independence.

When the ambulance arrived, he stood in the bedroom doorway with Emily in his arms and watched the paramedics assess Laney's condition: shining a light in both her eyes, prodding various places on her body, and asking her questions she struggled to answer. They had just assisted her onto the stretcher when Ray heard the front door open and Jim thundered down the hall, stopping abruptly to take in the scene before him.

"I'm okay," Laney assured him. "I just tripped."

Jim darted a look at Ray, who shook his head helplessly.

"Are you her husband, sir?" one of the paramedics asked.

Jim nodded, still too stunned to speak.

"In that case, you can ride in the ambulance with her, if you'd like."

"I'll take my truck," he replied gruffly. Turning to Ray, he said, "Meet us at the hospital" before trailing the first responders outside. There, the flashing red and blue lights brought back a swarm of memories from the night of Laney's stroke—a night that would change Ray's life forever, though he hadn't known it at the time.

Still holding his niece, he walked back to the bedroom, picked up his phone, and called Hannah to tell her the news.

Six

"I'm getting sick of this place," Ray said as he took a seat next to Hannah in the row of chairs lining the hospital hallway. He handed her a cup of coffee and folded back the tab on his own, bringing the scorching beverage to his lips for a quick sip.

Victor had declined Ray's offer for a coffee, although he thought he could've used a little pick-me-up with how much of a fuss Emily was making in his lap. He repositioned the squirming baby on his thigh and told his brother, "You guys can go home if you want. Addy and I don't mind staying."

"I'm not saying I want to go home. I'm saying I don't want to be here in the first place." Hannah nodded understandingly as Ray continued, "Hannah and I weren't going to say anything to you guys, but when we went to see Laney after we got back from Hawaii, she was in the kitchen with Emily and her cane was in the living room. She told me off for being concerned, of course. Like she always does." Ray's gaze drifted back to the door concealing his godmother from view. Time and time again, she went against the advice of her doctors and her family, convinced she knew better than everyone what she could and couldn't do. And perhaps she did, but until he saw some incontrovertible proof that she could manage her day-to-day affairs safely, Ray would continue to fret over her.

"We've talked to her about not using her cane," Adrianna explained, pinning a lock of blonde hair behind her ear. "Don't get me wrong: I'm super grateful that she wants to be involved in Emily's life. But we worry constantly."

"I lost my temper with her last week," Victor put in. "I told her that Emily is to stay in her playpen except when she's being fed or changed. Laney means well, but she's having a hard time accepting her limitations now."

"Did she tell you off, too?" Ray asked.

"Oh, yeah. Told me to stop treating her like a child."

The younger brother nodded and leaned back in his chair, the brown paper cup poised on his knee. For several minutes, all of them were quiet, the usual workday hum filling the gaps in their conversation. Hannah had taken her phone out of her purse and was scrolling through her Instagram feed, her thumb cocked over the screen and clearly aiming for every baby announcement and family portrait. Ray wasn't going to sit here and pretend he hadn't noticed a change in his wife's social media habits: whenever Hannah wanted something, her entire online demeanor pivoted toward its acquisition. Although he'd never found the photo-sharing app to be particularly useful, he had to admit it made keeping track of Hannah's desires that much easier. Besides, everyone needed a distraction from time to time, hence the coffee run.

When Jim eventually emerged from Laney's room, Ray stood up first, followed by Hannah. Victor shifted Emily to a more comfortable position on his hip as Adrianna moved to stand beside him.

"Well?" Ray prompted.

Jim met his gaze briefly before turning to look over his shoulder at Laney's room.

"Good news: she doesn't have a head injury like we feared." He gave the group a chance to release their breath. "Bad news: her wrist is broken."

"You've got to be kidding me," Adrianna said.

Jim shook his head. "Afraid not. It's minor, but it'll still take a few weeks to heal." His eyes took in the range of expressions before him— shock, disappointment, indignation, defeat. If he had a mirror, he was certain his face would reveal more than a hint of resentment at this wholly preventable accident, with just a twinge of compunction for holding Laney's misfortune against her.

"Are they keeping her overnight?" Victor asked.

"They don't need to. It's not a serious enough injury." Jim sighed. "I'm sorry for this. I know the timing is awful, but until Laney feels better,

I think it would be best if you found someone else to watch Emily during the day."

"This never should've happened," Ray muttered. "What next? She breaks her hip? Sets the kitchen on fire? How many more times are we going to meet up here before she realizes she can't do everything herself?"

"I know," Jim said. "I've been married to that woman for a long time, and she's never liked the idea of accepting help. But you're right that this can't go on. So, I'm considering putting her in a home."

Hannah repeated, "A home?"

"A nursing home," Adrianna clarified, and her expression shifted noticeably into something resembling dread. "What if you hired someone to come in a few times per week instead? I have some friends in the home healthcare business. Do you want me to talk to them before you make a decision?"

A rueful smile formed on Jim's face. He'd gone almost totally bald in recent years, the joke being that Laney and her precarious health had saved him hundreds of dollars in trips to the barber. He scratched at the thinning patch of reddish-brown hair on the back of his head and replied, "That's all right. I think having someone in her home, moving everything around, will only make the existing problems worse."

"She's not going to agree to move into a nursing home any more than you'll agree to wear a back brace," Ray spat out. "You two are the most stubborn people I've ever met. And stubborn people find solutions."

"Ray, it's fine. Just let them work it out, okay?" Hannah placed a hand on his arm. "Whatever they decide to do, they'll have our support."

"We appreciate that, Hannah. I know this is difficult to hear. Fitzgerald Farms has been Laney's home for close to forty years, and I know she won't leave it without a fight. That being said, at least a nursing home has aides around-the-clock, plus registered nurses and dieticians— a whole team of people trained to care for those with complex health needs. I've done my best to keep Laney safe and comfortable, but I'm not getting any younger… and the four of you have families of your own to look after, or will very soon." His focus switched from Victor to Ray. "You can go home now. I'll take it from here."

With the matter of Laney's fate temporarily settled, Jim turned and walked back to her room. After all this waiting, he hadn't even bothered inviting them in to see her. In Ray's mind, this could only mean one thing: his godmother's health had declined sharply, to the point that even a non-medically trained observer like himself would realize they'd passed the point of no return. And now, with Jim casually throwing around the idea of placing Laney in a more permanent healthcare setting, Ray was almost certain he'd seen the beginning of the end, like a fluorescent yellow sign warning him that the road ahead would be rough.

Adrianna let out a long breath, bringing her hand to her forehead as she turned away from the group. "Now what?"

"Now, I guess Jim's going to take her home," Victor said. Emily rested her head on his shoulder.

She lowered her voice. They'd moved several paces away from Hannah and Ray, but the couple could still hear them perfectly.

"Not that. I mean, what are we going to do about Emily?" Adrianna asked. "I hate to be so selfish about this, but we can't ignore the elephant in the room."

"I know. Can your mom watch her for a few weeks?"

"She has two jobs. She's practically never home."

"Okay, then what about Heather?"

"Working. As always."

Victor sighed and angled toward a painting on the wall. He hadn't realized how much of his time would go toward worrying about childcare until his daughter was born, and a bottomless pit of need had suddenly opened up in his life. He wasn't used to the lack of sleep, the lack of freedom, and the lack of answers, as if everything he'd once known was now a piece of artwork with countless ways of being interpreted.

Adrianna suggested, "Can you take the day off tomorrow to watch her?"

"You know I can't—I'm already on thin ice with my boss."

"Well, I can't take tomorrow off either."

"Then what are we going to do?"

She bit her lip, rubbed her forehead again as if it were a magic lamp containing a wish-granting genie, and dropped her arm with audible defeat.

Hannah darted a glance at Ray before chiming in, "Maybe we could watch her."

Adrianna faced them. "Are you sure?"

"Yeah, of course. I don't work until the afternoon, and Ray's home all day. I mean, it's only for a few weeks, right? Just until Laney's wrist heals."

"Oh, my God. That would be amazing," Adrianna said. She added, somewhat bashfully, "We didn't ask you guys only because we know how busy you are. But if you're available…"

"Yeah. Why not?" Ray forced himself to smile. It would be good practice, and besides, it seemed like Hannah already knew what she was doing.

"Thank you so much. Seriously, you just saved us a colossal headache. I'll text you later to let you know what time we'll be dropping her off." Adrianna faced Victor, who was trying to soothe Emily through her latest bout of tears, and said, "She's overdue for a nap."

"I know. Let's take her home." Adrianna once again addressed Hannah and Ray, who were still hovering around Laney's door. "We'll be in touch. And again—thank you." She then turned and fell into step with Victor and Emily, three figures blurring into one as they disappeared down the hall.

Ray was still trying to wrap his mind around everything—had it really only been a few hours since his conversation with Hannah in the kitchen? She must've been having similar thoughts, for he took one look at her face and saw only an empty husk where there had previously been a well brimming with hope for the future.

"I guess we should go home too," he ventured, trying to capture her gaze.

"Right. And check on Lucky."

Lucky. Shit, how could he have forgotten about that? All his emotions from this morning came flooding back in a white-hot rage.

Ray said, "Therese thinks we should report Curtis. I'll check the cameras when I get home and see if they yield anything useful."

Shaking her head, Hannah said, "This whole day has been hell. Well, except for the very beginning, I suppose."

"You mean, what we talked about in the kitchen?"

"Yeah."

"Is that why you offered to watch Emily?"

A tiny smile poked at Hannah's lips. She turned and led them down the hallway, her voice losing some of its edge as she imagined what it would be like to be responsible for another human life, even if it was only for a few weeks.

"I'm sure it'll be good practice for us," she started, wrapping her fingers around the strap of her purse. "How hard can it be? All we have to do is feed her, change her, put her down for a nap in the afternoon, and make sure she doesn't get into any trouble."

"But our house isn't really set up for a baby. Nothing's baby-proof. You saw how much trouble Lucky got into just by going into the drive shed."

"Do you plan on taking Emily into the drive shed?"

"Oh, yeah. I was thinking we might start by chopping some wood, then we'll spot check a few fences, then, for fun, we'll see if we can outrun the bull." Ray smirked.

Hannah crowed, "Gotta start 'em young, right?" She laughed. "But seriously, is that what your dad did when you were Emily's age?"

"Not those chores specifically. But he took me out as soon as he could. Mostly, I just watched him." He added, "Just so you know, I plan on raising our kids the same way my dad raised me: in the saddle."

They had reached the main entryway, where the white floors were gleaming in the afternoon sun. Quite naturally, any references to Bernard's parenting style filled Hannah with dread: he'd been a neglectful man in more ways than one, and although he'd succeeded in turning his youngest son into a fine cowboy, Ray had suffered plenty of bumps, bruises, and broken bones in the process—to say nothing of the emotional damage caused by being abandoned during his formative years.

Ray seemed oblivious to Hannah's discomfort in this moment. Instead, he seemed fixated on his vision for the future as they walked through the doors and out into the parking lot.

"Our kids are going to love living on a ranch," he said, "growing up around horses, working with their hands, getting dirty, sleeping under the stars on warm summer nights. It'll be great, you'll see."

"I'm sure it will, just as long as they also learn that life on a ranch isn't always glamorous. There are a lot of really hard days. Sometimes you get hurt. Money is often tight. And the cute baby cows end up being dinner."

Ray explained, "My dad only focused on the things you just described. He didn't want my brothers and me growing up with any delusions about our lifestyle." As the smile returned to his face, he added, "As hard as it is sometimes, I love my job. That's what being a parent is really about, isn't it? Being invested."

The longer he spoke, the more convinced Hannah became that her fears about history repeating itself were unfounded. Ray had long ago accepted his father's absence, and with that acceptance came the freedom to define his own future. She strode around to the passenger side of the truck and climbed in, her mind shifting automatically into planner mode as she considered what they would need to make Emily's visit go smoothly.

"We should probably stop at the store while we're in town and grab a few things for tomorrow," she said as Ray turned over the engine. "I'm thinking diapers, and maybe some child-proof locks for the lower kitchen cabinets."

"It's a small town. People might talk if we suddenly walk out of Walmart with a box of Pampers."

"Half the town was at our wedding. I'm sure no one would question it."

Ray smiled. Having Emily around was sure to be a lot of work, but with Hannah overseeing everything, he felt a little more confident. And for the first time in his life, he knew he was ready to be a father.

Seven

Before marrying Ray, Hannah had held plenty of misconceptions about life on a working ranch. She'd assumed anyone who grew up wanting to be a cowboy did so because it looked like fun, riding horses all day and avoiding the soul-crushing monotony of a corporate job. In reality, being a rancher involved everything people hated about their jobs, and more. The days started before dawn and demanded constant overtime, water cooler talk was replaced by everyone in town knowing everyone else's business, and Hannah had yet to meet a rancher who didn't fret about the economy. On days when the weather was bad, there was no telecommuting to the office: the animals still needed to be fed and watered, even when the snow was piled up higher than the roof. And yet, Ray had never talked about giving up his ranch. Beyond its obvious monetary value, this place was home, and he couldn't imagine living anywhere else.

Ray was deep in preparation for tomorrow's cattle drive, gathering essential supplies and touching base with some of his neighbours to discuss the logistics of their plan. Even though it was evening and Hannah's workday was over, Ray continued pacing around the house, checking last-minute tasks off his to-do list and worrying about whether they were going to have enough people to manage the herd.

"I don't care what he told you—that route isn't an option." Ray sank down on the couch and opened his laptop to scrutinize the map on his screen. He told the person on the other end of the phone, "I have too many calves this year to risk taking shortcuts. And if he insists on it, then he can compensate me for my losses."

Hannah looked up from the salad she was preparing. She assumed the "he" in question was Micah Abbot, considered by many to be an expert when it came to navigating the backcountry. He'd overseen countless cattle drives in his career, but his old-fashioned views on women and their "rightful place" on a ranch (usually nowhere near the cowboys, unless it was lunchtime) consistently left Hannah with a bad taste in her mouth. She added a handful of cherry tomatoes to the bowl as Ray went off on the caller again.

"But he says that every year! And every year, it isn't an issue. Look, if we just go a few miles west, we can avoid that area altogether. And since it's my herd, it should be my call." He set his jaw, staring at the multitude of potential routes as Hannah sat down beside him.

At last, Ray seemed to regain his composure. "Okay. I guess that works, too. I'll see you tomorrow." Hanging up the call, he chucked his phone on the coffee table and sank back against the couch cushions with a sigh of defeat.

"Micah?" Hannah guessed.

"Yeah. There's a river that cuts through our property—it's pretty wide, and around this time of year the water level's higher thanks to the runoff from the peaks. Anyway, Micah wants to change the route we originally agreed on because he thinks it's too long and the horses will get too tired, but the route he's proposing crosses the river at a point where the current is particularly strong. Darrel says there's a spot where the river bends a bit—if there's a bank to slow the current down, then we can get the calves across safely. He's going to run this plan by the guys and see if they have any objections."

"And if Micah doesn't approve?" Hannah prompted.

"Then he doesn't get to be point man. Simple as that." Ray leaned his head back as Hannah wrapped herself around his arm and breathed in the familiar scent of his old green sweater. "I don't know why I bother some days. When Marc was the boss, no one questioned him."

"Except you. And you bother because you love it. Being a rancher is in your blood."

His turned a pained smile on her, but didn't dispute this fact. He knew he wasn't the first person to contemplate whether he'd chosen the right profession, although in Ray's case, the decision had been made for him a long time ago. But he often wondered if he stuck around because of an honest-to-God passion for the trade, or because he didn't know how to do anything else.

She reached into her back pocket and pulled out her phone. Ray glanced over to see a notification pop up on the screen. *It's time to track!* the blue bubble declared. Hannah dismissed the prompt and reclined on the couch, thoughts of dinner momentarily forgotten as her mind shifted to their recent decision to start a family. Should they or shouldn't they? Her mind never seemed totally made up either way, and the uncertainty was becoming rather troubling.

"What was that?" Ray asked.

"My app. You know, the one you said we didn't need."

"Ah."

"Maybe you're right. Maybe we don't need it. I just like having a plan—kind of like you do." Hannah gestured to the laptop and notebook, both of which proved Ray wasn't a fan of leaving the future of his business up to chance. "Too bad you're going to be in the upper rangeland on the day we have the best chance of conceiving."

"You're right. Let me call Darrel back and tell him you and I are going to be too busy having sex to move the herd."

"Hard to imagine any man would argue with *that* change of plans," Hannah replied, amused.

Ray placed his hand on her thigh. He let it linger there, feeling the warmth of her body through the skin-tight material. Instead of musing over what their future could look like, he fell back into reminiscing about the very first time he'd touched her this way. It seemed strange now to think of how innocent they'd been back then, stealing kisses behind the barn and getting butterflies over the faintest brush of skin. All that excitement had paved the way for a much richer connection, even if the landscape of their intimacy had shifted to something a little bit easier to navigate.

"I know it's almost dinnertime," Ray began, a crooked smile taking over his face. "But do you want to go upstairs and see if we can make another baby?"

As a grin broke out on Hannah's face, Ray seized her hand and led her toward the stairs.

"Just so you know, it's not an exact science," Hannah told him as she stood at the foot of the bed and removed her shirt.

"I know."

"And we're not getting our hopes up," she warned.

"Of course not." Ray stepped out of his jeans and kicked the pants aside.

She couldn't help but smile. Right now, her mind seemed as made up as it was ever going to be. Reaching behind her back, Hannah unclasped her bra and tossed it into the pile of clothes on the floor. Ray had already won the race to get undressed, and when he took her into the shelter of his arms, she felt those same butterflies come to life all over again.

Hannah sank back into the softness of the old quilt. As Ray leaned over her, she reached for the lamp cord and pulled it, plunging the room into darkness.

*

The following day, Ray sat astride his sorrel gelding, sweat trickling down the back of his shirt. He would've given anything for some snow right now, or even just a drizzle of rain, but the sky was a spotless, sparkling blue, and so clear that he halfway expected to see his reflection on the horizon.

Russell came to stand next to him. For the past few hours, Russell had been riding alongside the herd, ensuring the cattle remained tightly clustered together. Micah, with his vast knowledge of the backcountry, rode up front, leading the way through the swooping valleys and scraggly brush that dominated the foothills. This had left Ray, the appointed trail boss, hovering somewhere in between, filling in for Micah when needed and keeping the herd in his peripheral vision at all times. It wasn't the worst position to be in, especially on a day like today: a cloud of dust followed in the herd's wake, thick enough to render the drag men nearly invisible. Even now, Ray could only make out a glimmer of red bandana and the silhouette of one rider's horse, plodding obediently through the suffocating clouds.

"I think you made the right call siding with Darrel," Russell confessed, his own bandana in a tight wad beneath his chin. "Micah thinks he's got all this wisdom—or that we don't know how bad his hip is."

"I was surprised he agreed to come. Even Laney thinks it's time for him to retire."

"Yeah, but he won't. He's a stubborn old bastard." Russell sniffed. "Speaking of, there's a rumour going around that Laney's thinking of selling Fitzgerald Farms. Apparently some developer is offering big bucks to buy her place and the lot next door." He turned to Ray, evidently having greater confidence in his knowledge of Laney's business plans than Micah's leadership skills. With a spark of hope in his voice, Russell added, "But that's just a rumour, right? Anyone who knows Laney knows they would have to pry Fitzgerald Farms from her cold, dead hands."

Ray tugged the brim of his hat down over his eyes and scanned their surroundings. Sometimes, rumours were just rumours, but sometimes they were like storm clouds in the distance, hinting at something that hadn't yet transpired.

He turned his horse away. "I need to talk to the wranglers about something. Can you keep an eye on the herd for a minute?"

"Sure thing."

A sense of calm fell over the valley as the last of the cattle moved in, escorted by the less experienced riders at their heels. As the dust settled, the sun was once again a blazing pearl in the sky, shrinking the shadows of the trees and weighing on the air like an invisible hand. Ray returned to the lookout to find Russell standing next to Micah a short distance down the hill, gazing at something in the woods. Upon noticing Ray, Russell raised a hand and waved him over.

"You're gonna want to see this," he said as Ray got closer.

"What is it?"

"A problem," Micah answered gruffly. He was stooped over examining something in the leaflitter.

Ray stepped forward. Underlying the cool scent of mulch was the sharp tang of a decaying animal carcass, lying in a pile amidst the ferns. A swarm of black flies congregated around the calf's head, laying their eggs in the pockets of soft pink tissue. The fur had been plucked out near the animal's ribcage, granting access to the thoracic cavity, except most of that had been plucked out too, leaving a gaping hole where the vital organs should have been.

"Do you think it could've been a bear?" Ray asked, turning to Micah.

Micah shook his head. "Not a bear. Bears don't leave the entrails."

"Maybe a smaller predator then," Russell suggested, "if the calf got separated from its herd and died, any number of predators might've nibbled on it. Looks relatively fresh, too."

"Gotta be a mountain lion," Micah said, swatting a rubbery maple sapling out of his face. "They go straight for the heart and lungs, where the nutrients are. And they tend to be private about feeding—either this calf died right here, or the lion dragged it into the thicket herself after making the kill. The big bones are crunched through."

Ray picked up a stick and used it to flick some leaves off the calf's rigid corpse.

"That's Dean Chase's brand, over at the Lazy K. I'll give him a call when I get home and let him know we found one of his calves." Ray straightened, stabbing the stick into the dirt at his feet as he mulled over their predicament. "So, you're saying we might have a cougar in the area."

"I'm saying you might want to keep an eye on your horses for the next few nights. Bring them inside if you have any doubts." Micah ducked beneath a branch. A few yards beyond the treeline, the valley was bathed in sunlight, painting a much more optimistic picture than the one Ray now had in his mind. As a rancher, he faced countless threats to his livestock every day: disease, bad weather, thieves, and of course, hungry predators. They would just have to keep moving, and remain alert for signs of danger lurking in the shadows.

"What do you want to do?" Russell asked.

Ray considered his answer. "We stick with the plan. When I get home, I'll see if anyone's reported any cougar sightings in the area. A lot of ranchers pass through this corridor at this time of year. The least we can do is give them a heads-up."

He lifted his gaze, suddenly remembering that cougars preferred to perch in high trees and rocky overhangs. In these woods, the big cat would be perfectly camouflaged among the natural browns of its surroundings. But he saw nothing to explain the chill at his back—no honey-gold eyes peering down at her prey with practiced patience. Ray tossed the stick back into the underbrush and led the way out of the forest, deciding to focus on his cattle instead.

"You know, Micah could be wrong," Russell said.

"Maybe. But in the off-chance he's right, I think we should keep moving."

Ray pulled himself up into the saddle, reined toward the herd, and set his horse in motion with a firm kick to its ribs, leaving the woods to her secrets.

Eight

Jim and Laney had visited six nursing homes in a two-week span of time, and none of them were quite what they were looking for—that is, until they discovered Alpine Terrace. The home had a white stucco exterior and a flat, concrete roof that underlined the summer-green mountains in the background. Flowerbeds rife with sunset-orange tiger lilies and violet clusters of gladiolus blooms curved along the stone walkway leading to the front doors, which zipped open with an inviting burst of climate controlled air.

Even as they were making their way toward the entrance, Ray was looking for reasons to hate the place. For one thing, there was no terrace in sight, or even the suggestion of a balcony extending from the awfully-narrow windows on the second and third floors. And even if Alpine Terrace somehow lived up to its promise to provide residents with all the comforts and conveniences of home, he doubted Laney would ever fully adjust to eating food prepared by other people. At this thought, his feet came to a sudden standstill in the broken shade of the pergola. He was never going to enjoy another one of Laney's meals again. The impact of this realization hit him like a fist to the stomach, the pain shooting up into his chest in a hot spear of agony.

A couple of steps ahead, Hannah sensed Ray's absence and turned around, a worried look creasing her expression. "Are you okay?"

Ray swallowed. "Yeah, I'm fine."

Hannah gazed up at the white façade, spanning across the clear blue sky like the wings of a gull. "It's kind of nice, don't you think? A little bit Mediterranean, almost, especially with the dark blue accents."

"Yeah, because I'm sure the residents love to be reminded of all the places they can't go."

She reached for his hand as he walked toward her. Jim and Laney had already arrived and were waiting for the couple just inside the front doors, which opened onto a foyer covered in dark laminate floors. A circular reception desk, positioned in the centre of the annular space, allowed for visibility in all directions. To the left and right were the resident rooms; straight ahead, an accessible dining area furnished with wooden tables and a large, painted mural overlooked a secured courtyard. As they approached the welcome desk, Ray forced himself to think of nothing, to feel only the cool air on his face and the bright sunlight cascading down on them from the skylight above.

At the sight of him, Laney broke into a grin.

"Here he is," she said to the woman behind the computer, "that's my godson, right there. I told you he'd be coming."

"You did," the receptionist, Nicole, replied in a friendly tone.

Sticking out his hand to her, Ray said, "Hi, I'm Ray. This is my wife, Hannah."

"Pleased to meet you." As Nicole went back to her work, she told the group, "Elsie will be out shortly. She's just wrapping up a meeting."

"Perfect," Ray replied flatly. He switched his focus to Laney, sitting in a wheelchair with her purse in her lap and her wrist cast gleaming brightly in the sun. The cane had been bad enough, when she remembered to use it. But the wheelchair was a one-way street to a town Ray had no desire to visit. The wheelchair meant the end of the road, for all of them.

Ray once again forced his mind to empty. Soon, footsteps clopped across the foyer, heralding the arrival of a woman wearing a creamy white pantsuit and matching peep-toe shoes. It was nearly impossible to discern where the spotlight ended and their tour guide began: everything about her was as delicate as a mist, right down to the pale blonde hair she'd fashioned into a neat bun. She greeted her guests with a smile and launched straight into her well-rehearsed sales pitch.

"Thank you for waiting," she told the group, her eyes travelling automatically to Laney. "I'm Elsie White. Welcome to Alpine Terrace. We're happy to have you."

Ray stiffened at the unintentional finality of Elsie's words. Nothing was set in stone yet, he told himself. They were just here to look and ask questions.

"I'm Jim, Laney's husband." As he stepped forward to shake Elsie's hand, Jim nodded to Ray and Hannah. "That's my godson and his wife. We've more or less made up our minds about coming here, but Laney wanted to see the facility for herself before we sign any papers."

"Of course. Well, I'm happy to show you around. Our residents just finished breakfast, but you'll have a chance to see the dining room and activities area, as well as our physiotherapy room upstairs."

"Excellent," Laney enthused. Looking at her now, Ray couldn't believe how white her hair had turned in only a few short years. He could see the bony outline of her knees through the coral fabric of her pants, and the knot of purple veins spidering across the tops of her feet as she adjusted her sandals on the wheelchair's foot pedals. "We've already been out to see a few other homes in the area. I've always believed in following my intuition, and this place feels right. Don't you think, hon?"

Ray snapped out of his thoughts, surprised to find Laney staring politely in his direction.

"If you like it…" he started to say.

Elsie led the way toward the resident rooms.

"I think you'll find this place to your liking, Mrs. Fitzgerald. Our home features 120 beds, and we have staff on-site twenty-four-seven. We understand that moving to a new home can be a difficult transition, so we've included plenty of amenities to promote your overall health and wellbeing."

They walked down a long, carpeted hallway, with Jim pushing Laney and Hannah and Ray taking up the rear. On one side of the hall was a row of windows affording a clear view of the gardens and parking lot. Ray concentrated on the sunlight glinting off the spokes of Laney's wheelchair as Elsie continued with her sales pitch, the clip-clop of her heels returning as the carpet gave way to vinyl.

"This is the A-side care centre," she explained, stopping next to a high desk staffed by a number of employees in scrubs. "All of our floors have been assigned a letter. Your room will have its own number as well, so you can always find your way home."

"How efficient," Laney remarked. She raised her hand, her lips hinting at a sly smile. "Not that I get lost easily, mind you, but at least everyone will know where to address the Christmas cards."

"Of course. As I mentioned earlier, we have nurses on staff at every hour of the day, as well as four registered dieticians and a team of physiotherapists upstairs. Working in conjunction with your primary care provider, we'll be able to come up with a care plan that meets—and hopefully exceeds—your expectations for holistic, compassionate care." Elsie paused. Her gaze drifted to each family member in turn before finally settling on Ray, who pretended not to notice by studying the fire safety plan posted on the wall instead. "If you'll follow me, I can show you some of our rooms. We have both private and semi-private rooms available. The cost will vary depending on which features you choose to include in your accommodation package, but we can discuss all those little details later."

Jim said, "We've already discussed the particulars. A semi-private room would be best, I think."

"Oh, yes," Laney agreed, peering up at Elsie. "I haven't had a roommate since college, but it's like I always say: you're never too old to make a new friend."

Ray leaned down to whisper in Hannah's ear, "Laney's going to hate having a roommate."

"You don't know that," she whispered back. "Laney loves people. She knows everybody."

"I know she hates it when someone else tries to take over in the kitchen. And I've seen her get upset whenever anyone tries to move her books or her knitting supplies. Do you really think she'll be able to handle not being in complete control of her environment?"

Hannah bit her lip, suddenly skeptical of the plan. It was true that Laney had good days and bad days. On good days, such as this one, she was receptive to just about anything. But what would happen after she got settled in here, and the novelty of the experience inevitably faded? How agreeable would she be if the staff couldn't create the perfect cocktail of medications to soothe her pain, or adjust the pillows precisely to her liking?

"Let's just focus on the positives for now, okay?" Hannah told him, noting the faint twitch in Ray's jaw as he clenched his teeth. "Maybe this will be good for her."

The tour continued, snaking through the halls and past the rooms in an orderly manner. Several of the doors were closed, but every time they passed one that wasn't, Ray couldn't help but peek inside. Most of the rooms were simple and spartan, like his room had been before Hannah moved in. Each one had the usual trappings of a healthcare facility: hospital beds with crinkly blue mattresses, forlorn plastic chairs with salmon-pink cushions sitting next to the window, and of course, a stock-standard box of scratchy, grey tissues, waiting for whoever was desperate enough to use them.

In one room, an old lady was napping in an armchair. In another, an elderly man with white hair was tipped back in a wheelchair beside the bed. His mouth hung open in vacant reverie, his dry, chapped lips caving in around his toothless gums. A slightly younger woman sat next to him, dabbing dolefully at his tongue and cheeks with a small, pink sponge dipped in a cup of water. Ray tore his eyes away, horrified by what he saw. Things may not have been perfect at Fitzgerald Farms, but at least there was still life to be found there. He followed the somber procession through a set of doors and into the dining room, where a housekeeper was tackling a stain under one of the chairs.

"And this is where the meals are served three times a day," Elsie announced, turning to her party. "Do you have any dietary restrictions, Mrs. Fitzgerald?"

"No. Although I do enjoy a nice cup of camomile tea before bed each night."

"That can be arranged."

"Why is it called 'Alpine Terrace'?" Ray blurted.

Elsie smiled, unruffled by the challenging edge to his voice as she crossed the dining room to a set of glass doors. After punching a string of numbers into the nearby keypad, the doors opened onto a wide landing decorated in raised flowerbeds and patio furniture. A series of stout, green peaks laced with ski paths and gondola cables lay just beyond the wooden privacy fence. Ray sized up the terrace, dumbfounded by the pristine beauty of the blue sky and how it seemed to make everything beneath it sparkle, Laney included.

"That's why," Elsie said with unwavering politeness. "Do you have any more questions?"

He shook his head, his cheeks reddening. "No."

"In that case, I've put together an information package for you to take home. You can pick it up at the front desk on your way out." Gazing down at Laney, Elsie said, "It was a pleasure meeting you, Mrs. Fitzgerald. I do hope you'll consider making our home, your home."

Laney must've replied, but Ray didn't hear it. In that moment, all he was aware of was the sun on his face and the steady breeze that blew in off the mountains. It wasn't until they'd made their way back to the parking lot that his self-inflicted numbness began to wane, and that familiar prickle of sadness moved in to fill the empty spaces inside him.

Hannah touched his arm. "I'm going to go wait in the car, okay?"

"Okay." He was standing next to Laney on the sidewalk. Already petite, she appeared no bigger than a child now, her head just barely meeting his elbow. If he had to, Ray thought, he could pick her up and carry her away—anywhere but here. But neither of them moved.

After Hannah left, Jim turned to his wife and said in his usual gruff timbre, "I'll bring the truck around." He then set off toward their vehicle, his broad shoulders swaying with each step.

Ray set his jaw. He felt, rather than saw, the subtle movements in Laney's hands as she clutched the strap of her purse. *Now what?* The

60

words pounded through him like a beating heart, pushing away the chill in his bones.

"Laney, I have to ask… is this really what you want?"

Her features softened, and the corners of her mouth poked up into a mild smile.

"What I want is irrelevant at this point," she said after a moment. She sounded neither defensive nor resigned, but spoke with a cool practicality normally reserved for only the gravest of choices. "What matters now is no longer being a burden on Jim. When we got married, we agreed to take care of each other. So, that's what I'm doing."

"Yeah, but he could take care of you at home. He's been doing it for years."

"He's tired, Raymond." Laney reached up to squeeze his hand. "On my wedding day, I took a vow, just like you did. In sickness and in health. And now my sickness is becoming too much for either Jim or myself to handle. As much as I'd love to spend whatever time I have left at Fitzgerald Farms, I know I'd be asking for more than my fair share in the marriage. At least if I came here, it wouldn't be so hard on Jim's back. I owe him that much, I think."

Jim pulled up in his truck and got out. As he opened the passenger door, Ray steered Laney's wheelchair toward the edge of the curb, feeling altogether useless as Jim hoisted his tiny wife into the passenger seat and helped her fasten the seatbelt. After loading the wheelchair into the pickup's bed, Jim turned to Ray, his expression inscrutable.

"Will we see you and Hannah at the house?" Jim asked.

"Maybe another time. I need to work with that new horse today."

Jim nodded once, then shuffled around the truck to the driver's side. As he climbed behind the wheel, Ray stepped off the sidewalk and crossed the parking lot to where Hannah was waiting.

"How's Laney?" she asked as he ducked into the passenger seat.

"She's worried about Jim's back," Ray replied as he slammed the door. "She always worries about everyone but herself. I just don't want her to feel like she has to come here."

"I know. But she seems to really like it."

"That's what worries me," Ray murmured.

Hannah put the car in gear and pulled out of the space. They drove home in silence, their thoughts turning toward two very different versions of the future. In Hannah's version, Laney moving into a facility like Alpine Terrace had several positives: staff to assist her around the clock, countless opportunities for social interaction, and of course, less pressure on Ray to be available at the drop of a hat. But she couldn't ignore how difficult this was for him either. Fitzgerald Farms had never existed without Laney, and although Jim would likely hold onto the property for as long as he could afford to maintain it, visits would never be the same.

As if divining her thoughts, Ray said, "Russ heard a rumour that Jim's thinking of selling the farm. He told me during the cattle drive."

Hannah glimpsed the passenger seat. The window was open, and a light breeze was combing through Ray's hair. "Rumours are just rumours, right? Besides, if Jim and Laney were thinking seriously about selling, I'm sure they would have said something to us or Victor and Adrianna." She smiled. "Look on the bright side: if someone else is taking care of Laney, then that gives you and me more time to focus on starting our family."

His expression darkened. "How can you think about that right now?"

Hannah felt stung. "I was just trying to be positive," she answered quietly.

"We don't always have to be positive. It's a weird habit, always looking on the bright side of everything." Ray turned his attention back to the window, trying to make sense of his own thoughts.

As a tense silence filled the car, Hannah wondered if he was right. When she was younger and still reeling from Cameron's death, seeking out the good in her life had kept the size of her problems in perspective. But maybe she was only imagining the silver lining this time: without

Laney, who could they count on for reliable childcare that didn't cost them the equivalent of a mortgage payment each month?

"You're right," she said, flipping on her blinker. "We're being selfish."

"Mainly you."

Hannah shot him a wounded look. "Maybe I should go back on the pill then. Because it seems like we have this discussion every week."

"I just don't think now's the time to be making big changes to our life. I mean, what if Laney hates living at Alpine Terrace? And do you really think Jim's going to be able to live without her?" When Hannah merely shook her head, Ray said, "I'm serious—I'm really worried about him."

"I'm worried too, but I don't appreciate you snapping at me like I've done something wrong."

Ray forced himself to take a deep breath. He'd been prepared to argue about... well, he wasn't sure, and it didn't matter. Hannah refused to look at him as they drove through the last intersection out of town and headed toward the mountains in the distance, to a place that had once seemed so sheltered from the world's problems. Perhaps that was where Ray's anger lay: in the knowledge that their life wasn't any safer out here than it was in the big city.

"I'm sorry," he said. "I was out of line."

"I'm sorry, too. I guess I'm just trying to cope with everything in my own way."

"For what it's worth, I don't want you to go back on the pill. No more pills, okay? I want to do this."

"You know, we still have plenty of time with her—and even if Laney does end up moving to Alpine Terrace, there's no way she'd miss out on the most important moments of our kids' lives," Hannah said. "Try to have a little faith in her. When has she ever not come through for you?"

The sign for the ranch finally came into view, and Ray, comforted by her reassurances, got out to open the gate.

The driveway stretched along the fence, bordered on one side by a wide, flat plain that climbed toward a trifecta of stony peaks. The drought had made its way here from California, scorching some of the smaller trees dry and bleaching the needles of the pines. Hannah drove toward the house, thinking of the sign out front and the children they hadn't yet conceived, her hope for the future tempered by more immediate concerns in the present. Ray leaned forward in the passenger seat, squinting his eyes in order to see through the faint scrim of dust coating the window.

"Where's Lucky?" he asked.

Hannah pulled up to the house, put the car in park, and turned off the engine.

"In the isolation paddock," she replied.

His body twisted in that direction. Hannah studied the slightly lighter hair on the back of his neck and felt a sudden chill creep up her arms.

"I don't see him." Ray undid his seatbelt.

"He has to be there. He was there when we left."

"Well, he's not there now."

Hannah scrambled to remove her seatbelt. By the time she'd exited the car, Ray was halfway down to the small paddock under the trees. He scanned the patch of shade behind the lean-to, but there was no sign of the grey horse to be found. A soft clanging noise came from somewhere on his left, along with the dusty percussion of Hannah's footsteps.

Ray went to the gate, picked up the chain that normally held it closed, and stared uncomprehendingly at the free-swinging metal clip.

"Maybe Curtis picked him up early," Hannah suggested meekly.

He let the chain drop from his hand and turned to her, his expression finally registering this turn of events.

"I don't think so. I think maybe…"

Hannah spoke carefully. "Are you completely sure you closed the gate?"

"Of course I closed the gate. When do I not?" Ray headed toward the barn with increasing urgency.

Hannah stood on the threshold with the sun at her back and watched as Ray paced the full length of the aisle. When he reached the opposite end of the barn, which overlooked the fields and forests to the west, Ray abruptly ceased all movement and let the weight of his carelessness crash into him. Checking the gates had become a daily habit on par with brushing his teeth, and now he couldn't recall whether he'd actually confirmed the gate was secure, or if he was simply remembering the thousands of other times when he was certain he'd latched it.

Hannah came up beside him.

"I'm sure he couldn't have gotten far," she began. "I'll saddle a couple of horses and we'll go out and look for him."

"No. I'll go alone." Ray doubled back on his tracks and swiped a lead rope off one of the hooks. "You came out to talk to me about Laney and I got distracted and forgot to double-check the gate."

Hannah faltered. "So you're saying this is my fault?"

"No. I'm saying it's my responsibility. We've only been gone a couple of hours. With any luck, he might still be nearby."

"Are you sure you don't want me to come with you?"

"No. I want you to stay here, in case he comes back."

She nodded stiffly. People had been bringing their horses here for years, and Ray had built his reputation on their glowing testimonials. If word of Lucky's escape got out, the entire foundation of his horse training business—and, by extension, their dreams of a family—would crumble to dust.

Hannah heard footsteps, both horse and human, and turned to see Ray leading a black mare from the main paddock.

"You're taking Abby?" Hannah asked incredulously. The swayback mare had more or less retired from ranch work, although her eyes and coat still gleamed with health. A years-old scar on her knee tightened and rumpled with each step.

"Why not? She knows the area, and she's fast. If I have to chase Lucky down, I'd rather do it on her." Ray handed Hannah the rope to hold, then disappeared into the barn to fetch his tack.

"I keep thinking of that calf we found," he said a moment later, the monstrous leather saddle tucked against his hip. "Micah said there might be a cougar in the backcountry. It's rare for them to prey on horses, but still—I'd rather find Lucky before she does."

Ray tossed the saddle pad onto Abby's back with a flick of his wrist, then heaved the saddle's mighty weight on top of it. He reached under her belly for the girth, pulling it snug against her ribs.

"What about humans? Do cougars prey on those?"

"Only when they're protecting their cubs." Ray's face contorted with the effort of tightening the cinch.

Hannah squinted at the hills in the distance, covered in miles of dark green Douglas firs. Plenty of places for a big cat to hide, although she knew they were equally at home in a rocky outcropping overlooking a grassy meadow.

When Ray emerged from the barn again, this time carrying Abby's bridle, Hannah said, "Any other dangerous animals I should be aware of?"

"We get the odd black bear, but they don't pose much threat to humans or horses." He crossed the reins over Abby's neck and glanced at his wife. "Now would be a great time to think positively."

Ray placed his left foot in the stirrup to pull himself up. Once he was settled, he told Hannah, "I should be back before sundown. Keep your phone handy in case I need to call you."

Hannah nodded and released Abby's reins. Ray turned her in a tight circle and urged her on at a lope, setting her on a course that would take them directly into the foothills.

Nine

Under ideal conditions, an average, healthy horse could travel up to thirty-five miles in a single day. Although it seemed unlikely that Lucky could've achieved such a feat in only a few hours, as Ray ascended into the high country, he began to question everything he thought he knew about the equine mind. Maybe they weren't the predictable, fear-driven creatures he'd been raised to believe. Maybe a horse like Lucky, bonded to a woman like Dolores, had set out on a direct path to her woodland oasis knowing only that he'd felt safe there, and wanted to feel safe again. Ray had heard of cats and dogs walking hundreds of miles to find their owners; humans went even farther, crossing entire oceans in search of a place to call home. And still these distances didn't compare to the gulf between a child and the parent who'd abandoned them.

As this thought came uninvited into Ray's mind, he urged Abby into a steady jog, taking advantage of the flatter terrain that unfolded across the rangeland. Just a couple of weeks ago, his cattle had been crossing this same plateau, unaware of the cougar or the river they'd eventually have to conquer. Could Lucky have followed their trail? Ray allowed himself to believe it was possible. Abby plodded along beneath him, her elegant black ears in ceaseless motion trying to pinpoint every tiny noise that emanated from her surroundings.

"See anything yet?" Ray asked, causing her right ear to flick toward him. As it swiveled back to the narrow path, he lifted his gaze and scanned the rigid grasses skirting the meadow. A younger horse might've bolted at the way the wind pressed down on their grey stalks, imitating the threatening approach of a predator, but the raven mare simply soldiered on, happily soaking up her chance to relive her glory days.

By mid-afternoon, Ray found himself in a wooded area. Despite the day's heat, the air was cool beneath the trees and rich with the smell of decomposition. Lodgepole pines pierced the hazy sky, their bows weaving random patterns across the scrim of pale blue. In the distance, he could make out the slightly plumper shapes of Engelmann spruce, with clusters of chokecherry scattered across the hills. These were trees his mother had loved, introducing them by name each time they passed, or sometimes reaching out to stroke their branches. At the time, he'd been too young to comprehend the extent of her illness. Instead, he'd simply walked with her along the winding trails around their house, picking the flowers she'd deemed safe to pick and presenting her with a bouquet that had wilted in his hand.

Looking back, he could see now why she'd been drawn to the woods: despite his lingering fears of a potential cougar attack, and the nerve-wracking realization that he'd lost a client horse somewhere in the mountains, Ray couldn't help but appreciate the stillness. He pulled on Abby's reins, stopping her briefly in a thicket teeming with birdcall, and gazed around at the forest's boundlessness.

"What do you think? Could Lucky have come through here?" Ray sized up the path ahead, the gaps between the trees barely wide enough to accommodate a horse and its rider. Nevertheless, he pressed on, giving Abby's flanks a light tap for encouragement.

She picked her way through the woods, her hooves crunching loudly in the deadfall. When a chipmunk darted out from the cover of a log, she snorted and skittered sideways three or four steps, causing Ray's thigh to smash against the side of the saddle. Wincing in pain, he straightened and prodded her sides with his heels.

"Walk on," he gritted. In that moment, he decided that horses really were the predictable, fear-driven creatures he'd been raised to believe, and that if Lucky had gone anywhere, it would've been to a neighbouring ranch. Another ranch, populated by other horses, would've offered the best hope of safety. Ray rode on at a brisk walk, chastising himself for questioning his instincts. The woods were no place for an animal designed to travel thirty-five miles a day.

And yet, Abby stopped. Her ears pitched forward, her body tense with concentration. She inhaled noisily, her ribs expanding under Ray's knees. With every breath she took, he grew increasingly aware of the woods around him, how the stillness from a few moments ago had been nothing more than an illusion. His shirt was damp with sweat: as it cooled, it left him chilled and shaking like the leaves of the aptly-named Quaking Aspens, their ghostly trunks unnervingly visible in the growing darkness. Abby snorted once, turned her head to look at something, then relaxed and waited for his cue to continue.

"Walk on," Ray said again. She started forward at a careful pace, her ears still erect on top of her head.

After a couple of minutes, the carpet of pine needles became thinner and eventually turned to soft, black earth. The distance between trees had widened too, until there was more than enough room for a horse and rider to pass. Ray ducked his head slightly to avoid a low-hanging branch. When he raised it again, he saw a blur of greyish-white in the distance.

Abby let out a small nicker. The greyish-white blur answered back, its choppy hello echoing through the forest.

Ray pulled Abby to a stop and dismounted. Lucky extended his nose toward him, then dropped his head to nibble on the ferns wreathing the base of the tree. Only he couldn't reach them—the rope that kept him tethered to the tree was too short, and he raised his head again, gazing placidly around at the bushes that concealed him from view.

Ray approached the gelding and ran his hand along the rope, then stepped around Lucky and into the small clearing. The area couldn't have been more than twenty feet across, with a blue tent on one side and a firepit on the other.

Scattered around the campsite was further evidence of human habitation: a single cooking pot and spoon cooling in the dirt, wood for that night's fire already assembled in a neat pyramid of dry timber, and clothes draped over thin branches to dry. Ray kicked some extra dirt into the firepit until it stopped smoldering. He was used to hikers cutting through the area—that was to be expected, given the size of the lot. But camping out on private property? Ray wouldn't tolerate that for even a second, even if he did have the space to entertain uninvited guests.

He started back toward where Lucky was tied. His hand was already reaching for the knot when he heard a crashing noise somewhere behind him, and a man came stumbling out of the bushes with a feral look on his face.

"Watch it! He's skittish," the man warned.

Ray jerked at the voice, grating like a chainsaw on the uneasy silence. Lucky threw back his head but quickly recovered his composure.

Ray turned toward the deranged figure. He had brown hair down to his shoulders, a wiry, unkempt beard streaked with grey, and remarkably blue eyes. His face could've been carved from wood, each sharp angle reminiscent of the marks cut by a hatchet's blade. Even his hands, held out in front of him in a gesture that implored caution, were calloused in all the same places, the skin as thick as the silence that had returned with an almost theatrical flourish to the forest.

What the hell? The words came thundering into Ray's head as if by divine intent. His eyes searched the man up and down, seeking and finding more details he couldn't ignore. The leather boots. The worn-out belt, cinched at the fourth hole. The way his mouth opened to utter a small, inquiring sound.

"Ray?"

Ray took a step back, shaking his head. The fire had finally, fully gone out. In his face, the heat was slowly beginning to build. His mouth opened, and a reply came tumbling out, no more a part of him than the man to whom it was addressed.

"Dad?"

Ten

"He's skittish," Bernard said again, nodding in Lucky's direction. "His halter was caught on a branch over there. I had a rope, so I figured I'd try and catch him."

Ray stood there, speechless. His father was alive. He was alive, and worse, he was living on the same property he'd abandoned twenty years ago, as if he had any business being here at all. Ray thought about asking him to leave. He thought about begging him to stay. In the end, he did neither of these things. Instead, he stood there taking in the scene around him, each scattered possession shrouded in an aura of desperation.

Ray snapped out of his stupor. "What are you doing here?"

"I lost my job. I got sick, and I lost my job, and before I knew it I was out on the streets. I didn't have any other choice but to—"

"To what, come crawling here begging for forgiveness? You left us. The night mom died, you walked out of that hospital and you never looked back. Jim and Laney ended up taking us in. And now here you are, and you expect me to feel sorry for you because you lost your job?"

"I'm not asking for your pity. I'm not asking for anything."

"Then why are you here?"

Bernard raised both hands again, his expression subsiding into defeat. He moved toward the firepit, around which he'd arranged a number of his sparse belongings, and took a seat on a stout, grey stump with a rattling sigh. His fingernails were black and the backs of his hands resembled old leather, just like Ray remembered. Reluctantly, he stepped forward as well, watching as Bernard lifted a length of beech off the nearby woodpile and placed it with due reverence into the ash-lined dugout at his feet.

"I'm here because I don't have a choice," Bernard said. "Can't get a place without a job. Got no friends who'd take me in. My plan was to lay

71

low here for a while, just until the winter, then head south where it's warm. I never meant to bother you."

"You are bothering me though. This is my place now, understand? Not yours—mine."

"I left it to Marcus." Bernard selected another log and leaned it against the first.

"And he gave it to me as a wedding present. The land is officially under my name now. My wife and I own it outright."

Furrowing his brows, Bernard met Ray's gaze. "Where's Marcus?"

"Why do you care? It's not like you wanted anything to do with us."

"I care because he's still my son, just as you are." Bernard looked him over. "Where is he?"

"He's in Wyoming."

"And Victor?" Bernard asked, already shying away from Ray's potential vitriol.

His youngest son didn't react with anything other than facts. "He's still in Aspen. Married with one kid."

Ray paused, debating whether or not to continue. He didn't owe Bernard anything, least of all information about the family he'd disowned. After a moment, Ray turned his focus to the campfire, listening to the clink of dry logs settling in their shallow grave.

From the pocket of his sweater, Bernard withdrew a red cigarette lighter and cradled it in his palm. "Boy or girl?"

"Girl."

Bernard nodded. He couldn't picture what either of his twins looked like now. Hell, seeing Ray had been enough of a shock, with his sandy hair darkened to a dignified bronze and his cheeks, once the smooth, plump features of a child, textured with coarse blond stubble. He let his regret slip through his fingers like sand, then held the lighter's flame to a brittle twig until the tip ignited.

"You shouldn't be lighting a fire," Ray said sternly, "we're in a drought."

"Who told you that?"

"It's all over the news!" Ray wrangled his anger back under control. If he squinted, he could see the ragged line of mountains in the distance, the sky beyond their shadowy peaks softening to the cool yellow of fresh custard. Dusk had arrived, and because he'd failed to think any of this through, he'd be riding home in the dark, at precisely the time when most predators came out of hiding.

The fire surged into brightness despite the remaining sunlight. Bernard said, "I won't be a bother here. I just need a place to stay for a while."

"Then come with me," Ray said, not knowing what he was going to say until the words left his mouth, "if you need a place to stay..."

Bernard paused, blinking up at his youngest son in disbelief, his eyes so ferociously blue against the muted greens of the sprawling tree cover that Ray was forced to look elsewhere.

"I can't," Bernard finally replied, his eyes shifting slightly. "I appreciate the offer, but... I can't."

"It's good to know you haven't changed. You couldn't accept help back then, and you still can't accept it now." Turning away from the fire, Ray approached the tree where Lucky was tied and gave a firm tug on his rope to free him. "Thanks for catching him."

"Ray, you know if I could, I would. If I could pretend none of this ever happened, if I could go back in time and make a different choice—"

"But you didn't make a different choice. You made this one. You chose to leave and miss everything. And I've spent the past twenty years trying to be okay with that." Ray's face was flushed from the heat and a desire to cry that didn't quite reach his eyes. "Marcus dropped out of school to raise me, and thank God he did because if he hadn't, I might've turned out like you. So, stay here as long as you want. Because as far as

I'm concerned, whether you're here or not doesn't change a thing. I meant nothing to you… and you mean nothing to me."

Ray led Lucky over to where Abby stood grazing in the shade of a tree. He bent down and picked up her reins, pulling her away from a patch of wildflowers that grew in weedy clumps around a decomposing log. Then he climbed into the saddle, his left hand wrapped tightly around Lucky's lead.

Bernard stood up. "Ray, wait—"

Ray tapped Abby's flanks with his heels.

"Walk on," he told her, and set off at a brisk pace into the woods.

*

Ray was on foot when he arrived home a few hours later, leading Abby in one hand and Lucky in the other. Their progress was slow, the light from the sickle of moon virtually non-existent. When Abby had refused to cross the river, Ray had had no choice but to ride half a mile downstream in search of a spot where the current wouldn't sweep them away, and wade into the icy alpine water himself, leading the black mare by the reins.

Soaked to the bone by sweat and the runoff from the mountains, Ray tried not to think about Bernard's campfire as he trudged along the old tractor path that paralleled the highway. He tried not to think about anything, really, but as the path widened and the sign for his family's ranch finally came into view, the conveyor belt of thoughts powered up again until his mind was humming like a factory at peak production.

His father wasn't dead. His father wasn't even missing. He was, somehow, precisely where Ray had left him: a lone figure lurking in the shadows, forever just a few steps out of reach.

Hannah saw movement in the driveway and rose from the couch to peer out the living room window. She spotted Lucky first, followed by Ray's tall, shuffling silhouette. She slipped into her shoes and opened the front door just as the trio passed the isolation paddock, causing a stir in the adjacent pasture.

"You found him," Hannah called out, prompting Ray to turn around. She jogged the last few feet and took Lucky's lead rope from his hand.

Ray winced and flexed the fingers of his left hand to loosen the joints. The skin on his palms was red and blistered, chaffed from the effort of controlling the frightened horse.

"He was in the woods," Ray explained. "I found him tied to a tree. Free rope, I guess."

He led the way into the barn. After hours of picking his way through the darkness, praying he wouldn't step on a snake or lose an eye to a low-hanging branch, the glow of the lights was almost torturous. Hannah led Lucky into an available stall at the end of the aisle, then closed the door and turned to Ray with an uncomprehending expression.

"What do you mean you found him tied to a tree?" she asked.

Ray didn't answer her immediately. For all his wool-gathering, he hadn't even begun to think of what he was supposed to tell his wife about her decidedly absent father-in-law. Instead, he loosened Abby's cinch. She sighed gratefully as the pressure on her girth eased, and Ray undid the fastenings on her bridle.

Hannah placed her hand on Ray's back, only to recoil a moment later. "God, you're soaked."

"I know."

"And you're shivering. Here—" She disappeared into the feed room. When she returned carrying the grubby green coat that had once belonged to Bernard, Ray's gaze dropped to the floor.

Hannah held open the garment, and he reluctantly slipped his arms into the sleeves.

"Better?" she asked as he wriggled his shoulders for a more comfortable fit.

Ray nodded stiffly and turned back toward Abby.

"Well, it was nice that someone caught him," she went on, taking a seat on the bench. "Although I'm not sure how they would've known who to call. Were they hikers?"

"No."

"Then who was it?"

Ray stared unseeingly at Abby's left rein, which he'd left on the floor in a loop of reddish-brown leather. How could it be that a horse could remain in one place better than a grown man with a family? he wondered. And when the wondering got him nowhere, he finally found the words to tell Hannah the truth.

He looked over his shoulder at her. "It was my dad."

"Your dad?" Hannah furrowed her brows, thinking she'd misheard.

Ray faced her. His cheeks were pale and his eyes sunken, like all the life had been sucked out of him with a straw. "I found him, Hannah. He's alive."

Her eyes widened as she stood up. "He's alive?"

"He recognized me. He lost his job and he's been living in a tent in the woods for God knows how long. All this time I thought maybe he'd died or changed his identity, but no—he's turned into a squatter. A filthy, deranged mountain man."

Hannah blinked several times, but she couldn't even begin to summon such an image in her mind. Ray had been only eight years old when Bernard had left, and the few pictures of him that Laney kept were at least twenty years out of date. So instead, she focused on the man before her, his face handsome but defeated, wearing a coat patched with duct tape around the elbows.

"Are you okay?" she asked. "This must be a lot to process."

"I'm not sure. I just walked over two hours in the dark and I'm cold and in pain. I'm too spent to even begin processing everything."

Hannah nodded, feeling almost relieved that his physical discomfort temporarily trumped his emotional unrest.

Ray removed Abby's saddle and set it on its wooden stand. Small eddies of steam wafted up from her damp black coat, filling the air with the distinct fetor of sweat and soggy wool. He spread a cooler over her back: the thin sheet was designed to retain body heat while wicking away excess moisture, ensuring her muscles wouldn't seize before her body temperature stabilized. This, like so many other things, Ray had learned from Bernard. There was no escaping this man, no way to deny their connection whenever he was around a horse.

He walked over to the bench and sat down with his back pressed against the wall.

Ray gazed down at his lap. "I offered for him to stay with us. I wasn't even planning on being that generous. It just… came out."

"Why would you do that—especially now, when we're trying to start a family?"

"Because he's my dad, Hannah. If it were your dad out there, you'd do the same."

"Ray, that man out there broke your heart. And after twenty years you're finally making peace with it… I know how hard it is to see him this way, but you can't help everybody. You have to accept that—"

"How?" He stood, looking down at her with bloodshot eyes. "How can I accept that I wasn't good enough for him? You had a dad growing up—I didn't. And I've always felt like a part of me is missing."

She bit her lip. Eventually, Ray sat back down and buried his head in his hands, his breathing echoing loudly in the quiet of their barn.

"So, what do you want to do?" Hannah asked at length.

Ray lifted his gaze and let it rest somewhere around her knees. "I don't know. But I think maybe we shouldn't tell Marc. Not yet."

Hannah nodded her agreement. "What about Victor and Addy?"

"That might be okay. They won't tell the whole town, at least." Ray sat up and almost immediately began to shiver. His waterlogged jeans and his soaked boots and his sweaty, rumpled shirt had only become more apparent under the coat, like he was dressed in a suit made of lead.

After leading Abby to her stall, Hannah returned to where Ray was sitting, pulled him to his feet, and said, "Come on. You need to get out of those wet clothes before you get sick."

They trekked up the driveway and into the house. By the time they made it upstairs, Ray was dizzy from exhaustion and the stress of the day's events. He was well beyond the ability to form coherent thoughts— most of what came to him were images of Bernard settling in next to the fire, his blue eyes blazing through the column of smoke. What if he'd insisted? Ray caught himself thinking. What if Bernard had meant to say yes instead of no? *What if I went back?*

Hannah twisted the knobs in the shower and let the spray of hot water fill the bathroom with steam. In the early days of their marriage, this space had been a source of unexpected intimacy: on chilly winter mornings, it became an extension of their bed, a place where their damp bodies met in a sleepy embrace. But then the newness of marriage had worn off, they'd stopped showering together, and mornings had become mundane once again.

She turned to look at Ray, holding onto the edge of the sink with one hand. A combination of exhaustion and emotional upheaval had caused his skin to turn grey beneath the thorny stubble on his cheeks. Hannah approached him and cupped her hands around his face.

"You're a good man, Ray Fisher," she whispered, brushing her thumb along the ridge of his cheekbone. "And you did a good thing, even if it didn't have the outcome you were hoping for."

She undid each of the buttons on his shirt and pushed the wet fabric back off his shoulders. Underneath it, his skin was ice-cold and clammy.

Ray reached his free arm around her waist and pulled her against his partially-undressed body as the steam erased them from the mirror. Her head fit perfectly into the groove under his chin, allowing him to feel every breath entering and leaving her lungs.

"Thank you for taking care of me," he whispered.

"Of course. I'll always take care of you." As Hannah drew back, her hands moved to the button on his jeans, popped it free, and slid down the zipper. "You should get in before you get a chill."

Ray nodded absently and lowered his jeans, inviting a draft to cross his thighs. He tossed his pants and underwear into the pile of dirty clothes on the floor, then slid back the curtain and stepped into the warmth of the shower, his preoccupations temporarily melting away as the hot water stripped the dirt and sweat from his body. Today had been a rollercoaster: he was used to the uncertainty of running a commercial ranch, but each year brought new challenges. Bernard's return, while shocking in its own right, was just one more storm brewing on the horizon. Tomorrow would bring clear skies and a clearer mind; Ray would know what to do in the morning, once he'd had a chance to sleep and digest everything he'd learned tonight.

"This goes without saying, but we can't tell Jim and Laney either," Ray said as he worked the soap into a lather on his skin, "especially Laney."

"I know, but it's only a matter of time before she finds out."

"Then I want to be the one to tell her. I just have to figure out what to say."

Hannah collected the soiled clothes from the floor, then reached for the door and left Ray to his shower.

Eleven

Ray felt Hannah's breathing on the side of his face. She'd somehow managed to wriggle over to his half of the bed, leaving him with nothing but a narrow strip of space at the edge of the mattress. Not that he really needed it: he hadn't slept all night, and now, on the doorstep of dawn, he felt more awake than ever.

He noted the softness of her features in the pale light. She clearly hadn't made a harrowing discovery in the woods the day before, or walked several miles with a horse in each hand. None of this was her fault, of course, but lying next to her felt painful in a way it never had before, and not just because of how he was forced to position himself so he wouldn't fall out of bed.

In less than twenty-four hours, Ray's entire outlook had changed. He didn't have to be the object of anyone's pity anymore: he had a father (albeit a terrible one) and, moreover, he knew where he was. All those questions about himself that he could never answer in his teens reverberated with an irrepressible urgency deep inside of him. In the light of day, he didn't see his father as a filthy, deranged mountain man, but as someone whose travels lent unique insight into Ray's past. Whoever Bernard was, and wherever he'd been in the two decades since he'd disappeared, Ray sensed a new pattern emerging in the shifting kaleidoscope of his life.

Ray lifted his head from the pillow. Very slowly, he slid his right leg out from under Hannah's knee and extricated himself from the sheets. As he rose to a sitting position, Hannah stirred and turned onto her back. She sank back into a peaceful sleep as Ray crossed to the door, opened it, and slipped out into the hallway.

*

Hannah had slept in—sort of. The clock on the nightstand read 6:15, which was late by working ranch standards, and the sun was already intruding on the room through the crack in the curtain. As she slid her left hand across the mattress, she found the wrinkled sheets cool to the touch. Ray had probably gotten up at dawn, wanting to complete morning chores before the heat of day made being outside unbearable. He'd be halfway done by the time she got down there, so instead of rushing, Hannah remained in bed, feeling the faint cramping in her lower abdomen. Disappointment flooded through her. Even though they'd sworn they wouldn't get their hopes up, she had been reasonably confident in her ability to get pregnant a second time without too much preamble. When she hadn't wanted to be a mother, her body had provided the perfect environment for a growing fetus. And now that she wanted a baby, the old rules didn't apply. It was all guesswork from here on out. *Better luck next month*, she thought.

Hannah rose, at last, at 6:45, opened the curtains, and headed to the bathroom to shower and prepare for the day. By the time she finished, Ray would be on his way back to the house for his second cup of coffee. They'd fall into their usual routine, his workday stretching well into the afternoon and evening, until he finally came inside for good sometime after dark.

At 7:10, Hannah went downstairs. The coffee maker had not been refilled. She didn't see Ray's boots by the front door. She called out to him, but her inquiry went unanswered in the empty house.

She descended the last few steps and walked over to the living room window, brushing the curtains aside. As sunlight poured onto the pinewood floors, she looked toward the barn and saw that the door was still closed. Ray normally kept it open during the day to air out the stalls, but she didn't see him anywhere—not in the paddock, doling out hay for the horses, or in the round pen, lunging a skittish yearling. He wasn't even in the isolation paddock, where Lucky was scratching his neck on the corner of the lean-to.

But his truck was gone from the driveway, and that told Hannah everything she needed to know.

*

"Wow," Victor said after Ray had told him everything that happened the day before. They were sitting on the patio in the backyard, two cups of coffee growing cold on the table between them. Victor flicked a tiny, scurrying beetle off his pajama pants and gazed out at the wall of trees shielding their house from the road, wondering what else to add.

"Yeah," Ray replied. He stretched out his fingers and wrapped them around the chair's armrests. "I hope I didn't wake the baby with my knocking earlier."

Victor waved his hand. "She sleeps like a rock." He met his brother's gaze. "Does Marc know about you finding dad?"

"No."

"That's probably for the best. You know how he can be."

"Funny thing is, I can't stand the thought of keeping this from him." Ray chuckled, scanning the treeline unseeingly. "Out of all the secrets I've kept from him over the years, this is the one that might just kill me."

Victor nodded.

"But he should know," Ray went on, "it's only right. I know he hates dad, but dad's as much a part of Marc as he is a part of you and me."

A cold wave of dread washed over the older brother. Every time Addy had gone back to Jason in high school, he'd secretly wondered if it was the last time he'd see her alive. And then Doug had come along, and Victor had worried for her safety all over again. But this—this was something else. A new kind of fear that locked onto him and wouldn't let go.

"I don't like the way you're talking," Victor admitted. "Look. I know dad leaving sucked. But you were eight years old, and I don't think you really understood what was going on at the time."

"Of course I did. I remember all those sleepovers at Jim and Laney's, and I especially remember Marc telling us that he was the man of the house now, and we had to listen to him or else."

"Right, which sounds just as ridiculous now as it did then. Marc shouldn't have had to step up the way he did—and the craziest part was, he did a better job of parenting us than Bernard did. That should tell you what a shitty dad he was, that a thirteen-year-old could take over." As the fear took root in him and grew, Victor pleaded, "You don't need him, Ray. I am begging you—do not go out there thinking you can talk Bernard into coming home."

"But if I just try—"

"No. It's not worth it."

Ray wasn't known to surrender so easily. Most days, that sort of determination was admirable, but Victor only feared for him now, and found himself fighting off the charged silence.

"Remember when Addy was seeing Doug? She believed that if she stuck around, she could fix him. Her intentions were pure but ultimately misguided, just as yours are now."

"Dad never abused me," Ray argued.

"He abused mom."

Ray's denial deepened. "No, he didn't."

"What do you think abuse is? Just hitting? It's so much more than that. Denying someone affection, leaving them to rot in bed all day—those are quieter forms of abuse, but they kill a person all the same." As Ray averted his gaze, Victor continued, "Like I said, you were eight years old. You got up on Saturday mornings and ate cereal in front of the TV while Marc and I made mom breakfast. You fell asleep in dinosaur pajamas while Marc and I stayed up listening to mom and dad fighting through the bedroom door. Near the end, right before mom killed herself, dad disappeared for two days and didn't tell anyone where he was going. Just because you don't remember any of this doesn't mean it didn't happen."

Ray shook his head. If what Victor was saying was true, then why did he have so many fond memories of Bernard? His father had taught him how to approach a fractious horse without losing his nerve, and how to gauge a cow's temperament by the way it held its head or carried its tail. He'd taken him out of his bed on countless chilly mornings to watch the sun rise over the mountains and, when it was just the two of them, allowed Ray to have a tiny sip of coffee. It had been their delicious little secret, and spending time with Bernard had made Ray feel safe, like a prized trophy in a glass display case.

Victor stood up, placed both hands on Ray's shoulders, and gave him a light shake.

"I'm trying to protect you. Please, just trust me."

Shrugging off his hands, Ray maintained, "I just want to talk to him. What could go wrong?"

"What's going on?" Adrianna asked as she appeared in the doorway.

Rather than answering her, Ray ducked toward the stairs and tromped down the steps with audible frustration. As he rounded the side of the house and disappeared, Adrianna stepped fully onto the deck and waited for Victor to provide some sort of explanation.

He rasped, "Ray found our dad living in the woods. He wants to go back and talk to him."

"Why?"

"Because he's naïve. He thinks he can reunite the family or something."

As they heard Ray's truck drive away, Adrianna exclaimed, "We have to stop him somehow, right?"

"How? He's an adult. He can do whatever he wants."

"This is ridiculous. He's putting himself in danger for a man who…" She trailed off as Victor's somber expression settled on her. Her voice bristled defensively. "There's no comparison between this and what happened with me and Doug. I was—"

"You were in love. Or at least scared of being alone."

"Still, it's not the same."

"Not exactly."

"So, let's call someone. I'll go get my phone and—"

"Addy." Victor sighed, closing his eyes. "Let him go."

She whispered, "Marc wouldn't."

"Marc's not here. Ray is either going to come to his senses, or he won't. But either way, we can't tell him what to do." Picking up the coffee mugs, Victor told her, "I should hurry. I'm already late for work."

Twelve

Hannah had spent most of the morning floating in and out of sleep, her mind and body finally feeling the effects of last night's developments. She woke up fully when she heard the sound of Ray's truck pulling in, only instead of coming inside, he headed down to the barn. Maybe now everything would be okay, Hannah hoped as she trekked down the laneway in search of her husband. Ray's biggest question had finally been answered (and he'd found Lucky, which was the primary reason for his journey into the high country). At last, they could move on, create the family he'd never had, and live happily among the pines and the mountain vistas, just like they'd always talked about.

When she stepped into the shade of the barn, she found Ray saddling Jack, his sorrel gelding. A pair of leather saddle bags, normally reserved for long-distance trips, hung on either side of the horse's flanks. Hannah proceeded cautiously down the aisle as Ray added another item to the off-side saddle bag before turning and reaching for the bridle.

"Going somewhere?" Hannah asked, deliberately keeping her tone light.

He lifted the headstall off the hook and took a couple of steps toward her.

"I'm going to go look for my dad. I've thought about this a lot, and I want him to be a part of our life."

She blinked a couple of times. "I'm sorry, what?"

"I know it seems crazy—"

"It *is* crazy. You said so yourself last night—he's a filthy, deranged mountain man. And you want to bring him *here*, where we plan to raise children?"

Ray held up his hands. "He's my dad, Hannah. I know you understand how much this means to me to finally know him."

Hannah lowered her chin and stared at one of the buttons on his shirt. When she'd wanted to postpone their wedding to get her degree, he'd let her go off to Vancouver knowing she'd never have closure without checking that dream off her bucket list. There could be no marriage without trust, and if this was what Ray thought he needed to feel whole, then she was willing to set her reservations aside.

"Okay," she whispered. "But promise me—"

"I'll be careful." Ray smiled. He wrapped his arms around her until she felt the steady, metronomic rhythm of his heart in the pit of her stomach. "Thank you."

As he slid the bridle over the sorrel's face, Hannah walked over to the chalkboard and reviewed the morning's unfinished tasks. Back in Canada, when she still worked at *Ruth's*, she'd looked forward to the days when the delivery truck came to drop off bags of fertilizer and potting soil. Something in the act of performing physical labour made even the most troubling thoughts temporarily disappear—what the mind created, the body overcame. She picked up the stub of white chalk and added a couple more items to the bottom of the list at the same time that Ray was tightening Jack's cinch. When they were both finished, they turned and looked at each other in silent understanding.

"I should be home before dark," he said, lowering the stirrup into position.

"Do you have enough water? It's supposed to be really hot today."

"I have water. I plan on refilling it at the river."

Ray picked up the reins and led Jack outside. The sun hadn't quite reached its zenith, but it was getting there, and Hannah could already feel the effects of its stunning indifference on the exposed skin of her face and arms. Ray placed his left foot in the stirrup and swung his right leg over Jack's back, settling into the leather seat with a faint creak.

He pushed his hat down onto his head, shading all but the very tip of his chin. "Try not to worry too much, okay?"

"Okay," Hannah replied.

The saddle shifted sideways as Ray leaned down to kiss her.

"I love you," he said. Then he straightened, arranged the reins in his hand, and set off in search of Bernard.

*

Ray had ridden this route countless times in his life. From the point where the trail connected to the backside of the north pasture, it serpentined in a continuous upward fashion, gaining more than a thousand feet in just under a mile. He'd seen hikers cut through here on several occasions, small bells intended to deter bears jingling on the frames of their enormous backpacks. Most of the time, if they saw Ray coming toward them on horseback, they gave him a berth. But today, the trail was deserted. No ringing of bells or marching of feet disturbed the chorus of birdcall that blanketed the woods. If it weren't for the heat, Ray might've even enjoyed himself.

Eventually, the trail evened out when it met up with the valley where Ray's team had camped out with the herd during the cattle drive. It was early afternoon, and the blue sky was dabbed with white clouds. Without any wind to propel them, they hovered above the rocky peaks like cartoon thought bubbles. Surely, if a mountain could have an opinion on anything, it would consider Ray's excursion to be nothing more than a fool's errand. Bernard had never been particularly forthcoming even when he was a part of Ray's life (Laney had once joked that he talked to horses more than he talked to people). What could he tell Ray now that he didn't already know?

He rode through the field at a jog, imagining different versions of this long-awaited conversation. In one, Bernard was telling him about Ray's mother—how they'd met and who she'd been before her depression wrung her out. In another, he was telling Ray about his plans to head south. Maybe he'd go to Texas, find a job on a ranch somewhere the way so many travellers did. Or perhaps he'd wander down to Louisiana and fall in love with one of the locals from the French Quarter. Both possibilities disgusted Ray. What was wrong with Colorado? What was wrong with staying right here, in the land their ancestors had claimed and cultivated generations ago? Sure, the winters could be brutal, but was that fact any worse than running away from something he knew he could never escape? Whether he was the hero or the villain didn't make much difference at this point: Bernard was still a part of Ray's story, as permanent as the Rockies piercing the sky in every direction.

Fueled by his rage, Ray cut off the main trail and headed toward the screen of pines in the distance. The river lay just ahead on the left; he could hear its thunderous torrent over Jack's laboured breathing. If he continued in this direction, Ray knew he'd locate Bernard's campsite by sundown. Then he'd have no choice but to talk to Ray—or risk any number of potentially life-threatening injuries trying to run off into the woods at night.

Ray ducked beneath a low hanging branch, feeling the feathery caress of a white pine against his cheek. As they ventured deeper into the wilderness, the sorrel gelding swung his head from side to side, his nostrils flaring bright pink with each breath. At least it was somewhat cooler in the forest, although navigating the densely clustered trees in his wide leather saddle was exactly the kind of problem Ray didn't need right now. But if he continued on his current trajectory, the woods would eventually open up to reveal Bernard's hideout. Then the real work would begin—for both of them.

Suddenly, Jack stopped. The drumming of his nine-pound heart reverberated through the saddle into Ray's backside. He stared between the tips of Jack's ears and spotted nothing but prickly red tree trunks as far as the eye could see.

"What is it? A chipmunk, right?" He dug his heels into Jack's sides. "Walk on."

Jack snorted and took an obvious step back.

Ray squeezed the horse's flanks harder. "Walk on."

Again, Jack refused. He made a low, fretful whinnying noise as he lowered his head to reverse course on the narrow trail.

Ray gave the sorrel a firm kick with both legs, only to end up two steps closer to the tree they'd just passed under. Waxy green needles swarmed around them, stabbing Ray all over the side of his face and the back of his neck. He batted the branches away from his eyes and jerked the reins sideways, untangling Jack and himself from the net of branches.

"What's wrong with you? I said walk on." He put more power into his next kick. Surprised by his aggression, Jack threw back his head, nearly clipping Ray in the nose.

"Walk on!" Ray cracked his right rein against Jack's hide.

The sorrel retaliated with another frantic shuffle.

Sweaty and frustrated, Ray turned his horse in a tight circle to get his feet moving again. For a second, it seemed to work, but once he was facing the path again, surrounded on all sides by prickly red trunks with thick, conical bows, Jack planted his hooves in the bed of pine needles and rounded his neck, refusing to go any farther.

Ray lifted the rein again. As it came down on Jack's rump, the gelding lifted both front feet off the ground, causing Ray to fall backward out of the saddle. He landed hard on the forest floor, his body crumpling on impact. Before he knew it, he was rolling in an uncontrolled fashion down the side of a ravine littered with rocks, trees, and jagged stumps.

The fall was eternal. At first, it felt as if he were merely sliding on the slick layer of needles. His hands grabbed fruitlessly at clumps of moss and dirt. Over and over he rolled, the world spinning violently around him in a blur of black and green. If there was some way to stop himself from slamming into every lump of rock and gnarled tree root, Ray didn't know it. All he knew was that he was going down, very far down, and very quickly. A hint of blue sky streaked through his field of view as he tumbled another ten feet toward his unintended destination.

In those harrowing moments, time lost all meaning. He could've been falling for twenty seconds or an hour—he didn't honestly know. But then somehow he leveled out, the forest skidded into focus, and Ray ended up flat on his back in a place he didn't recognize.

The trees rose like the bars of a cage all around him, their canopies whispering high in the air above his head. His eyes were open, but his vision was blurry. *Breathe*, he ordered himself.

Ray took a sudden, sharp breath and nearly blacked out from the pain.

He put a hand to his ribs, where a wildfire ache was spreading through his bones. He lay perfectly still, gasping for air as he stared up at the clouds. They drifted aimlessly across the sky, light as air and totally unencumbered. Not like him: everything hurt, like his body was entombed in hot lead.

One spot in particular was pulsing with psychedelic intensity. Ray struggled to sit up on his elbows and tracked the strobe of his pain down his right leg.

He took one look at his calf, then rolled onto his side and proceeded to puke his guts out.

Thirteen

So, this was how it ended: at the bottom of a ravine in the middle of nowhere, with a laceration on his forehead and a broken tree branch buried in his leg. Of all the possible endings to his life, Ray had dared to believe he was going to go quietly in his bed when he was old and grey. But this conclusion seemed more fitting. More merciful, too, since Hannah wouldn't have to face the pain of watching all his memories disappear as his body broke down. Okay, he could accept this. He was going to die alone in the woods. He'd had a good run. Marcus would say some nice things at his funeral. Everything would be all right.

Except that—no, this wasn't how it ended. He was hurt, and hurt badly, but he was still breathing. He wasn't going to die down here and leave Hannah wondering what had happened to him for the rest of her life. That was cruel.

Ray lay very still for a moment, trying to decide what to do. He turned his head slightly and stared at the branch that had penetrated his lower leg. A stain the colour of Bordeaux encircled the wooden shank. This was bad. Really, really bad. If he tried to remove it himself, he risked bleeding to death. But what was the alternative? No one was coming to his rescue, and he couldn't move his leg without feeling as if someone had taken a cheese grater to bare skin.

Say he removed the branch... Ray mulled over this thought as his eyes drifted upward again, settling on the wink of blue sky overhead. If he could control the bleeding, if he could somehow stabilize the wound and climb to his feet, maybe it would be okay. It was a long shot, but if he could get back to the main trail, maybe he'd encounter day hikers. One of them had to have a satellite phone. Or first aid training. Preferably both.

Ray fingered the slick red line on his temple and wiped the blood off on his shirt. Every time he blinked, the world faded in and out of focus. A monstrous headache was brewing behind his eyes, signaling the onset of a concussion. Never mind the branch—how long would he last out here with a head injury and no water? Hannah had warned him about the heat, and Ray could feel it rising despite the tree cover. Hot, dry air mixed with unremitting sunshine was a recipe for severe dehydration: the tourists were warned about it, and the locals took no chances. *Welcome to Colorado—the state that wants to kill you!* That had been the unofficial slogan for years around here, and Ray had laughed along with everyone else whenever some hiker collapsed from elevation sickness or a family in a minivan got stuck on an ATV trail.

Well, he wasn't laughing now, was he?

Ray surveyed his surroundings, trying to find something he could use to pull himself into a sitting position. High above him he could see the top of the ravine, with its dark crown of trees waving in the wind. Scraggly pines with clumps of fragrant green needles grew out of the narrow crevices that lined the slope. Ray had landed on a bed of dirt and dead leaves on a patch of rock where the mountain flattened out for a few feet before dropping off again. Past that point, a shallow black creek carved a shining path through the older trees that made up the majority of the forest.

Ray spotted a juvenile pine and dragged himself close enough to wrap his hands around the slender trunk. From there, he maneuvered himself into a sitting position so he could examine the broken branch more closely. It didn't appear to have gone all the way through his leg, but it had penetrated deeply enough to make every touch feel like a red-hot branding iron against his skin. Ray clenched his teeth, biting back the sour taste of bile filling his mouth. Looking at it now, it was clear he had only one choice: if he couldn't tolerate the pressure of his fingers on his calf, how did he expect to climb out of this ravine by nightfall?

The branch had to come out. One way or another.

Blood-tinged sweat dripped into his eyes. Ray wiped away the mess on his brow, wrapped his fingers around the exposed end of the branch, and tugged. The branch glided backwards, pulling his skin with it.

He let go, shaking his hand as if he'd been burned. Slow and steady would simply prolong his agony. The extraction would have to be quick, like ripping off a band-aid.

Ray fumbled for his belt buckle. Yanking the strip of leather through the loops, he guided it toward his mouth, bit down on the pliable material, and shut his eyes.

He grasped the branch in his fist and pulled.

Teeth marks formed in the belt. Less than a minute later, the branch slid out covered in blood. His hands were shaking as it fell to the ground.

Ray removed the belt from between his teeth and looped it around his leg above his right knee. Threading it through the buckle, he pulled the belt as tightly as he could, fashioning a tourniquet out of the strip of leather. The seepage from his wound had coloured his pant leg a deep plum-red. Ray allowed himself a minute to catch his breath—just sixty seconds of rest, then he'd conquer the ravine.

He swallowed. The inside of his mouth felt sticky, and for the first time since abandoning the trail, he became aware of the depths of his thirst. He'd had a full bottle of water in his saddle bag when he left—that amount had dropped to half within the first thirty minutes of leaving the ranch. He'd planned to stop at the river, drink to his fill on the bank, and top up his bottle for the next leg of his journey. But none of that was possible now, though he could hear what sounded like a dripping faucet somewhere nearby. Or was it just his head playing tricks on him?

Ray slowly maneuvered onto all fours, groaning in pain with each sluggish movement. Using the same tree from earlier to pull himself up, he rose unsteadily onto his feet, then stood teetering for a moment until the world stopped spinning in circles.

Ray looked straight up to the top of the ravine. The slope had to be at least a hundred feet long, the path his body had taken in the fall faintly reflected in the displaced leaves and pine needles. There were several trees growing out of the side of the hill, including a handful of saplings he could employ as handholds if necessary.

He took one step on his right leg, and his knee buckled like a table in a wrestling match. The belt had prevented profuse blood loss, yes, but it had also put a pin in his strength.

Moving on hands and knees, Ray wrapped his hands around a stony protuberance and pulled himself up the embankment. With each inch he advanced, more soil came loose and rolled past him to the bottom of the gorge. Ray struggled on his abdomen to cover six feet, using his feet to propel his lower body over the debris in his path. Horribly inefficient, this mode of travel, but at least he was finally moving.

His hand slipped, missing the next handhold, and he skidded backward down the slope. His right knee smashed into a tree root and he cried out in pain, the belt coming loose as he instinctively twisted his body sideways and slid all the way down to where he'd started.

In a fit of anger, Ray grabbed the belt and flung it into the woods. He'd been stupid to come out here alone to look for a man who wanted nothing to do with him. And now he had no water in the middle of a drought, and his leg was bleeding like some God-sent flood all over his boot and the forest floor.

Rationality returned to him, albeit not without considerable willpower. *Jesus Christ, Ray, get it together.* Now wasn't the time for a meltdown.

He had to staunch the bleeding again, somehow. Ray rummaged through his pockets, certain these were the jeans he'd worn on the cattle drive. He'd stuffed his bandana in here somewhere, thankful Micah respected him enough to let him ride ahead of the herd instead of behind it.

He found the blue and white paisley fabric, along with his phone. The screen was cracked, but still functional. Hope welled up inside him.

Ray set the device on the ground and shook out the bandana. It was stiff with dirt and sweat, but with enough flicking he was able to lay it flat on his lap. From there, he folded a two-inch strip up from the bottom until he had a length of cloth about ten inches long and two inches wide. He leaned forward and wrapped the bandana around the wound, concealing the tattered hole in his jeans from view. He fastened a tight knot in the fabric, reintroducing some much-needed pressure to his lower limb, then leaned back against the tree and tried to relax.

As his panic ebbed, Ray picked up his phone. He'd call Hannah first, explain what had happened, and tell her not to worry. Even though it made no difference to his physical injuries, the sound of her voice would soothe him long enough to come up with a plan for surviving the next few hours, or however long it took for help to arrive. He selected her name from the call log and brought the device up to his ear, only for the call to drop before it had connected.

Ray lowered the phone and glanced at the upper left-hand corner of the screen. *No service.*

"Come on," he muttered, and tried Hannah's number again, without success.

He tried 9-1-1 and was relieved when the call seemed to connect, but a moment later the line went dead.

He'd keep trying until he got through to someone, or until his battery ran out. But the one thing he absolutely was *not* going to do was start crying like a baby.

"Come on," Ray said in a choked voice, and raised the phone above his head. He panned the device from side to side, but the results were the same. No service.

If he could just get to the top of the ravine, then maybe he'd get a bar or two. Who was he kidding? He'd already tried that and failed. He'd failed so terribly that his belt was now lying twenty feet away from him, and he'd been forced to dress his wound in a piece of cloth meant for nothing more than keeping the dust out of his nose.

The reality of his situation was finally starting to sink in. He was trapped in a ravine in the middle of the woods in a remote area of their property with no water, a banged-up leg, and a bleeding head. His phone had no service, Hannah didn't know where to look, Bernard didn't know he was looking for him, and there were probably no day hikers coming to his rescue any time soon.

The reality was, he was probably going to die out here.

Ray wasn't sure if it was possible to be more uncomfortable than he already was. Propped up against the nearest sturdy tree, with the nubs of its bark digging into his back, he stretched out his left leg and reminded himself that dawn was only a few hours away. His head was still pounding and his tongue felt like sandpaper. If he squinted, Ray could make out the creek bed past the lip of his perch. The heat had evaporated most of the water, but the loamy fragrance told him there was some moisture in the soil, or maybe a muddy little pool he could drink from nearby.

He leaned sideways, wincing at the pain in his right leg as he pinned his weight on his knee. Stiff, yellow needles pricked his palms as he placed his hands on the cool rock and advanced precariously toward the water source. The woods were pitch-black in every direction: even the most experienced search and rescue team would be hard-pressed to traverse the wilderness at this hour, and his thirst couldn't wait.

Ray had barely made it five feet from the tree when a sharp object pierced the flesh of his thumb. He yanked his hand back to find fresh blood beading up on his skin.

His gaze ventured back to the creek. There was an eight-foot drop between him and the ground that he would've hesitated to attempt even if he wasn't injured. With his head wound, battered ribs, bound leg, and bloody thumb, there was no way he'd make it down safely. He'd have to wait for rescue and tolerate the dryness in his mouth just a little longer.

Frustrated and resigned, Ray scooted back to the tree and tipped his head against the trunk. So much for being home before dark. So much for thinking he could do anything other than make an already bad situation worse. He stuck his thumb in his mouth, tasting blood, dirt, and the sour remnants of his own sweat.

He'd never been so thirsty in his entire life, but just having something in his mouth seemed to bring some much-needed relief. It gave him an idea.

Ray reached his hand up, plucking a few grey needles off the branch bobbing above his head. He'd spent enough time in the great outdoors to know a bit about foraging, and he seemed to recall that, with few exceptions, the spiny leaves of most coniferous trees posed no threat to human health. He sniffed the resinous needles in his fingers, then placed them in his mouth and chewed slowly, releasing their citrusy taste. It wasn't much, but he'd take anything he could get at this point.

Hannah had to have been worried sick by now. Ray wondered if she was waiting up for him. He pictured himself stumbling into the house, his clothes filthy and torn, dried blood crusted on the side of his face, and his leg looking like a horror movie prop. She'd take him upstairs and run the shower as she undressed him, and it would be like nothing had changed.

But things had changed between them. He'd felt it on the drive home from Alpine Terrace, when she'd dared to think of anything other than Laney. While Hannah had always had her sights set on the future, he'd been hopelessly wrapped up in the past—complicated grief masquerading as tradition and nostalgia. And look at where all that pining had gotten him—trapped in the middle of the woods in the dead of night, chewing a mouthful of pine needles so his thirst wouldn't drive him insane.

Ray took out his phone. Might as well examine his leg, since he clearly wasn't going anywhere.

He shone the flashlight on his wound. The bandana had turned almost totally black with dried blood, with faint glimpses of the paisley pattern visible in the folds of fabric. Despite the ongoing pain, it didn't appear that any fresh blood was leaking through. Ray carefully lifted one edge of his makeshift bandage. As the sticky material peeled away, he saw the wound underneath as nothing but a hole fringed with black clots. Blood, blood, and more blood.

A branch snapped somewhere on Ray's right. His head whipped in that direction, but when he shone his phone's flashlight on the trees, he saw nothing unusual. He panned the light over the slender grey trunks, shuddering at their resemblance to old, faceless ghosts. The blackness was deep and endless between them, and filled with faint crackling noises high and low.

Ray lowered his phone. *Get a grip!* he told himself. He was a grown man, and grown men weren't afraid of the dark.

He glanced at his battery and switched off his flashlight. He didn't know how much longer he'd be stuck down here, after all. Slipping his phone back into his pocket, Ray settled against the tree, ripped off another bunch of pine needles, and chewed the flavour out of them while he waited for help to arrive.

Fourteen

By five o'clock the following morning, several of Ray's neighbours had gathered in the kitchen to hash out a plan for finding him. Russell had jumped into action the moment Hannah told him about Ray's disappearance. Darrel had come equipped with a fleet of ATVs, as well as a pair of long-range radios and detailed topographical maps of the area around the ranch. Micah, as always, would be leading the expedition.

"So, here's what I'm proposing," Darrel said, spreading one of the maps flat on the table. "We split up. We know that Ray was headed for the river, so that's our landmark. Russ and I will ride upstream. Micah, you and Victor will go downstream toward the sandbar."

"I really think we'd be better off doing this on horseback," Micah protested, "a horse is more nimble than one of your quads. And there's a decent chance Ray might've crossed the river, rather than just going downstream."

"The quads are faster. Every second counts."

"I agree with Darrel," Hannah said. As the focus shifted to her, she added, "Ray's lost in the woods with nothing but the clothes he was wearing. Now's not the time to tire out the horses."

Russ nodded his agreement, Darrel went back to tracing the lines on the page, and Micah merely stared at her, his bushy white eyebrows furrowing at her audacity.

"And what are you planning to do, sweetheart, while we're out looking for your husband?" he drawled.

"I'll be trying to get the word out. Someone had to have seen him," Hannah reasoned. "It's a lot of land to cover. Are you sure you're going to be okay?" she asked Darrel.

"I think it's a good start. If I know Ray, he'd stay out in the open— better visibility that way."

Russ recalled, "He was pretty concerned about the dead calf we found on the cattle drive. I doubt he'd have ventured too deep into the woods if he thought there was a cougar in the area."

Hannah considered this logic. If only Ray were the kind of person who took these types of risks into account, then maybe they could count on him sticking to the beaten path. But the way he'd described Bernard's campsite had made it seem like his father didn't want to be found, which made sense seeing as he was technically trespassing. Realistically, Ray could have been anywhere—and on five thousand acres, locating him would be like trying to find a needle in a haystack.

Darrel gathered up the maps and said, "We're wasting time. The sooner we head out, the better our chances of finding Ray alive."

Hannah felt like she'd been punched in the gut. As the men exchanged a few final words, Adrianna wrapped her arm around Hannah's shoulders.

"It's going to be okay," Adrianna whispered. "We know Ray. He's a fighter."

"I know." Hannah turned to Victor. "I'm glad you're going with them. I'd go too, if Micah let me."

"It's better if you don't. ATVs are dangerous if you don't know how to handle them." Victor waited until Micah, Russ, and Darrel had filed outside before putting a voice to the thought that had been swirling around inside his head ever since Hannah called them to say Ray had not come home. "Have you called Marc?"

"No. Should I?"

"It might not be a bad idea. Keep him in the loop, you know."

"Maybe we should wait for the guys to come back," Hannah said, wanting to delay the inevitable. "With any luck, Ray might be close by. Do you really want to make Marc worry for nothing?"

Victor pulled on the black-and-lime-green ATV gloves and spread his arms. "It's his little brother. He's going to worry one way or the other."

"Victor's right." Adrianna met Hannah's fretful gaze. "He's going to find out eventually. He won't be upset with you for telling him the truth."

"I wouldn't go that far. His hatred for Bernard runs deep. Maybe you can just leave that part out for now—tell him Ray was checking on something and got thrown from his horse. It's believable enough," Victor said.

Micah stuck his head back in the house and rumbled, "Are you coming, or what?"

"Coming." Victor turned back to Adrianna. "I'll see you soon."

Within moments, the usual early-morning silence was lost to the quartet of off-roaders powering to life. Micah rode up front, straddling the black seat of his wasp-yellow four-by-four in a way that wouldn't aggravate his already griping hip. Russell purred up behind him, raising his voice to be heard over the noise. After getting a quick refresher on gear shifting from Darrel, Victor mounted the bulky blue quad and joined the mountain-bound queue. They fell into formation somewhere near the paddock gate, prompting a few of the horses to look up from their grazing.

As the sputter of their engines faded, Adrianna turned away from the window to find Hannah staring at her phone, too paralyzed with trepidation to call Marcus and tell him some watered-down version of the truth.

"How about this—I'll call Marc, and you go get some sleep," Adrianna suggested.

"Thanks, but I don't think I'll be able to sleep until Ray's found."

"That could take hours. Once Ray comes home, he's going to need you to be at your best in order to take care of him." Adrianna smiled and set Hannah's phone in the corner of the counter, where she wouldn't be tempted to Google the survival rate for people missing in the woods. "I'll wake you the moment I hear anything," she promised.

Hannah crossed to the stairs. The bed was still made up when she stepped into the room and shut the door. She glanced at Ray's belongings on the dresser, which seemed to glow as sunlight filtered through the trees outside the window. Hannah ran her fingers over the knobs on the drawers, recalling her very first exploration of this space: she and Ray had only been dating for a year, and there was so much they hadn't known about each other. Nine years later, Hannah knew him better than most people ever would, his life like a book she'd read and reread countless times. But the past twenty-four hours had been the start of a new chapter, and so far, she didn't like where the story was headed.

Hannah crawled into bed, curling up on top of the familiar-smelling quilt. She'd been planning on using these private moments to plan the next stage of their search, but fell asleep the instant her head hit the pillow.

Ray's tree had made an awful bed, but somehow, he'd managed to fall asleep. As the trilling of birds heralded a new day, he rubbed the stiffness out of his neck and gazed blearily at his surroundings. Last night, he was sure something had been stalking him, the only evidence of its existence being the snapping of twigs as it moved invisibly through the forest. Whatever it was, it seemed to prefer the cover of dark. Now, with the sun coming up, Ray was about to face an entirely new threat: dehydration.

He shifted uncomfortably, a small groan slipping past his lips. Yesterday he'd been thirsty, but his thirst had been overshadowed by the pain of his injuries and a blinding sense of panic that he'd be trapped in the woods overnight. His head was still beating like a drum this morning, but he could live with that. His leg was another matter: swollen and sticky with dried blood, it didn't look capable of bearing weight. If he could fashion a crutch out of a sturdy branch, he might be able to hobble out of here. The movement would promote circulation, and hopefully take away some of the numbness that had resulted from spending the night sleeping on a cold slab of rock in the middle of the woods.

Ray awkwardly dragged his leg into the sunny patch on his perch before leaning his head back against the tree and letting out a breath. His teeth were sticky with pine sap: turns out, eating the needles was more trouble than it was worth, and he couldn't stomach the idea of scarfing down another handful despite the nauseating jabs of hunger.

He needed water desperately. He hadn't urinated since yesterday afternoon and felt no urge to do so now. Still, there was hope: earlier, he'd heard a faint rumble that was definitely thunder, which meant there'd soon be rain. Unless he was hallucinating. Ray rubbed the goose egg on his head and decided he'd had enough of sitting here. He was a cowboy, for God's sake—a born-and-bred, red-blooded American who'd grown up eating dirt from all the falls he'd taken trying to ride his father's half-broke horses. And if there was one thing he'd learned, it was to get up, wipe the tears off his face, and get back on the damn horse.

Ray leaned sideways, his face contorting in pain. His left leg was stiff, but movable. His right leg, which had been speared by the branch, quivered as he attempted to flex the knee. Perhaps he'd tied the bandana too tight—not that he was going to risk bleeding to death by loosening it.

His body was shaking as he crawled toward the base of the slope, watching where he placed his hands this time. After a few feet, Ray reached for the nearest tree root and made his first real attempt at being upright since he'd fallen off Jack the day before.

To his surprise, his right leg seemed to tolerate the change in position. He'd broken this ankle years ago trying to ride one of Mickey's rejects. At the time, he'd been concerned that the fracture wouldn't heal properly, and he'd have to give up working with horses due to chronic pain. But when the cast had come off, the ankle had looked no different from before, aside from a little paler than the rest of his leg and a little foul-smelling from not being washed in six weeks. And on that day, Ray had sworn he'd never do anything as stupid as not double-checking his cinch ever again.

Ray sized up the challenge before him, mapping a path for himself through the leaflitter and fallen logs. How was he supposed to scale this? There had to be a way around. Getting to higher ground would make him more visible, and possibly allow him to use his phone to call for help. He tightened his hold on the tree root and pulled, digging the toe of his left boot into the dirt for added stability.

His ascent began in earnest. Grappling from one handhold to the next, he dragged himself over the debris until he was six feet off the ground. He'd never been much of a climber, but he'd started climbing up on Bernard's horses from the time he could walk, and it had never crossed his two-year-old mind that he couldn't.

Left foot rock, right hand tree. Like the world's most treacherous game of Twister, Ray thought. Only in this version, losing had much graver implications.

Failing to gain a toehold, his left foot slipped and pulled the rest of his body down with it.

Ray hit the ground and landed on his back. Pain exploded across his body. His headache threatened to split his skull open. And his leg—God, his leg. Ray extended a trembling hand toward it as if attempting to console a screaming baby and ended up feeling like he was going to break down crying himself.

Instead, he rolled onto his side and promptly started dry heaving. He was too dehydrated to vomit, or even spit, but his body insisted on some kind of reaction. He retched a couple more times, then crawled toward the tree and sat down at its base with his back against the trunk. It wasn't much, but it was everything he had in this moment. That, and his faith that someone would come.

Ray closed his eyes, his chest heaving in a fierce sob. But his eyes didn't shed a single tear.

Fifteen

Hannah jolted awake, startled by a clap of thunder so loud that the walls of the house shook. For several seconds, she lay in the middle of the bed with her heart in her throat, waiting for the rain to wash away the dust of the last few weeks.

Then she heard it: the whisper of an overdue downpour making its way over the mountains. It descended on the front yard in a cloak of grey, showering the old wooden barn and its metal roof in a deafening spray. Sand turned to mud within minutes. The horses that hadn't sought shelter beneath the trees stood in a drenched clump on the hill, the rain rolling off their coats in dark rivulets. Hannah watched the droplets streaking down the window, thinking of Ray. If he was somewhere in the path of the storm, then that meant he'd have water. The odds of being found alive were greater if he wasn't battling dehydration.

Hannah rose from the bed and made her way into the bathroom to freshen up. She could hear Adrianna talking to someone downstairs, the words spilling out of her in a garbled rush. Hannah quickly dried her hands on the towel and opened the door, her heart racing as she headed toward the conversation. By the time she reached the main floor, Adrianna had already hung up the phone.

"Who was that?" Hannah wondered, her footsteps creaking on the stairs.

"My mom. She's babysitting Emily."

Hannah nodded, unable to disguise her disappointment. "I see."

"Were you able to get any sleep?" Adrianna asked. She led the way to the kitchen, where a fresh pot of coffee awaited Hannah and the crew. Taking down a pair of mugs from the cupboard, Adrianna filled each of them to the top and offered the first one to Hannah, who sipped it with alacrity.

"A bit." Hannah slurped another mouthful and checked the window. "The storm woke me up."

"Hopefully the guys are okay. The last place you want to be during a thunderstorm is on a mountain."

Hannah nodded and pulled in another sip of the coffee. Wherever he was, Ray would know to hunker down and ride it out, just like the cows did.

Adrianna nursed her own drink in thought. Victor was out there too, and she was equally concerned for his safety. He had never really considered himself a rancher, despite being raised under the same roof as Ray and Marcus. But being the kind of person he was, he couldn't sit by while someone he loved was in trouble. That sort of soft-hearted determination had saved her from a life of misery with an abusive partner. With any luck, perhaps it would spell salvation for Ray as well.

"By the way, I called Marc," Adrianna began.

Hannah lowered the mug. "Was he upset?"

"He seemed more worried than upset. Anyway, he thinks we should organize a search party on horseback. I told him I'd run it past you first, but it seems like a good idea."

Hannah nodded firmly. She had just sat down at the table to make a list of supplies when the rumble of an engine interrupted her planning. She looked up and spotted the first of four pairs of headlights as its rider dipped out of sight beneath the hill. When the ATV reappeared, she abandoned her note-taking and ran outside to meet the searchers.

To her amazement, it wasn't Micah leading the pack, but Victor. His pants were caked in mud up to his knees, and dark speckles of dirt coated his helmet, goggles, and gloves. He steered his vehicle into the parking area, switched off the engine, and peeled off the various pieces of protective equipment as Hannah bounded over to him.

She opened her mouth to speak. Victor merely shook his head.

Hannah stopped short. Micah, Russell, and Darrel each arrived soaked and splattered in mud, their somber expressions revealed the moment they began to undress.

She pinned a desperate look on Micah. "Did you reach the river?"

"We did."

"And?"

The oldest member of the team dismounted his quad with an involuntary groan of pain. He left the helmet on the seat and strode toward Hannah stiffly. "We turned around."

Her eyes widened. "You turned around?"

"We had to," Victor told her softly, "the weather was changing so quickly, we had to get off the mountain before any of us got struck by lightning."

"What about Ray? What's he supposed to do to avoid lightning?" Hannah's focus zipped back to Micah. "You know, I actually had some faith that maybe *you* would find him, since you're so familiar with the backcountry. But all the sudden we get a little rain and you run straight home?"

"Don't blame Micah," Russell cut in, "we all agreed to return to the ranch. And not because we didn't want to find Ray."

"It's a basic rule of search and rescue: don't endanger the searchers," Darrel put in, his ATV sputtering rudely as he rode in a wide arc around the paddocks toward his trailer.

Hannah gazed wildly from one face to the next. She could hear Adrianna approaching from behind, walking over to Victor, and pulling him into a hug. The patter of rain on the leaves drowned out whatever murmured words she poured into his ear.

Hannah knotted her fingers in her hair. She was suddenly faint, and realized she hadn't taken a full breath since she'd stepped outside.

"Hannah?" Adrianna was directly in front of her now, her face wavering in and out of focus. "I need you to take a deep breath, okay?"

"You left him out there," Hannah seethed, her bloodshot eyes veering toward Micah. "If you can't find him, then I will."

"You're not going out there. No one else is leaving this ranch." Micah nodded to his gaggle of defeated rescuers. "From now on, we leave this one to the professionals. We get the word out. But no one, and I mean *no one*"—his gaze settled pointedly on Hannah—"goes out there alone. We're dealing with an honest to God missing person case here. Have you called the police?"

"No. I was counting on Ray coming home today, with all of you," Hannah said.

"Then you better get on that. The sooner, the better."

No one dared to challenge Micah's authority this time. The reality of Ray's disappearance was setting in faster than the chill in the air; what had previously been a blessing was now an added complication. Without adequate shelter or proper clothing, the risk of succumbing to exposure increased exponentially. He would've had the good sense to pack warm clothes in his saddle bag, but those bags were currently propped against the wall of the storage room, where Hannah had dropped them after removing Jack's tack the night before.

Everything Ray needed was right here on this ranch, which meant that he was out there with no food, water, or way to keep warm. No matter how hard Hannah tried, she couldn't seem to catch a single breath.

"He's going to die out there," she whispered.

Adrianna shook her head. "No, he's not. We're going to find him. Okay? We're going to call the police and they're going to find him."

"For what it's worth, Russ wanted to keep looking," Micah said as he walked over to them. "If you need someone to be mad at, be mad at me. I saw those storm clouds and I got a bad feeling, just like the cows do. I didn't want to risk losing more men."

"He's right," Victor agreed softly. "We all want to find Ray, but we have to do it properly. I think it's time to involve the police."

Hannah nodded, a stiffness brought on by fear and the dampness in the air rendering the rest of her body immovable. "Of course. Whatever it takes."

Ray didn't believe in miracles, but if he had, this would have been one of them.

Thunder rolled overhead, ushering in a layer of thick, grey clouds that blotted out the sky. Up until the rain started, there'd been no relief from the heat other than the patch of shade at the base of the pine tree where he was sitting. After a full day without a single drop of water, Ray was having difficulty thinking clearly, his skin was hot to the touch, and his head felt like a ten-pin bowling ball attached to his shoulders. He'd been drifting in and out of sleep for hours, only for a crack of lightning to bring him back to his senses.

The deluge commenced, delivering a week's worth of rain in the span of ten minutes. What the ground couldn't absorb it stored up in mirrorlike puddles. But the true miracle wasn't the fact that it was raining—it was in where Ray was sitting. The fall had positioned him on a shelf of rock several feet above the forest floor. And covering that patch of rock were dozens of small indentations, each one capable of collecting water.

Ray dragged himself over to the nearest depression and eagerly slurped up the shallow puddle. Sweet-tasting and a little gritty between his teeth, the water instantly filled him with relief. Thousands of warm, stinging droplets pelted his face as he moved to the next puddle and drank that too, then emptied the one beside it without a second thought. After slaking his thirst at the fifth pool, he ran a hand down the right side of his face to wash away the dried blood before rolling onto his back and opening his mouth. This rock, the rock that had nearly killed him in the fall, had just saved his life.

Still sprawled on his back at the bottom of the ravine, Ray watched as the clouds glided over the treetops, off to shower a different part of the forest. Hints of blue came into view around the edges of the sky, and soon the sunlight returned, unbothered by the storm's interruption.

His thirst was still immense. As the smile faded from Ray's face, another thought dawned on him: his clothes were wet, and at night, the woods got cold. With no way to build a fire, how was he supposed to stave off exposure? This threat, along with his existing injuries, promised another uncomfortable sleep.

He should have been found by now. He should have been on his way home to Hannah and the house where they planned to raise their kids.

Growling in pain, Ray grappled to a sitting position to inspect his leg again. The bandana was soaked through. Maybe if he removed it, he could attempt to clean the wound using the leftover rainwater, or simply sponge off the blood around his ankle.

He unwound the material cautiously, his blood rushing to the surface of his skin as the pressure on his calf eased. This would be his first real chance to get a look at the damage the branch had caused. His stomach clenched as his hand made its final turn and the bandana fell away to reveal the carnage underneath.

Ray could just make out the edge of the wound through the tear in his pantleg. He'd expected it to look worse, but he wasn't holding out hope for a smooth recovery just yet.

Picking up the bandana, he dipped it into one of the only puddles he hadn't drunk from and dabbed at his leg, trying to rub around the wound instead of across it. He cleansed a bit more dirt from the cut, then wrung the excess water out of the bandana and snapped it dry. He refolded the cloth and bound his leg again before leaning back on his hands and turning his face skyward, silently imploring some higher power to send him the help he desperately needed. Not that he was a praying man, but now that he was, quite literally, at rock bottom, it seemed that the only way to go was up, even if it was only in spirit.

The last grey puff of cloud sailed over the trees, signifying the end of the storm. Ray laid his aching body down, spread his arms flat on the rock, and let the sun wick the moisture from his clothes. With any luck, he'd be in fresh ones tonight, with Hannah sleeping peacefully beside him.

Sixteen

Word of Ray's disappearance had gotten out, and there was no stopping its spread. Hannah had learned early on that the ranching community, though often distant in geography, was closer than most families when it came to taking care of their own. Neighbours called her at all hours of the day, asking how she was doing or for more details about what Ray had been wearing or the path he might've taken. Chris and Connor Bernheimer, a father-son hunting duo who knew the wilderness better than most, agreed to comb the woods around their place for signs of human trespass like boot prints or broken branches. In a Facebook group dedicated to local cattle ranchers, members were urged to be alert for anything out of the ordinary on their land. And of course, when word reached Laney, the local church came together in a way it never had before, putting aside their differences to pray and comfort one another, or prepare meals to keep the family going through the long, daunting days that followed.

Ray had been missing for more than forty hours when the wilderness search and rescue team was brought in to scour the woods around the ranch. The patch of gravel in front of the house, where Ray's truck was still parked, had become home base for law enforcement and good Samaritans alike—a place to organize and regroup. Hannah was sitting in the living room when a knock came at the front door. She rose from the couch to answer it, leaving the laptop open on the coffee table.

A paunchy, middle-aged man stood on the porch wearing a bright red t-shirt with the words *Search and Rescue* printed in white across the front and back. He gave her a sympathetic smile and said, "You must be Hannah. I'm Mike. I'm with the local police department."

Hannah shook his hand, his warm, firm grip tightening uncomfortably around her own. "Nice to meet you. Come in." She stepped aside and motioned for him to enter.

"First off, I'd just like to say I'm sorry to hear about your husband's disappearance. I know it's not easy, not having any answers," Mike began.

"It doesn't feel real. Ray's grown up here and he knows this land so well. To think he's out there alone, and possibly hurt..." She reined in her emotions. Sometimes she felt nothing at all, and other times she felt everything at once. Grief was unpredictable like that, although she refused to call it what it was—grief for the time they'd already lost, and for what they may eventually find.

Mike nodded understandingly. "I know. It's overwhelming. But we've got a great team, and we're willing to do whatever it takes to find Ray and bring him home." He indicated the multitude of vans parked outside. "We've brought in a team of search and rescue dogs in hopes of picking up Ray's scent. Two of them will be scenting the air. The third one is a trailing dog—that means she'll be sniffing the ground, trying to figure out which way he might've walked."

"Ray was on horseback when he left. Is that going to interfere with the search?"

"Not if the dogs have a strong scent trail to follow. That's mainly why I came up here—to ask if there's anything Ray might've worn recently that still has his scent on it."

Hannah immediately thought of Ray in his favourite green sweater—the one with the frayed sleeves and the hole in the pocket, which he wore almost exclusively from late fall to early spring. Every time she did laundry, the ratty pullover was conspicuously absent. She'd been begging him to let her wash it for weeks. Now, she was glad she hadn't.

She trekked into the laundry room. If someone had punched her in the stomach, it would've hurt less than seeing the sweater sitting on top of the pile of dirty clothes in the corner. She'd finally convinced him to part with it last week, when a spray of mud had covered him from head to toe. "Happy now?" Ray had laughed as he'd pulled the sweater over his head.

Yes, she was happy now. Thrilled, in fact. If there was anything in this house that gave off Ray's smell, it was that damn sweater.

Hannah presented the green garment to Mike, who took it outside to show the dogs. Circumstances aside, it was a beautiful, clear day—warm, but not oppressively hot like the preceding weeks had been. A calm breeze blew through the trees around the house, creating a near constant white noise that Hannah had been using to block out any unsavoury thoughts. She watched as Mike crouched to the dogs' level, inviting them to congregate around the object of their search.

"The air-scent dogs have GPS collars," Mike explained as he stood up and handed back Ray's sweater. "We like to let them go off-leash when searching for missing persons. If one of them finds Ray, it'll come back and get its handler."

"What if they don't find Ray?" Hannah wondered.

"Then we'll come back tomorrow and try again."

The handlers of the air-scent dogs set off down the trail leading to the woods. The branches rustled and settled back into place, and soon Hannah lost sight of their bright red t-shirts and bulky backpacks in the endless sweep of shadowy green trees.

As the group spread out to cover more ground, Hannah prepared to return to the house, even though it was the last place she wanted to be in this moment, with so many reminders of Ray lurking in every room. If he didn't come home, could she really stand to live here without him? She hadn't wanted to ask herself this question, but it formed inside her anyway, crystalizing in an icy mass of dread that sat in the pit of her empty stomach. And the answer was no, she couldn't. The ranch may have been their home, but it was Ray's legacy. She'd see him everywhere and in everything: pressed into the soft light of early morning like a thumbprint in wet clay, swinging from the hooks in the storage room where they kept their tack, or simply as a figure in her periphery that vanished when she turned her head.

"Hi, I'm Justin. And this is Daisy."

Hannah stopped and faced the source of the voice. The man standing before her couldn't have been older than twenty-two, wearing the same red *Search and Rescue* shirt as all the others, his hair neatly trimmed around his ears. Seated at his heel was a tan and black Bloodhound in a fluorescent orange vest. The dog blinked slowly up at Hannah, then laid down on the ground and let out a heavy sigh.

"I take it she's the trailing dog?" Hannah ventured.

Justin nodded, clutching the leash that kept him tethered to his canine partner. "She's really good at her job. And she gets pretty depressed if she can't find the person she's looking for."

"I guess we have that much in common."

"Yeah. Anyway, I wanted to introduce myself. I'm not supposed to promise you that we're going to find Ray, but I can promise you that Daisy will do her best to trail him." He added, "She found a kid a few months ago that was missing for three days. That's the thing about Bloodhounds—they don't let up when they detect a scent."

"A few months ago there was snow on the ground. You expect me to believe that a small child could survive in the wilderness for seventy-two hours in sub-zero temperatures?"

"Kids are more resilient than you think. When there's no other choice, most people choose to fight."

Hannah set her jaw. Ray was a fighter, all right—she'd seen him fight for all kinds of things, but he'd never battled the elements before.

"Justin! We're on the move," Mike called from the treeline.

Justin faced her again and smiled. "It's going to be okay."

On his signal, Daisy leapt to her feet and dropped her nose to the ground. Like the two previous dogs, her sniffing led her to the barn entrance and the paddock gate—places where Ray had recently left scent pools—before luring her toward the trees. Even if Ray had been on horseback when he left, Hannah supposed it was possible that his scent was closer to the ground as well: he'd walked those trails on foot often enough, when he went out to check fences or ward off coyotes.

She walked back to the house, then closed the front door and stood alone in the foyer, all too aware of her own breathing. Hannah stared at the sweater in her hands. It was filthy and dank-smelling, like an old, flooded basement. There was also, amazingly, the faint, lingering scent of Ray's deodorant and the soap he used in the shower. Leather, hay, and bonfire smoke tied the memory of him together. He was all right here in her hands, so close and supple and warm.

Hannah turned the sweater over, slipped her arms into the sleeves, and pulled it over her head. It was too big for her, but it didn't matter. She climbed the stairs and strode down the hall to their room. Crawling into bed, Hannah turned away from the window and curled into a fetal position, letting the blade of her grief cut deep into her core.

4:12PM

Cold.

That was the word running circles in Ray's mind. He was freezing out here, with nothing but his thin, cotton shirt to guard against the chill of the forest. It seemed impossible, now, to recall the heat of the past few days, a force so oppressive it had caused the skin on his lips to peel and the bridge of his nose to blister from sunburn. The rain had been heavenly for the few minutes it lasted, but the hours that followed were filled with discomfort as his wet clothes stuck to his skin and leeched the warmth from his body. Looking back, Ray wished he'd had the presence of mind to remove his shirt and spread it on the rock to dry in the sun, but he could barely move as it was. Instead, he'd curled up at the base of his tree, wrapped his arms tightly around his body, and focused on staying awake as darkness descended. What if hikers happened to be walking by and he was asleep? How would anyone know he was down here if he couldn't call for help?

His eyelids grew heavy and slipped shut. *Just a few minutes can't hurt…* He was tired. So tired, and so, so thirsty.

When a bird alit from a nearby tree with an urgent twitter, Ray jerked his head up. Every inch of him hurt: head, ribs, backside, legs. The inside of his mouth was sore from chewing pine needles and—

Water. The word manifested in his mind with jarring clarity. Ray licked his lips and stared up at the sky again, hoping to spot a rain cloud or two. But the ceiling was clear and orange, the only clouds he could see gilded in the departing rays of sunlight. As desperation set in, shivers itched across his body again.

Cold. Water.

Ray opened his mouth to test his voice. It came out gritty and weak, inaudible to even his own ears: "Help."

His phone had died sometime this morning. He wrapped his fingers around it and brought the device up to his mouth as the urge to cry peaked inside him.

Hannah deserved better than this.

His heart fluttered erratically in his chest. Though not painful, the arrhythmias had been another sign that his lack of water was growing critical. What a way to go out—alone, freezing, and in pain. Like a fool. And his leg—Jesus, he didn't even want to think about *that*. How the blood was throbbing beneath the bandana, how the skin was burning hot from ankle to knee. And yet, he was shivering, yearning for the crackling comfort of a fire, a thick blanket, or just to curl up in bed with Hannah, whose body was always a couple degrees warmer than his. In the depths of his misery, he clung to the memory of her bare skin beneath the covers, his fingers tangled in her hair, and the tickle of her breath against the side of his neck. He closed his eyes and tried to dream her into existence, but his brain had gone too long without water, food, or a way to tend his wounds to conjure more than a faint likeness to the woman he loved.

As her face faded into the darkness once more, Ray's hand, the one that held his phone, dropped to his side, the last of his strength disappearing with the sun.

Seventeen

"The search continues for an Aspen, Colorado man believed to have gone missing in the woods near his home. Police say Raymond Fisher was last seen on Thursday morning around 11:15 when he left his ranch on horseback and headed into the mountains."

A photo of Ray appeared on the TV. After partnering with Mickey for a local colt-starting clinic, Ray's social media platforms were suddenly rife with photos of him in various settings. But the reporters had needed a headshot, something that clearly displayed his most prominent features for instant recognizability.

"On Saturday, police expanded their search area and deployed a canine search and rescue unit in hopes of finding clues that may explain Ray's disappearance. Meanwhile, neighbours have been scouring the area on foot and ATVs, and hanging posters along popular hiking trails."

The story cut to Laney. Jim sat silently beside her, with his head bowed over his lap and his pants still dirty from working in the garden. Despite their familiarity, they were like strangers to Hannah, who was watching TV in the living room after declining to be interviewed that morning.

"When we heard about his disappearance, we thought the police were talking about someone else. We desperately wanted it to be a coincidence, until they showed us the picture." Laney dabbed at her nose with a tissue before continuing. "The whole town's come together to look for him. These are the moments that restore your faith. We're a community, and we're going to find him—"

Hannah picked up the remote, switched off the TV, and sat alone in the pitch-black house, the memory of Ray's face painted indelibly on her mind. *These are the moments that restore your faith*, as if faith were one gigantic blanket that could cover everybody with the same comfort. But for Hannah, who was somewhere just outside of that warmth, there was no sudden intrusion of light in the dark tunnel of her grief. Her faith, which was shaky at best, was now completely shattered.

*

"I think I hear a helicopter," Victor said.

Hannah heard it, too. The sound of its rotors sliced through the chatter of the SAR dogs' handlers, who'd gathered for a second day of searching. Justin had already freed Daisy from her kennel and was scratching the spot behind her ears, earning himself an enthusiastic tail-wag.

Adrianna shielded her eyes and peered up at the sky in time to see the chopper sailing over the house. It was Sunday morning, and rather than joining the Fitzgeralds at church, where thoughts and prayers would be doled out like Halloween candy, they'd dropped Emily off with her grandmother before heading to the ranch to partake in the search party. Hannah had already loaded up a backpack with a day's worth of supplies and was sitting on the porch steps, her foot tapping anxiously on the wooden boards.

"I think it's a media chopper," Addy said as she lowered her gaze, "they probably want to get some aerial footage of the SAR dogs."

"Capitalizing on a family's suffering. Very classy." Victor sneered.

Hannah stood up and hoisted the backpack onto her shoulders. The police had checked the obvious places, including the cattle corridor that Micah's team had combed with ATVs, but there were plenty of other, more obscure paths Ray might've taken, like the trail to the lookout where he'd proposed. In the same way that dogs could detect smells that eluded human noses, Hannah would be able to see places that held sentimental value to him. It was her one advantage over everyone else: the x-ray vision of an adoring wife.

As the group prepared to set out—they'd be flanking the dogs today, hiking side-by-side in adjacent search lanes—a red truck with Montana plates came around the bend and parked outside the house.

Mickey got out, his face already twisted into an expression of mounting worry.

"Mickey," Hannah said, surprised. "What are you doing here?"

"I was hoping I might be able to help. Ray's disappearance is all over the news." He spread his arms in a helpless gesture. "How did this happen?"

"I don't know. All I know is that I'm not solving anything by sitting around."

Mickey turned back to his truck and pulled several bottles of water out of a cooler in the backseat.

"You'll need these," he said, handing them to Hannah, Victor, and Adrianna. "To be honest, I didn't have much of a plan when I decided to drive down here. I just knew I had to do something, and I figured keeping the search party hydrated would be a good place to start. I can make some calls too, if that helps. Or hang posters. Anything you need."

Hannah steeled herself against an unexpected rush of emotions. For days, she'd willed herself to be strong: acknowledging her emotions would only make it harder to run the ranch or talk to police, so she'd packaged her sorrow and put it on a high shelf at the back of her mind. But there was something devastating about random acts of kindness: just when she thought there was no hope, that her faith was truly and irreparably broken, Mickey arrived to prove her wrong.

Hannah excused herself and stole around the side of the house to break down in relative peace. After a few moments, Adrianna followed her.

"The dogs will need water too," Victor told Mickey. "It's supposed to be hot again today."

"Good. I've got plenty."

Victor nodded. What more was there to say?

"I really am sorry to hear about this. Ray's a dear friend of mine, and I respect the hell out of him for the work he does. He's one of the real ones, you know."

"I know. He's my brother." Victor glanced sideways as Hannah and Adrianna reappeared, then lifted his backpack off the ground and swung it over his shoulder. With a parting look at the Horse God, he trailed the dogs and their handlers into the wilderness, with Adrianna on his left and Hannah, her face blotchy but determined, on his right.

Day three of the search operation had officially begun.

There was a strange noise coming from the east, and Ray was struggling to focus on it. His dehydration had reached a critical point, forcing his breaths to come in shallow gasps. Maybe that was what he'd heard: his organs singing their swan song. He wasn't sure what death was supposed to sound like, much less what came after it. But he was dying, wasn't he?

Ray opened his eyes and gazed gloomily at his leg, a pulverized mass of flesh and bone that was rotting away in the heat. He couldn't say he felt afraid of the inevitable—he had Laney to thank for that, and all her promises of an afterlife filled with warmth, joy, and the chance to reunite with his mother. But what about Hannah? Ray wasn't sure what worried him more—that she'd move on, or that she wouldn't. Everything he had was hers, including the ranch that had become their home. The thought of someone else moving in, of filling the hole he'd created, made Ray's empty stomach twist with jealousy.

It wasn't fair to expect her to grieve forever. It wasn't fair to make her grieve, period.

Ray thumbed his wedding band. The metal was cool against his hot skin, just as it had been the day he'd put it on and promised to... What? Had he really forgotten his wedding vows only three years into his marriage?

Even if I have to break a hundred horses or drive a thousand miles, I'm always going to come home to you.

He would wait for her, he decided now. No matter how long it took, or who she chose to loan her heart out to after he was gone, he'd be patient and look forward to being with her again.

Bringing his left hand up to his mouth, he kissed the ring before letting his hand fall back to his lap. He closed his eyes and let the sounds of the woods sing him gently off to sleep.

Eighteen

"We'll keep looking, Hannah. Ray has to be out there somewhere."

Hannah nodded absently. After four gruelling hours of hiking on a mostly upward slope, they'd been faced with a difficult dilemma: continue on their current path and risk becoming stranded in the woods overnight, or retrace their steps back down the mountain and hope that the SAR dogs were having better luck tracking Ray. Like humans, though, even the most devoted canine searchers needed their rest. Justin had noticed Daisy's energy flagging by midday, but promised they'd keep looking so that Hannah, Adrianna, and Victor didn't have to.

This would be Ray's third night lost in the wilderness. As much as she tried not to think about this, Hannah knew what that meant: the chances of finding him were rapidly decreasing, along with his odds of survival.

Her voice was hoarse when she spoke. There'd been no answer when she called out to him today, but she'd called out nonetheless, desperate to hear the husky pitch of his voice in the cruel infinity of the woods' silence. "When's Marc going to be here?"

"As soon as he can. He was just leaving Cheyenne when I talked to him." Victor assumed a seat in the armchair, equidistant from both the sofa and the hearth. It wasn't particularly cold tonight, but he'd lit a fire anyway, needing any excuse he could find to stay busy.

Hannah said quietly, "What if it's too late? What if Ray's already…"

Victor's attention drifted back to her. "Do you really believe that?"

"He's not," Adrianna said firmly. "Look, we all know Ray. He's a survivor. Whenever life tries to knock him down, he comes back swinging every time."

"I appreciate that you guys are trying to be optimistic," Hannah mumbled, looking at both of them in turn, "and I want more than anything to see Ray again. But we have to consider the facts: he has no water, no way to keep warm, and if Jack came back without him, then that means he's probably hurt, otherwise he would've gotten up and walked home."

"What we know for sure is that he went looking for Bernard," Victor said gently. Hannah went back to staring at the fireplace, her eyes dull and sunken. "He might've found water somewhere, and he might've made a shelter out of whatever's around him. Although I agree with you that he's likely injured—he's always been a bit accident-prone."

"He's not 'accident-prone'. He's a goddamn magnet for disaster!" Hannah exploded. Bracing her arms at her sides, she stood up and walked to the bathroom to splash some water on her face.

After the door closed, Adrianna looked at her husband. He was hunched over his lap with his head cradled in his hands, looking more vulnerable than she'd ever seen him before—a small, defenseless child trapped in a grown man's body. Her instinct, like any mother's, was to shelter, to comfort, to protect, even as she knew that her ability to ease his suffering was limited by her own pain. Ray was her family too, and losing him would have the same effect as losing a limb. Life would go on, but it would never look or feel the same again.

"I should've stopped him," he said quietly.

"You did what you could."

"Did I? I could've offered to go with him, since I knew there was no changing his mind. I could've stepped up the way Marc did, but I was more worried about not getting involved in family drama. And now our family drama is plastered all over the town."

She shrugged. "It was tell the whole town, or risk losing Ray forever. Personally, I prefer the first option."

Adrianna stood up, crossed the room, and perched on the chair's armrest. Her arm encircled Victor's shoulders as she rested her chin on his head and gazed into the fire.

"We're going to find him," she whispered. "Just like you found me."

*

"The dogs are getting tired. We have to call it a night," Mike said.

Justin turned, Daisy's lead wrapped around his wrist. "We still have a couple of hours until sundown."

"I know that," Mike countered, stopping to catch his breath. "But this search has gone on longer than it should have. And you owe it to her to turn yourself around and begin descending." He pointed to the Bloodhound, her reflective vest soon to be the brightest thing in these woods. Since Hannah had contaminated Ray's sweater by wearing it, she'd had to provide a new scent source this morning. But it had been a good one, and Daisy had been nose-down all day, sniffing herself into a frenzy.

Justin glanced at his canine partner, then back at Mike. "I just need one more hour. She's never been this interested in a trail before. That means he's close."

"We don't have an hour. In forty-five minutes, it'll be dark in the woods. Damn it, we talked about this: search and rescuers are not heroes. They're ordinary people trying to do a good thing—but if you keep insisting on pushing your luck, one day I'm going to be out here looking for *your* sorry ass."

Justin nodded grimly and reeled Daisy in.

"Understood?" Mike asked, clearly needing some kind of verbal confirmation.

Instead, Justin told him, "Twenty minutes. Then you drag me out."

"God damn it," Mike muttered. "Were you even listening to a word I just said? We're done. Get your dog and let's get out of here."

"I know my dog," Justin argued, "last winter, when we found three-year-old Casey, it was after everyone else had gone home. They told me it was a lost cause. To Daisy, that's a dare. She sniffs until the person is found. And if my sorry ass ever ends up turned around in these woods, I sure hope Daisy's on my trail."

Mike scrunched his brows. From police chief to volunteer search and rescuer, he'd seen the worst in people on countless occasions. But sometimes the most dangerous thing a person could do was perform an act of unrelenting goodness. Whether it was the bystander who jumped onto the subway tracks to save another commuter, or a local teen pulling their elderly neighbour from a house fire, the world was full of people like Justin McClintock—the ones who reached out and embraced the darkness with both hands, fearless and dog-loyal to the bitter end.

Mike took one look at Daisy and let out his breath.

"Twenty minutes," he muttered, "and not a second longer."

Justin turned to Daisy. "Search," he said in a firm, clear voice. She surged ahead of him, disappearing in a red-and-black blur through the screen of leaves.

Ray didn't know this, but Justin was a huge fan of his—not because he liked horses, but because he loved his twelve-year-old sister, Jordan. Jordan had been a typical horse-crazy tween up until her leukemia diagnosis. Now, she was a horse-crazy tween who spent entirely too much time in hospitals, alternating between vomiting and sleeping, or playing Super Mario World on her big brother's Nintendo Switch. But on the worst days, when nothing could ease the pain of her disease or quell the uncomfortable side effects of the chemo drugs, Ray's YouTube channel had proven to be the distraction the McClintocks needed. And for that, Justin would be forever grateful.

Daisy snuffled loudly, pulling Justin out of his thoughts and back to the woods. He staggered after her, the orange leash bobbing like a telephone wire in a hurricane. Darkness was falling to the east, but there was enough light to see the ground directly in front of him, covered in pine needles and other forms of kindling.

"Do you smell something, Daisy?" Justin asked, his heart taking up an erratic rhythm. "You smell him, don't you?"

The Bloodhound raised her head, cocked an ear toward the trees on their right, and pulled hard into the leash. Something had caught her interest, and she was barrelling toward it with her nose to the ground and the harness digging into her shoulders. A tingle of anticipation washed over Justin as a dark object came into view on the trail in front of them. Daisy plunged her nose toward it, then dropped onto her haunches and waited for Justin to catch up.

"What's that? What did you find, girl?"

His hand went out and fell on the stiff brim of a cowboy hat. He showed it to Daisy, who took one sniff before springing into action once again.

"This is Ray's, isn't it? Where is he, Daisy?"

Daisy inspected the ground where the hat had fallen, took a few steps toward the ravine, probed the air with her nose, and let out a low, gravelly bark.

Justin gathered up the slack in her line and peered over the edge. The drop had to be a hundred feet, if not more, with vegetation so thick that it was hard to discern a human form among the profusion of tree limbs. But in the dying light of afternoon, he spotted a distinctly human shape sitting motionless amidst the incessant movement of the forest. He fumbled for the whistle looped around his neck and blew into it with all his might.

"Hey! We found him! He's down here!"

75 HOURS AFTER THE FALL

Victor seldom answered the phone when it rang. Given a choice, he preferred to receive news in written form. But some things couldn't wait for the right words.

Hannah and Adrianna were talking over the six o'clock news. Victor thanked the caller and hung up the phone before walking into the living room.

"Hannah," he said.

She turned to him and stood abruptly, her face filled with a mix of hope and dread.

"They found him," he whispered. Victor saw her take a breath and hold it, her body stiffening with the effort of maintaining her composure.

Hannah repeated, "They found him."

Victor nodded, unable to believe the words poised on the tip of his tongue. "They found him, Hannah. Ray's alive."

PART 2

Nineteen

For the first time in her life, Hannah understood what it meant to be worried sick. The dry hospital air made her throat feel raw, and though she hadn't cried much when the rescuers were loading Ray into the ambulance, her eyes continued to water under the harsh fluorescent lights. Even now, in the quiet of the ICU, she found it impossible to rest: her legs continued to carry her through the long hallways, past the nurses stations and supply carts, until she had more or less memorized the layout of the floor.

But her wandering always brought her back to Ray's room. Two chairs, one slightly closer than the other, sat next to his bed. Hannah had thrown her jacket over the armrest of the nearer one, claiming it as soon as she was able to, then helped herself to a cup of water from the plastic pitcher that had been left on the bedside table. For the first couple of hours, she'd merely sat with him, trying to reconcile the bruised, bloodied, and dehydrated man in the bed with the one who'd run off to look for his father only three days ago. Thankfully, Ray was breathing on his own, but the infection in his leg raged on, indifferent to the salvo of antibiotics and other medical interventions.

Hannah leaned over the bed and gently kissed his brow before letting herself out of the room. This time, her feet led her to a waiting area near the end of the hall. The TV was muted, and Marcus was sitting beneath it with his phone pressed to his ear.

"We're waiting to see what the doctor says. I know the timing is bad, but I don't see myself coming back before Wednesday at the earliest... I understand that, but my brother is very sick right now..." Marcus heard Hannah's approaching footsteps and raised his gaze to hers, a combination of exhaustion and frustration surfacing on his face. She sat down next to him as he told the person on the other end of the call, "Okay, thank you. I'll keep you posted." He hung up, a sigh fleeing his lips as he stared at the device between his knees.

"Is everything okay?" Hannah asked.

"That was my boss. He wants to know when I'm coming back to work."

She bit into her bottom lip, resisting the impulse to lash out at her brother-in-law's employer. In her sleep-deprived state, it was all too easy to forget that for most of the world, Ray's recovery was nothing more than a minor inconvenience. "I hope you're not in too much trouble."

"No. It's just that if I lose my job, I also lose my health insurance."

Hannah kept a straight face. No one had told Marcus about Ray discovering Bernard's campsite: all he knew, so far, was that Ray had gone out to "check on something" in the high country and been thrown from his horse. But the eldest brother had developed a keen intuition as a result of having parental duties foisted on him as a teenager. It was only a matter of time before he began asking the right questions, or before Ray, compelled by pain or exasperation, blurted out the truth.

"How's Ray looking?" Marcus asked.

"The same, I think. It's hard to tell with the bad lighting."

"Did they say anything more about his infection?"

Hannah shook her head. "A nurse came in a while ago. She took one look at his leg and left without saying anything."

"It's usually not good when they don't tell you what they're thinking. It's like this wall goes up in front of their face, and the truth is on the other side of it."

She studied him for a moment. Clearly he had some experience with this metaphorical wall—Hannah had, too, on the night of Cameron's accident. She shoved the thought away as a muscle in her throat tightened and her eyes once again began to tingle.

Suddenly, Marcus stood up and slipped his phone into his pocket. "I could use a coffee. Do you want me to bring you anything when I come back?"

"That's okay, I had some water in Ray's room."

"You need more than just water. By the way, when was the last time you got any sleep?"

"I'm fine," Hannah argued, "really, I don't want anything."

Marcus shot her a deadpan look as he took his leave. "I'll bring you a sandwich. Just in case you change your mind."

As Hannah watched him leave, feeling both grateful that he'd insisted and miffed that he thought he knew best, her mind turned to the hours and days ahead. Right now, Ray was stable, which was hospital code for having normal vital signs. But the leg wound, like so many things in life, was deeper than it appeared. If the infection spread to his bloodstream, it would put him at risk of becoming septic. He'd try to fight it off the way he fought for everything else, but sometimes the battle wasn't enough to win the war.

And tonight, the battle had only begun.

*

Ray wasn't too far gone to know he was in a hospital, surrounded by machines that generated incessant noise. The nurses station was visible through the glass door on his left: every now and then one of them would pop up from behind the desk and come check his vitals, or confirm the IV needles in his arms were still in place. He flexed his right hand, hating the bulky feeling of the plastic butterfly they'd taped to his skin. It wasn't nearly as painful as being propped against a tree with a mashed-up leg and a head wound, but being bedbound came with its own discomforts and irritations.

Ray's eyes flickered back to the door. One of the nurses glanced up as Hannah strode past them, a small knot of worry between her brows. As she entered his room, she shifted her gaze to the bed and her face relaxed into a veneer of relief.

"Hey. You're awake," she said softly.

Ray replied in a gravelly voice, "My head's killing me."

"The nurse gave him some Tylenol," one of the aides said on her way out. "I'll drop by again in a little while and see if it's working."

Hannah nodded and turned her attention back to Ray. He still looked awful, even after being cleaned up and stabilized. The skin on his nose and cheeks had been ravaged by sunburn and his lips were cracked in about ten different spots. She approached the bedside table and poured some water into one of the plastic cups before holding it to his lips.

Ray forced himself to take a sip. When the searchers had discovered him at the bottom of the ravine, he'd been so dehydrated that even the slightest movement felt like broken glass gliding beneath his skin. After a couple minutes of them rubbing his sternum and saying his name, Ray had regained consciousness enough to accept the water someone held to his lips. It was the most divine thing he'd ever tasted, so cool and fresh on his dry, aching tongue. He would've guzzled the whole bottle right then and there if they'd let him, but moments later he'd drifted off again, just in time to hear one of them comment on the grisly state of his leg.

Hannah took a seat in one of the chairs. Each time Ray stirred, he stayed awake a little bit longer. By this time tomorrow, maybe he'd be ready to have a proper conversation about his father and what exactly he was trying to accomplish by looking for him.

"How are you feeling, besides the headache?" she asked.

Ray drew in a breath and closed his eyes. "Tired."

"Me too." Her expression lifted. "Guess who's here." Ray quirked a brow inquiringly, prompting Hannah to say, "Marcus."

His eyes widening, he lifted his head somewhat to stare at her. "Marc's here?"

Hannah nodded. "He drove straight from Cheyenne to Aspen without stopping, apparently."

Ray swallowed thickly, his eyes glazed with fear. She'd only seen this look a handful of times since meeting him, and it always took her by surprise, including right now.

"He's just across the street getting a coffee," she added as she settled into her seat. "I'm sure he's going to be really happy to see that you're awake."

"What did he say when you told him about my dad?"

Hannah sobered as understanding came to her at last. "Marc doesn't know about Bernard. No one's had the heart to tell him."

"Then what does he think happened to me?"

"I told him you were checking on something in the backcountry and you fell off your horse. On Victor's advice, I mentioned how you and Micah found the dead calf… and I guess Marcus bought it."

"So, Victor encouraged you to lie to him," Ray persisted, his brows furrowed against the sudden spike of pain behind his eyes.

"Like you've never lied to Marc about anything."

"I know I have, and that was wrong of me. You don't think he deserves to know what's really going on, especially after I almost died out there?"

"We didn't think it mattered right now. What matters is *you*. There will be lots of time to have that conversation later, don't you think?"

Ray was silent, his fingernails scratching the rough linens as his hands tightened into fists. It was hard to think straight when so much of his body hurt. He was becoming aware of his leg again, wrapped up like a mummy beneath the sheets. The Tylenol didn't seem to put a dent in that throbbing mass of beat-up flesh—if anything, Ray felt the pain was getting worse, although he knew better than to make Hannah aware of that fact.

She leaned toward him and clutched his hand, brushing her thumb over his knuckles while being careful to avoid the needle embedded in his skin.

"It's going to be okay," Hannah whispered as Ray lifted his gaze to hers. "As soon as you get out of here, we'll find a way to tell him together."

She stood up, tucked her hair behind her ears, and picked up her jacket.

"Where are you going?" Ray asked.

"I need some air. I haven't been outside since you were admitted last night." She faced the bed, and the shock of seeing Ray in such a haggard state hit her once again. It didn't feel right, leaving him like this, but neither did wandering the halls like a ghost.

Hannah crossed to the door and let herself out of the room. It had been years since this feeling had taken over her body, and yet she could feel it spreading through her like an electric current. From her fingertips to the soles of her feet, she felt nothing but numbness. Marcus was right—she needed sleep, but every time she closed her eyes, all she saw were the faces of the search and rescue team as they carried Ray out of the woods by the light of their headlamps. She'd fallen in love with a man who didn't give any thought to his own safety, and mixed in with that love was a quiet, seething anger she could never bring herself to face.

A tepid breeze rose and surrounded her at last. She walked to the edge of the parking lot and breathed in deeply, her lashes damp against her cheeks. She was always here—always in a hospital, and in a state of worry about those she loved. When did it end? Would it ever?

"I'd ask if you're okay, but I think I already know the answer," Marcus said as he approached carrying a coffee in one hand and the sandwich he'd promised her in the other.

Hannah peered over at him, debating whether to speak her mind. As her breathing evened out, she wiped the moisture from her cheeks and said, "Ray's awake. He has a headache, but he seems to be okay otherwise."

"Ah. Well, I guess that's good." She nodded absently. "So, why are you out here and not inside with him?"

"I had to get out for a moment. I couldn't breathe in that stuffy room."

Marcus gestured to a small garden on Hannah's left, its circular ecosystem surrounded by a stone wall about three feet high and one foot wide. "Do you want to sit down for a minute?"

She took him up on his offer without comment. They sat side by side in front of the hospital, the sky sprinkled with stars above them and the traffic streaming lazily along the highway in the distance. If she'd had the guts to tell Marcus about her anxiety attacks, he would've probably listened without judgment. Instead, Hannah indicated the paper-wrapped package and asked, "What's that?"

He handed it to her. "Turkey club. You're welcome."

She smiled as she accepted the sandwich. "Thanks."

"Not that we have to talk about it, but I get why you came out here. I don't know how people like Addy do it, being surrounded by illness and death all day."

"I guess she's learned to dissociate from it all. I can't, especially when it's someone I care about."

Hannah unwrapped the sandwich, lifted it to her mouth, and took a small bite. She wasn't particularly hungry, but she'd need all her strength in order to confront the ramifications of Ray's actions.

There it was, again. A white-hot flash of anger erupted behind her eyes as she thought about all the times he'd tried to be a hero, often at the expense of his own happy ending.

She murmured, "Sometimes I wonder if all this was a mistake—marrying Ray and moving to the US, I mean."

"Do you mean that, or are you just saying it because you're wiped out and haven't eaten anything today?"

Hannah considered her answer as she stared at the bun's flaky crust. "I don't know," she replied honestly.

Marcus picked up his coffee, took a sip, and set it back on the wall.

"The husbands always leave. That's what one of the nurses was telling me," he said. "She said, 'When the wife gets sick, ninety-nine percent of the time the husband doesn't know what to do, so he leaves.' But I know Ray—if it were you in that ICU, he'd be by your side day and night. I hope you know that."

"I do." Hannah lowered the sandwich. "And I know I should be up there with him. It's just... the way he lives sometimes makes me wonder if he loves himself as much as he loves me. I had hoped that after Wilbur shot him, he'd realize he can't always be saving the day—" She broke off, just in time to prevent herself from revealing the real reason they were here.

After a beat, Marcus asked, "Did you guys lose any calves this year?"

"No. At least, I don't think we did."

"That's good. One less thing."

Hannah hastily re-wrapped her sandwich and stood up. "I should probably head back inside."

"Good idea. I'll be in soon."

Turning toward the glow of the hospital, she steeled herself and walked up to the doors. They parted with a rush of cool air, and before long she was back in the entryway, surrounded by the same pale walls and flat, antiseptic odor she'd sought to escape. Marcus remained outside, studying the night sky as if it held the key to his future.

Twenty

"Excuse me. I think this belongs to you." The nurse, newly graduated and glowing with hope for her future, extended the plastic bag toward Hannah just as she and Marcus were preparing to leave.

Hannah exchanged a look with her brother-in-law and held out her hand to receive the items.

The young nurse explained, "It's your husband's personal effects. We thought you might like to have them back."

A smile crossed Hannah's face at the words *personal effects.* Definitely the language of the still-peppy-and-eager-to-please club. "Thank you."

As the nurse returned to her station, Marcus ran a hand over his chin. They'd been at the hospital for nearly twenty-four hours, and he was long overdue for a shave.

He indicated the plastic bag, which Hannah was holding by the neck like some kind of thief who'd just looted the hospital. "What do you think he had on him?"

"I don't know. I'll look through it when we get home."

They drove the backroads in silence. With no streetlights for miles, the truck's headlights provided the only source of illumination outside, and Hannah didn't have the heart to turn on the cabin light to investigate the contents of the bag. Instead, she cradled it gently in her lap, her fingers absently kneading the soft corners of Ray's clothes. When they'd extracted him from the woods, it had been too dark to see much of anything: he'd been wrapped in blankets for the long walk home, with only his face sticking out of the grey cocoon. She knew he'd been injured in the ravine, but she wasn't sure what state his clothes would be in until she unpacked them.

Another part of her wanted to burn everything and forget this "accident" ever happened. How was she supposed to confront Marcus with the news that their father was back—or that Ray had insisted on reconciling with him?

"You can use the shower first," Marcus said when they pulled up to the house a few minutes later, triggering the security light above the barn. "I'll bring in the horses."

"Lucky stays outside. He's the grey one in the small paddock out front."

Marcus craned his head to look through the passenger window. Sure enough, he spotted the light-coloured gelding standing by the gate, distinctly visible in the sea of shadows. The other horses were sure to be hovering somewhere in the background, waiting to see if the sudden presence of a vehicle coincided with the appearance of food.

"Ray's alive," Hannah whispered. She still didn't believe it, despite all the evidence to the contrary.

"He is. And he's going to live a long and happy life with you. Whether or not he's going to learn from this experience remains to be seen, but for now, let's just celebrate the fact that we're not planning his funeral." Marcus looked like he wanted to say more—Hannah could practically see the unspoken *yet* floating in the air between them like a spectre, but maybe, like the nurse, he still had some hope.

They both got out, with Hannah making her way into the house and Marcus travelling in the opposite direction until she could no longer hear his footsteps. She unlocked the front door, set the bag containing Ray's belongings on the bench, and walked into the kitchen, unsure if the hollow feeling in her gut was hunger or despair. She brushed her hand over his sweater, hung on the back of his chair after the rescuers had deemed it "contaminated," before collecting the garment and the plastic bag and carrying both upstairs to the privacy of their bedroom.

After shutting the door, the first thing Hannah did was open the window. Cool, damp air flooded in, along with the zesty scent of pine sap and diesel that wafted up from the nearby drive shed. In the distance, she saw Marcus's silhouette moving between the barn and the paddock, escorting some of the more vulnerable horses to the warmth and safety of their stalls. To say the work never stopped was far from being an exaggeration: around here, it was the one thing she could always count on. That, and Ray acting on impulse with no thought to his own welfare.

She faced the bed. Besides the clothes he was wearing, what could Ray have had on him that contributed to his survival? Certainly nothing useful like a matchbook or a satellite radio, she thought. Hannah took a seat on the edge of the mattress and reached into the bag for the first item.

It was a shirt—a dark green plaid with black buttons and a frayed collar, covered in splotches of mud. Beside the rancid odour of the damp fabric, Hannah couldn't help but notice the black stain on the right shoulder. She scraped at it experimentally, and dried blood came off on the tip of her fingernail.

She set the shirt aside and pulled out his jeans.

More blood. The entire right leg below the knee was black with the stuff, the fabric torn clean through by the branch. There were still bits of tree bark embedded in the denim, and Hannah felt a cold sweat break out all over her body as instinct compelled her to look away.

She uncovered his belt, boots, and the bandana, all stained or soaked with blood. Then she found his phone. To think he'd had access to the outside world whilst being simultaneously cut off from it entirely... maybe he and Bernard had more in common than Hannah was willing to acknowledge.

In spite of everything—the media coverage, the search and rescue dogs, the ATVs, and the no-man-left-behind solidarity that this community was built on—Bernard was still nowhere to be seen. Only now, Hannah couldn't muster the energy to be angry about it.

Setting Ray's phone on charge, she dug a change of clothes out of the dresser and went to the bathroom to take a shower.

*

The next time Hannah awoke, it was 1:30AM and her phone was ringing. She reached across the nightstand and picked up the device, the late-night shot of adrenaline bringing her into full-consciousness in seconds.

"Okay, thank you for calling. We'll be right there," she said less than a minute later. Swinging her legs out of bed, she crossed to the door and stepped out into the drafty darkness of the hall. The guest bedroom lay behind the first door on her left. She knocked three times, shocked that the persistent buzzing of her phone hadn't been enough to wake Marcus, then threw common courtesy out the window and turned the knob.

"Marc. Marc, wake up," she hissed into the pitch-black room.

At first, she heard only the faint creaking of the bedsprings. As her eyes adjusted, she saw him lift his head, and his upper body twisted toward her. "What's wrong?"

"The hospital just called. Ray has a fever of a hundred and two and he's struggling to breathe." Her chest tightened as she returned to her room, running through a mental list of everything she'd need to survive the next stint at Ray's bedside.

She'd just stuffed a change of clothes, both phones, and her charger into a tote bag when Marcus emerged, fully dressed, from the spare bedroom.

As he came to stand on the threshold, she told him, "They think he might have sepsis. They didn't tell me very much—probably don't want me panicking, which of course I am."

"Panicking won't help anyone. Is he alert, at least?"

"I don't know." Hannah kept her back to the door. "We might lose him, Marc."

"Last I checked, you're not a doctor. So, let's leave the speculation to the professionals and go do what we do best, which is comfort Ray." She heard his footsteps on the old wooden floorboards, the sound fading as he moved away from her.

For several moments, Hannah was frozen in place, her limited knowledge of infections holding her hostage in the room where Ray should've been sleeping. But Marcus was right: knowing just a little bit was as good as knowing nothing at all. She rounded up a few more necessities, then headed downstairs to find Marcus waiting in the truck, his headlights blinding her as she stepped onto the porch.

"Don't Google anything," he told her as she climbed into the passenger seat.

"Who said I was going to Google anything?" she asked, offended that he'd jumped to conclusions so soon after advising her against taking the same mental leaps.

"I'm just trying to spare you unnecessary anxiety. You can't plan your way out of this—just wait and see what the doctor says."

She nodded and wrapped her arms around her bag. She'd never been a *wait and see* kind of person, but sometimes that was the only option life gave her. Hannah stared out the window, watching the night rewind itself as they drove back toward town.

Twenty-one

"It's not sepsis, at least not yet," the doctor assured them. His gaze settled on Hannah, sitting directly across from him in the stuffy room that smelled like paper and leftover ravioli.

"Then what is it?" She spoke softly in hopes her voice wouldn't shake, although just about every other part of her body did. Ray had already been moved to another part of the hospital when they arrived, his condition critical enough to warrant immediate action.

Dr. Johansson explained, "Ray is having what's called a systemic inflammatory response. Basically, the infection in his leg is sending his immune system into overdrive, causing the high fever and increased respiratory rate. It often precedes sepsis, but with early intervention, we might have a chance of beating it."

"What kind of chances are we looking at here?" Marcus put in. He was standing off to the side, his face contorted in an involuntary grimace. "I'm guessing they're pretty slim, since the antibiotics don't seem to be having any effect."

"Ray hasn't even finished his course of antibiotics yet," Hannah said, turning back to the doctor. "Shouldn't we wait a few more days and see if this... inflammatory response settles down?"

"We could, but I'm concerned the situation will get worse before it improves." Dr. Johansson locked eyes with Hannah across the grey desk. There was a teddy-bear like quality to his face that she found difficult to reconcile with the words that came out of his mouth—words she was tempted to trust because of the white coat, grey hair, and frameless glasses resting on the bridge of his nose.

He went on, speaking calmly but without hesitation. "There's a reason antibiotics revolutionized modern medicine. However, sometimes drugs alone aren't enough. We know the infection originated in the soft tissue of Ray's right leg, but what we're discovering now is that those bacteria have begun to proliferate in the bone tissue, as well. If left untreated, Ray faces numerous potential health complications. As I said, there's a chance we can still beat the infection, but we need to act quickly."

Dr. Johansson reclined in his chair, removed his glasses, and polished a smudge off the lens with a corner of his lab coat.

"The way I see it," he told them, placing his glasses back on his face, "our best bet is to amputate."

Hannah pictured a mallet connecting with her gut, knocking the wind out of her in a single, bruising punch.

"No way," Marcus put in, "we're not cutting anything off. Ray will get better with the drugs. I know you don't know my brother very well, but believe me when I say he's come back from worse."

"Is there any other option, besides drugs or amputation?" Hannah wished she'd ignored Marcus's advice about not using Google. Terrible as it was for her mental health, the research would've given her a better understanding of Ray's condition. How was she supposed to advocate for his care when she lacked the language of the well-informed?

"I'm afraid not," Dr. Johansson replied, "but if we use those treatment options together, I'm confident Ray will make a full recovery."

"Full recovery." Marcus had started pacing the room; Hannah felt the zipper of his jacket brush the back of her chair as he reached the opposite wall and pressed a hand against it to steady himself. "Does anyone ever fully recover from losing a limb? My brother is a rancher. His whole life depends on being able to break horses and raise cattle, and I don't picture him doing any of that with only one leg."

His hand went up to cover his face—mainly his eyes. In all the years she'd known him, Hannah had never seen Marcus cry: he'd come close a few times when Laney received more bad news, but it had been baked into his DNA to never show emotion in front of other people.

The doctor waited a moment before speaking again, "I understand how hard this must be to hear. And I wouldn't suggest it if I didn't think it was the best possible course of action—"

"You think, or you know?" Marcus taunted. His eyes were bloodshot, but instead of letting his tears flow, he resorted to anger—anything to protect himself from the knowledge that his baby brother's life was teetering on a cliff. "I don't mind getting a second opinion. In fact, point me toward one of your colleagues. Because while you're over here thinking about how much you can bill the hospital for butchering a patient, I'll be making sure Ray's back home in one piece."

"Marcus," Hannah spat, turning to him abruptly, "calm down, okay?"

His eyes practically froze over as he stared at her. Darting an icicle at the doctor, he rubbed the lower half of his face and stalked toward the door, throwing it open. As it banged closed behind him, Hannah faced the desk again, all too aware of the chill that lingered in the wake of Marcus's hasty exit.

Her gaze sank to Dr. Johansson's wrinkled palms, wondering about all the people whose bodies he'd touched over the years, feeling for lumps and bumps and broken bones. If she had to place Ray's fate anywhere, at least she could count on Dr. Johansson handling him with care.

"Mrs. Fisher?" he prompted.

Hannah looked at him. "I'm sorry?"

"Do you have any other questions for me? Have you thought about what you'd like to do?"

She let his voice wash over her, feeling each word like a cold drop of rain on her face. Marcus was still somewhere outside, pacing the halls or maybe calling Victor and Adrianna and trying to persuade them to take his side. But at the end of the day, there was only one person who could legally make decisions on Ray's behalf.

Save the leg, or save her husband. What should've been the hardest decision of Hannah's life was suddenly crystal clear.

"I have," she replied. "Everything Marc said was true—Ray's a cowboy, and I know how hard it's going to be for him to adjust. But I know he'll move forward because I'm going to be there for him every step of the way." Hannah took a deep breath. "Let's do it. Let's amputate his leg."

*

By 9:30AM, Hannah was exhausted and Marcus was nowhere to be found. Hunkered down in the corner of the waiting room, she watched a parade of faces pass by while she waited for the rest of the family to arrive. She'd called Victor and Adrianna first and explained as best she could about Ray's inflammatory response and the need to remove his affected limb. Their reaction to hearing this news had been stunned silence—they'd talked to Ray on the phone the night before and noticed nothing out of the ordinary. But at least they hadn't chastised Hannah for choosing to go forward with the surgery, and for that, she was grateful.

Jim and Laney had been less supportive. While she understood their reaction was rooted in fear over their godson's future, it bothered Hannah to think that they doubted her judgment. Then again, when had her judgment ever been totally clear? Certainly not when she'd conceived a baby out of wedlock, or drunkenly called off the wedding at the engagement party.

But a few hours ago, when she was sitting in Dr. Johansson's office and Marcus was pacing furiously around the room, Hannah had experienced a flash of clarity. She'd made a promise on her wedding day to love and honour Ray in good times and in bad. In good times, it was easy to uphold her vows, but the real test of a marriage's durability came during moments like this, when the urge to run away eclipsed the promise to stay. It was a test many people failed every year.

Across the waiting room, Hannah saw Victor and Adrianna walking toward her, the baby sleeping in her car seat between them. Hannah sat up straighter and smiled a little, hoping a flicker of optimism might shine through the dark clouds of anxiety and regret.

"How are you doing?" Adrianna asked. She took a seat next to Hannah.

"Not very well," Hannah admitted. "Ray's operation was scheduled for eight o'clock. I think they should be almost done by now."

"Where's Marc?" Victor asked. He lowered himself into a chair across from his wife and sister-in-law, where he could keep an eye on the doors. There was no telling what kind of mood his twin brother would be in this morning, but hopefully this seating arrangement would allow Victor to see trouble coming.

"I don't know. He said he needed to clear his head." Hannah shrugged. "That was almost forty-five minutes ago. Do you think he might've gone home?"

"Not with Ray in surgery. Did you try calling him?"

"I just opted to cut off his little brother's leg. I'm not totally confident he'd answer me right now," Hannah said. She turned to Adrianna and asked, somewhat reluctantly, "Does Marc have any vices I should be aware of?"

"Vices? You mean like, poor coping mechanisms?"

Hannah nodded. "I'm getting kind of worried. He hasn't left Ray's side since he got here. I just don't—" She cut off, her throat filling with an unexpected surge of emotions. "I don't want him to do anything stupid, that's all."

"You know, he does smoke sometimes," Victor said, reaching into his pocket for his phone. "He never does it in front of Ray, of course. I'll text him and see where he is."

The waiting room was beginning to fill up. A family with two small children descended on the row of chairs across the room, with the youngest child cutting a beeline to the box of toys tucked under the table. Hannah watched the little boy with brown hair rummage around in the assortment of colourful blocks. In only a few days, she and Ray had gone from talking about kids to this. A whole life, transformed in the blink of an eye.

"Marc's okay. He spilled coffee on his jeans and had to go to the store to buy a new pair. He should be here soon," Victor reported.

Hannah sighed with relief. "Good. I know Ray's going to want to see him when he wakes up."

"Does Ray know he's losing his leg?" Adrianna asked. "Was he part of the care conference?"

"No. I mean, I don't think they told him. Or maybe they did. What's a care conference?"

"It's a meeting between health care providers and a patient's family. The patient is usually present, if they're alert and oriented."

"But I don't know if Ray was alert and oriented," Hannah protested, feeling suddenly angry that Ray's mental status had been kept from her. "All they told me was that he had a fever and shortness of breath and that the infection was spreading to his bone tissue. I didn't even get a chance to see him before he went in to the OR."

"Can they do that?" Victor asked his wife.

"If it's an emergency and there's no time to obtain consent, then yes." Adrianna turned back to Hannah and explained, "You're Ray's POA. If they were asking you for consent to perform the surgery, then that means Ray wasn't medically competent at the time."

"So he's not going to know what happened until he wakes up," Hannah concluded. Her voice cracked. "This never should've happened."

A glimmer of movement near the doors drew Victor's eyes in that direction. As soon as Marcus appeared, he stood up and crossed the room to meet his sibling.

"You had us all worried," Victor said. "It's not like you to disappear without saying anything."

"But when you do it, no one bats an eye," Marcus pointed out. "Did you just get here?"

"About ten minutes ago. No word on Ray yet."

"Is that good?"

"I don't know." Victor lowered his voice. "I just want to make sure everything is okay with you. I know you're mad at Hannah for what she chose to do."

Marcus's expression darkened. The bags under his eyes were more apparent than ever in the sallow light of the hospital hallway—obviously, whatever coffee had made it to his bloodstream was not having the desired effect. Marcus shot a glance at the nurse's station, then pocketed his hands and leaned against the wall just around the corner from the waiting room.

"Would you have done anything differently?" Victor wondered when Marcus remained silent. "We're talking about saving Ray's life here."

"I don't know what I would've done. I needed someone to blame, I guess."

"Well, that person shouldn't be Hannah. She's under enough stress as it is."

"I took care of Ray for years. He was *my* responsibility. Now, he's married and he doesn't need me anymore."

Victor smirked. "Of course he does. He never calls me for advice." Which was a lie, of course—Ray had come over to his house the day he'd gone missing. Victor and Adrianna had agreed to leave the task of telling Marcus about Bernard up to Hannah and Ray, but with everything else going on, their father's whereabouts were the least of the family's concerns.

Marcus snapped, "What do you want me to say? That I'm handling this well? Because I'm not. Hannah made a very bad choice, and I have to go along with it because she's Ray's wife. Even though I know him better than she does and I know that when Ray wakes up and sees part of his body is missing, it'll destroy him."

"You think you know him better than I do?"

They both turned to find Hannah standing a few feet away, with her arms crossed and her brows furrowed. Her gaze fixated on Marcus, who merely looked away.

"I've known him for longer," he said as he focused on her once again. "I was there during the worst years of his childhood, and I was there for him when you were away at university. I think that puts me firmly at the top of the list of people who can make decisions regarding his care."

"The antibiotics alone weren't working," Hannah reminded him. "Good to know you don't trust my judgment either, though."

"I never said I don't trust your judgment. It's just hard to look at you right now knowing what you did."

"That's not fair," she whispered. "If you'd been in my position, I would've supported you even if I didn't agree with your choice. That's what families do."

"Well, our family's a bit different, Hannah. You've always known that. Ray's worked his whole life to take over the ranch, and now that might not be possible."

Adrianna materialized from around the corner. She set down Emily's car seat and raised her hands, calling for a truce.

"I think we all need to take a step back here. The fact is, Ray's leg is gone—it doesn't matter who gave the okay for that. We all agree that we wanted to save his life, right?" She turned to each member of the group, watching as all three of them nodded their heads. "Okay. So now, we focus on moving forward as a family. No one gets to play judge, jury, and executioner here." Adrianna directed a pointed glance at Marcus.

Victor said, "She's right. Now's not the time for us to be fighting. Are Jim and Laney coming?"

"Jim said they'd try," Hannah answered, leading the way back to the waiting area. She sank into her seat as Marcus, Victor, and Adrianna settled into nearby chairs and Emily was placed in an empty seat between her parents. "Laney was really upset on the phone. Apparently she was already having a bad night before I called."

Victor nodded. A minute later, Adrianna leaned toward Marcus and gave a firm yank on the pocket of his jeans, causing him to look scandalized.

"You had a tag," she said simply, holding up the small paper label as proof. She chucked it into the trashcan.

"I always knew you liked me more," Marcus teased, shooting his brother a cocky look. "And who could blame you? I'm obviously the more handsome twin."

Adrianna shrugged, wrinkling her nose. "You're not my type."

In response, Marcus placed a hand over his chest, feigning a blow to the heart.

A smile waxed over Hannah's face at this brief moment of levity. But a few minutes later, right as Marcus was making faces at the baby on Victor's lap, a nurse rounded the corner and panned her gaze over the waiting room.

"Hannah?"

She stiffened. Her hand closed on the strap of her bag, but she couldn't bring herself to stand up and walk across the room.

Adrianna reached out to touch her other hand, bringing Hannah back to the present moment. "Did you want one of us to come in with you?"

Hannah surveyed the faces before her. All the playfulness had vanished from Marcus's expression, but he didn't volunteer to accompany her as one might've expected. Victor, as always, was quiet as a stone, his hands wrapped protectively around his daughter.

Hannah let out a breath and forced herself to rise. "I'm the cause of this. I think I should go in alone."

"You don't have to face this alone, Hannah. No one's blaming you," Adrianna said.

Hannah nodded. "I know. I just need a moment alone with my husband, if that's okay with everyone else."

"Of course. We'll be right here if you need us."

Hannah stepped around the chairs and walked toward the nurse, who led her through the maze of hallways. Soon, the nurse disappeared into a room consisting of four beds separated by green curtains. When Hannah caught up to her, she could see that Ray was in the first bed on the left, with new tubes feeding into his arm from the IV pole in the corner.

For several moments, Hannah could do nothing but linger at the foot of the bed, taking in the scene before her: Ray wore a loose gown, and the skin on his arms and face was still marred by scratches from the ravine. She moved toward the bed and wrapped her hand around his limp fingers, tracing the small scabs on his knuckles with her thumb. But the one thing she didn't do was remove her eyes from his face, because if she had, she would've noticed how the blankets that covered his body sloped down toward the mattress on the right hand side sooner than they should have.

"You can't trust the lighting in here," the nurse said, "his colour's great. And he started breathing normally as soon as he was extubated. Dr. Johansson's really pleased with how smooth the surgery went."

"How long does he have to stay here?"

"Just for a few hours. We want to make sure the wound drains properly and he has no post-op complications." The nurse retreated, reaching to pull the curtain closed behind her. "I'll be at the desk outside if you need anything."

Hannah thanked her, feeling cold and numb as she faced Ray again. There was knowing he had lost his leg, and then there was seeing it for herself.

Releasing his hand, she skated her fingers along the top of the blanket toward his right knee, only to encounter a soft, fleshy lump where the joint should have been. Beyond that, there was just an empty pocket of air draped in the rough, green fabric of hospital linens. Steeling herself, Hannah grasped the edge of the blanket with both hands and lifted it, unveiling the stump of Ray's residual limb wrapped in layers of soft, white gauze.

She wasn't imagining it: the leg was really, truly gone.

Hannah replaced the covers. She had expected the sight of his leg to move her to tears, but tears were the language of the grieving. Instead,

157

she went straight to acceptance, letting the anger and sadness bleed out of her in a single, deep breath.

"I'm sorry," Hannah whispered.

His eyelids flickered in response to her voice. A second later, Ray woke up.

Twenty-two

The plan had always been to head south—it was the getting there that Bernard had not given much thought to. His legs still worked well enough to carry him a few miles a day, and he didn't mind hitchhiking when the weather was bad. With any luck, he'd be in Texas by summer's end, just in time to find a job selling longhorn cattle. Or bartending. Or perhaps the winds would blow him in a different direction entirely, just as they had been doing for the past twenty years.

His mother used to call him a wanderer, although every time she said it, a small wrinkle of disapproval would form on her nose. Bernard had been the eldest of Josie and Dustin's three sons, and instead of following faithfully in his father's footsteps, Bernard had been more interested in blazing his own trails. He'd never wanted to take over the ranch, but tradition dictated that the homestead be passed to the firstborn son on his eighteenth birthday, and he'd inherited the lot in due time. His brothers grew up and eventually moved out—one to New York to take a job in finance, the other to California to work in the film industry. This had left Bernard solely responsible for the running of the family ranch, a job he'd accepted grudgingly after Dustin had made him promise he'd never sell.

"You never had much common sense," Dustin had said on his deathbed, "and you sure as shit have no business sense, but you'll figure out soon enough that you can't always be quitting things. I keep asking God to send you someone so that you'll finally settle down."

And send someone, He had. Emma Lynn Westley had come into Bernard's life as uneventfully as his brothers and parents had left, his growing awareness of her eventually culminating in what could rightly be considered a relationship. Unlike him, Emma had wanted desperately to settle down: as the only daughter in a military family, she'd known nothing but moving for the first eighteen years of her life, drifting from state to state before finally landing in Colorado for school. She'd been on her way to a party, Bernard on his way to his part-time job at a local bar, when they'd stumbled into the same 7-11 and fallen into conversation over a can of Pepsi.

"Why would you ever want to leave Colorado?" she'd asked when he told her his plans to catch a bus to Nevada and get a job somewhere in Vegas.

"Have you seen this place?" he'd replied, waving a hand at the horizon. "The state's haunted, you know. The mountains are full of old ghost towns and ghost stories."

"I don't believe in ghosts."

Bernard had smiled. They'd been sitting on the hood of his Chevy Silverado, talking by the glow of the convenience store behind them. Emma had been wearing a white sundress and matching white sandals, and every time she laughed, her smile practically lit up the parking lot. Bernard didn't believe in ghosts either, but that night in particular, he'd believed in angels.

"Well, good luck in Nevada," she had said, rolling her eyes as she added, "not that there's much to see there."

"You've been?"

"I lived in Reno for a bit. It's nice, but nothing like here."

Bernard had smiled. *Nothing like here* was exactly the kind of thing he was looking for.

Hopping off the truck, Emma had said, "I should get going. Don't want to be late for the party."

"I hope I see you around sometime," he'd replied, sliding to the ground as well.

"Does this mean you're *not* going to Nevada?"

"I go where the spirits lead me," Bernard had told her, trying to sound nonchalant about his wanderlust. It wasn't like he had a chance with her, this girl from everywhere who had dreams of settling down in the same town he was trying to escape. "Maybe Nevada, maybe Oregon, possibly Mexico."

"Well, then. Safe travels…"

"Bernard," he'd said, belatedly offering his hand.

"Emma."

"Enjoy the party, Emma."

Her face had split into a grin. "I always do."

She'd turned and started across the parking lot toward her destination. She had been a bright spot in the endless dark of the mountains, and his heart had followed her like a northern star. Two years later, they were married and living on the ranch, and for a time, Bernard had felt "settled down." But his soul had always secretly longed for the freedom of the open road, even after his twins were born and needed the stability of a family unit. Ray had been a surprise, and because he possessed an inclination toward horses from an early age, Bernard had hoped he would stay and help Marcus run the ranch.

Judging by their short reunion in the woods, it seemed Ray had never lost his gift. Which was good, Bernard thought now, because he'd already lost so much.

Bernard was walking on the shoulder of the road, his worldly possessions strapped to his back and his right thumb hooked toward oncoming cars. A green Subaru rumbled past him without slowing, so he dropped his hand and walked on, old memories churning like sediment in his mind. Yes, he'd go to Texas (he had his sights set on Amarillo), and from there… who knew?

But the one thing he wouldn't do is stay here, where his past was as inescapable as it was painful.

He knew this road he was on—he'd driven it a million times, in rain, snow, and unrelenting Colorado sunshine. He was on his way home, or what had once been home. The old, three-board fence stretched alongside him, and the field beyond it was in bloom with prairie-fire and yarrow, but their vivid hues weren't what caught Bernard's eye.

He approached the sign mounted to the front of the fence. Ray was still here, doing the one thing Dustin had hoped for all those decades ago.

He'd settled. More importantly, he'd flourished.

Bernard sidled over to the gate and stared at the driveway beyond it. Like the open road, it called to him. So many memories lay on that mile-long stretch of dirt and gravel, and before he could think of a reason not to, he unhooked the chain and invited himself in.

His boots crunched loudly on the stones littering his path. His cooking pot, which furnished the outside of his backpack, made a light pinging noise as it swung with each of his steps. Once, when the twins were toddlers, he'd hooked up a wooden toboggan to one of his old geldings and they'd spent the afternoon gliding up and down the driveway while Bernard led the horse by a lead rope. Emma had still been well then, and though Bernard had indulged occasional thoughts of what his life might've been like if they hadn't met, the joy on his sons' faces had convinced him he'd made the right choice. In fact, it wasn't until Marcus and Victor were in school that Bernard had noticed the changes in his marriage. Emma had admitted to feeling overwhelmed after Ray was born, but he'd chalked it up to hormonal changes. Who *wouldn't* be overwhelmed with three rambunctious boys in the house?

Emma hadn't gotten better. A lifelong artist, she'd tried to heal herself with a paintbrush, only for Bernard to claim that her macabre self-portraits were too frightening to keep in the house. She'd spend days holed up in her studio, slathering acrylics onto canvases and ignoring his complaints about their filthy house. That had been their agreement when they'd wed: Bernard would run the ranch and teach the boys how to ride and tend livestock, and she'd manage the household tasks and ensure they did their homework each night. And yet, as her mental state had deteriorated, his only concern seemed to be that he had to wait a little longer for dinner—or break out the cookware and make it himself.

The barn came into view as Bernard rounded the bend. There was the old tractor shed, a little worse for wear but still standing, and the round pen where he'd broken hundreds of young horses, not to mention a few bones. The paddocks were filled with bay and chestnut horses grazing under the trees, their tails swishing away the flies that hummed monotonously around the piles of manure that laced the field. Lucky emerged from behind his lean-to and plodded over to the fence, his elegant, grey head rising over the top board with ease. Bernard smiled and reached out a hand to stroke the animal's cheek.

"That's a good fella," he said. He saw his reflection in Lucky's left eye and was shocked by how much his hair had grown, and how much his beard had greyed, since he'd found himself living in the woods. Bernard glanced back at the house, but no one had come out to chastise him for communing with the livestock.

As Lucky circled back to investigate his hay pile, Bernard continued on a separate path that ended at the barn. Taking a breath to calm his nerves, he grasped the handle and slid open the door.

Nothing about the barn had really changed in the time Bernard had been gone: the aisle was a little tidier, and the old leather halters had been replaced with colourful nylon ones, but much of the workspace was just as he remembered it, crowded and covered in dust. This was where he'd come to be alone in the evenings—a place to think about the life he'd given up when he agreed to settle down. At least it would have made his father happy to know he hadn't sold the ranch. Even then, when it seemed like he'd inherited paradise, Bernard had counted down the days until Marcus turned eighteen and could take over the work for him. Then he and Emma could travel the world together—maybe go somewhere warm and sunny to alleviate her perpetual sadness.

Bernard stepped out of the storage room, walked to the end of the aisle, and stood in the doorway gazing out at the yard. This had all been his once, before his desperation and cowardice had compelled him to run away and leave his family behind. In the two decades since Emma's death, he'd never found another place that felt like this one. He closed his eyes, breathing in the scent of pine shavings and alfalfa. He pictured Emma shortly after they'd started dating, standing by the paddock fence in a blue dress and leather cowboy boots, her hair as free as her spirit.

"Do they all have names?" she had asked of the horses, who came over one by one to acquaint themselves with her scent.

"We don't name things around here. Saves us getting too attached," Bernard had explained.

"That seems a bit silly."

"Does it?"

"I've lived in thirteen different cities. I called every one of them home at some point."

"But you never got attached, did you? Knowing you would have to leave one day, I mean."

She'd smiled and wrapped her arms gently around the head of a red roan gelding who'd taken introductions a step further by snuggling up to her like a great, big puppy. "Everything is temporary. Why not love it while it's still here?"

Bernard felt his chest tighten as her memory faded. He loved her now as he'd loved her then. And when her brightness had begun to dim, he'd stumbled around in the dark, full of anger and resentment. Maybe she wouldn't have been so sad if he'd been a better husband and father. If he'd taken her complaints seriously, if he'd listened to her instead of running off to the safety of the barn every time she burst into tears, if he'd just stayed by her side like he promised to do, then maybe Emma would still be here, turning grey with him.

His eyes drifted toward the house. It wasn't too late to make things right with his sons, he realized as he started in that direction. What was the past but a blueprint for the future?

As he climbed the porch steps and prepared to knock on the door, he hoped Ray would be able to look past his unkempt appearance and see just how truly sorry he was for everything. And if forgiveness wasn't possible, then Bernard would settle for simply seeing his boy again, and go on his way once more. No hard feelings.

His knock went unanswered, despite the truck parked out front. Taking a couple of steps sideways, he peered in through the living room window. A reddish-brown leather couch, matching loveseat, and sagging recliner were crowded around the stone fireplace, and scattered across its mantle were numerous pictures featuring a young couple. Bernard withdrew, not wanting to intrude further. He tried knocking on the door again, but only silence came forward to greet him.

Perhaps Ray had gone out on horseback to check some fences or talk to his neighbours. As Bernard rounded the side of the house, he noticed the chopping block where he used to split wood, surrounded by a dense thicket filled with a variety of softwood trees. If he had to, he could make camp close by. He looked back and forth between the house and the woods for a minute, then set his feet on the well-trod path that led to the forest. For twenty years, Ray had waited for him to come home. Now, it was Bernard who would be waiting for him.

Twenty-three

Ray had been struck numb by grief over his amputated leg, just like when his mother had died and her absence had taken over the house. At night, after Hannah went home, he'd stare at the wall across from his bed, thinking about how he should have been prepared for this and wondering how he was supposed to face the weeks and months ahead.

They should've left him in the woods, Ray thought.

He heard Marcus before he saw him, chatting up one of the nurses outside Ray's room. His eyes flickered over to the door as his brother arrived with his usual flourish, carrying a paper bag in one hand.

"Good news," Marcus stated, setting the bag on the table next to Ray's bed. "The nurses said you can have food from outside the hospital, so I stopped by that burger place you like and got your usual."

"I'm not hungry," Ray muttered, his eyes once again returning to the TV. His breakfast tray hadn't yet been collected, and the semi-congealed lump of cold oatmeal wasn't helping his appetite.

Marcus grimaced at the tray. "I don't blame you. I wouldn't eat that either." He opened the paper bag and asked, "Where's Hannah?"

"She went to the bathroom." Ray darted another look at his brother, doling out the contents of the bag. "You're in a good mood."

"Beats the alternative," Marcus answered with a shrug. A tiny smirk wrinkled his cheek as he lowered his voice. "Besides, have you seen your nurse?"

"You mean, Alyssa, the one with the tattoos? Yes, I've seen her."

Marcus arched a brow. "Nothing, eh? You sure they took just your leg when you were under?"

"I'm married," Ray replied coldly, "and I'm not really in a mood to listen to your inappropriate sexual fantasies right now."

"Not so loud. Jeez. Here, eat this." Marcus tossed the burger into Ray's lap. As he turned to throw the bag in the garbage, Hannah walked through the door, her troubled expression smoothing away as Ray came into view.

"Speak of the Devil," Marcus said as she removed her purse and placed it on the chair. "By the way, did you find the health insurance papers?"

"Not yet, but I'm sure they're in the office somewhere."

Marcus gestured to Ray and said, "I brought him food. I would've gotten something for you too, but you weren't answering my texts."

Hannah ignored him. She and Marcus had been fighting for the past couple of days over her decision to remove Ray's leg, and while they'd agreed not to bicker in front of him, she sensed they weren't doing a great job of hiding their animosity toward one another. Pasting a smile on her face, she sat down next to Ray's bed and helped herself to a sip of the cherry cola from the takeout cup on the nightstand. "Has the physiotherapist come by yet?" she asked him.

"He did."

"And did you do your exercises with him?"

"No. I didn't see the point."

Hannah made a sound of disbelief. "The point is to regain your mobility and independence. You want to get out of this hospital, don't you?"

Ray said nothing. The burger was still warm, its wrapper leaving his fingertips shiny with grease. He peeled back the corners knowing he had no intention of taking a single bite as Marcus and Hannah traded looks across his bed.

Their silent standoff ended when Marcus announced, "Since you're here now, I was thinking of stepping outside for some air."

Hannah nodded and felt the weight of his presence lift off her shoulders. "Okay."

Marcus took his leave, his voice rising as he passed the nurses station once more. Ray shifted his attention to Hannah, who'd taken her brief visit to the restroom as an opportunity to freshen up and brush her hair. He set the burger on the table next to the untouched oatmeal, wiped his hands off on the blanket, and took a breath to speak.

"So, who's winning?" he asked.

"What?"

"The temperature of the room dropped about five degrees the moment you walked in. When Marc's pissed off about something, he does a terrible job of hiding it." Ray sobered. "It's about me, isn't it?"

Hannah sighed. "He blames me for amputating your leg. He wanted to keep going with the antibiotics, but I was worried that you'd become septic if we didn't do something to curb the infection. We've been sort of prickly with each other ever since."

"Huh. Well, I guess I'm not surprised."

Hannah watched as Ray's attention drifted back to the TV. Ever since waking up in post-op, he'd gone through the usual reactions to discovering he was an amputee, and she'd done her best to ride those emotional waves with him, while also acting as an anchor in this storm. When he wasn't groggy from the painkillers, he was nearly catatonic with boredom. This was the first time he'd actually been alert and oriented enough to talk about the accident, and Hannah was torn between enjoying his company and chipping away at his veneer of indifference to gauge the depths of his trauma.

"You should've left me out there," he whispered.

Her eyes widened. "Are you crazy? I wasn't going to let you die."

"Well, you should have," he pressed, "it would've been better for everyone."

"Don't say that," she seethed.

"I'll say whatever I want."

Her fight with Marcus forgotten, Hannah rose to pace the room. In a way, she understood where his anger was coming from, but that didn't mean he was justified in taking it out on her.

"Do you have any idea how many people it took to find you?" she asked. "How hard everyone worked trying to get the word out about your disappearance? Micah rode an ATV, for crying out loud! The least you could do is be grateful."

"For what? For being stuck in a hospital bed with only one leg? I'm probably never going to be able to ride again, you know that?"

"That's not true. The physiotherapist said it's totally possible that you will ride again, but you *have* to do your exercises."

"Oh, what does Terrance know?"

Hannah's shoulders sank. "Ray, please. You're better than this."

"Better than what? I was at my peak—and you brought me down." He looked around the room, seeing the same four walls that had been holding him prisoner for days. His gaze settled on the overbed table, covered in plastic dishes and food he couldn't bring himself to eat. "Why do I keep ending up here?" he whispered.

"Ray, it's okay. It's not your—"

As she was about to say *fault*, he reached for the table and shoved it as hard as he could. It crashed to the floor, prompting Alyssa and another nurse to come running into the room.

Appalled by his outburst, Hannah could only stare at the coffee splattered across the floor and up the wall. The overturned bowl of oatmeal had remained more or less contained, but the utensils had scattered in every direction.

There was a sudden clarity to Ray's expression as tears formed in his eyes. He stared at her, then down at his trembling hands as bright red blood beaded up on his skin where his IV needle had been.

"I'm sorry," Ray shuddered as Alyssa stepped carefully around the chaos. "I didn't mean to do that."

"I know. Can you take a deep breath for me?" Alyssa urged, her gloved fingers assessing the injection site on his right hand. To the other nurse, she said, "Page housekeeping and I'll get him fixed up here."

As Ray struggled to pull in a lungful of air, Hannah bent down and attempted to clean up the mess.

Alyssa told her, "You don't have to do that."

"I know." Hannah righted the table and set the spoon and empty coffee cup on top of it. There was little to be done about the oatmeal, which lay in a gooey puddle at her feet. As she tossed the burger in the trash, she felt it again—that hot feeling that preceded every anxiety attack. As Alyssa dabbed at the back of Ray's hand with a bit of gauze, Hannah said, "I should probably get out of the way here. I'll check in with Marc and come back in a few minutes."

She didn't wait for Ray's reply before grabbing her purse and beating a hasty retreat out of his room.

Marcus was on his way back inside when Hannah bumped into him outside the elevator. One look at her face was all it took for him to put aside his grievances, and he grabbed hold of her arm just as she was about to brush past him and sprint out the front doors.

"Whoa, hang on. Where are you going?"

"Outside," Hannah replied briskly. "Don't you think it's about time that I 'got some air'?"

He furrowed his brows. "What happened?"

His lack of vitriol was all it took to break down her wall. They moved to the side of the hall, close to a planter brimming with artificial bamboo, and let the usual hospital traffic continue to flow past them.

Hannah's heart was racing. As she struggled to meet Marc's gaze, she whispered, "Ray said we should have left him out in the woods. I told him that was crazy talk, and he reacted by pushing over the tray table and pulling his IV out. I didn't know what to do, so I just ran out of the room." An involuntary shiver went through her. The worst of her anxiety was behind her, but she still felt like the world was moving too fast and the air was too thin, making everything around them look blurry.

Marcus lowered his voice too. "How long has this been going on? The anxiety attacks."

She took a deep breath. "A few years."

He nodded, then surprised her by admitting, "I had one a few months ago. I was on my way to work. It was so bad that I had to pull over and wait for it to pass."

Hannah replied only half-jokingly, "I thought cowboys weren't afraid of anything."

"I wish that were true. Do you want to go home for a bit? I don't mind staying here with Ray if you need a break."

"Are you sure?"

"Of course. Someone has to tell him how to behave." Marcus smirked, and just like that, the tension of the past few days dissolved. "Go. I'll tell Ray you had to take care of something back at the ranch."

Hannah dried the last of her tears, then stepped around him and headed for the exit.

*

It was nearly dark when Hannah arrived at the ranch. With how much time she'd been spending at the hospital, there hadn't been many opportunities to take care of the house, much less shop for groceries. A paper bag filled with essentials like milk, eggs, and bread sat on the passenger seat beside her. It wasn't much, but it would tide them over for a few more days, if Marcus didn't offer to replenish their pantry sooner.

Hannah gathered up the bag and exited the car, the driver's door echoing as she shut it behind her. She hadn't given much thought to what the summer would look like, with Ray in the hospital and Marcus driving back and forth between Wyoming and Colorado every weekend for the foreseeable future. Tomorrow, she would have to call up Ray's clients and explain to them what had happened—give them a chance to take their horses elsewhere for training. This would inevitably leave their bank account short, but what choice did they have? It would be weeks before Ray could be fitted for a prosthetic leg, and another chunk of time on top of that spent learning how to function with it. The earliest he could hope to get back to work was sometime in the fall, and Hannah wasn't sure if their savings would last that long, even with her paychecks propping them up.

She switched on the lamp just inside the front door, causing the living room to fill with a welcoming glow. Slipping off her shoes, Hannah tossed her purse onto the bench, carried the groceries into the kitchen, set the bag on the counter, and glanced at the flashing red light on the answering machine. As the messages played, she emptied the bag and thought about the nature of this business. She didn't totally regret moving here, of course, but even in good times the ranch demanded constant upkeep—far more than she'd anticipated when Ray had proposed. If there was a silver lining to this seething cumulonimbus cloud that now towered over their life, it was the lack of snow and ice: with the horses on pasture for the summer, Hannah could get away with putting out less hay during the day, and thank God she didn't have to worry about winter blankets and water pumps suddenly freezing up.

After putting away the food, Hannah spent a bit of time tidying the place up. The wooden crate in the living room that held their firewood was down to a couple wedges of pine and a few ribbons of birch bark, so she trekked into the mud room and unlocked the back door. Like a squirrel stockpiling acorns for the winter, Ray had extra firewood stashed all over the ranch: there was a stack of it covered in blue tarp behind the house, another in the drive shed, and a third wall built up at the bunkhouse, where an antique woodstove provided the only source of heat for the cozy cabin.

Hannah had just folded back a corner of the tarp when she noticed the flicker of light in the distance. She squinted into the dark, past the chopping block and into the trees that bordered their backyard. A campfire, its sweet smoke riding the gentle breeze, grew visible amongst the evergreens.

Her heart kicked into overdrive. No way was she going to confront this person alone. Hannah's hands were shaking as she reached into her back pocket for her phone and clicked on Marcus's name to shoot him a text. *When do you think you'll be back at the ranch?*

She was weighing her options when he replied a few seconds later: *Probably another hour or so.*

Hannah lowered the phone and stared at the pulsing inferno. A lot could happen in an hour. Hell, a second had way too much potential for her liking, and she didn't fancy the idea of hiding in a closet while she waited for her brother-in-law to show up and take control of the situation. She slipped her phone back into her pocket and took a deep breath, knowing too well what she had to do.

She started toward the campfire, but stopped when she reached the chopping block. Hannah eyed the axe, the light from the mudroom behind her teasing the edges of its long wooden handle. Taking it with her seemed like overkill, but how stupid would she look if her uninvited guest had some lethal force of his own, and she showed up unarmed? *Better to look a little crazy than to end up dead*, she figured.

She yanked the axe out of the block, wrapped one hand around the handle near the blade to balance its weight, and walked toward the trees with steely resolve.

The fire was well-contained and well-fed. Tucked under the trees across from it, Hannah noticed a blue tent with a rain cover. This didn't strike her as an amateur setup—whoever had made camp here clearly knew what they were doing. She tried to see if her visitor had had the good sense to hang their feedbag between two trees, but between the darkness and the smoke, her eyes couldn't make out more than a hint of indigo sky. She loosened her grip on the axe, only for her fingers to tighten as she heard footsteps coming toward her.

Bernard emerged from the woods carrying an armful of dry branches.

"Stop," Hannah blurted.

"Jesus!" He staggered back a couple of steps, as surprised to see her as she was to see him. His wild eyes settled on the axe and he instinctively raised one hand. "I'm not armed."

Hannah didn't move, save for the rapid rise and fall of her collarbone as she breathed in the smoky air. She looked him over swiftly, clearly not convinced.

"I'm not armed. See?" Bernard set down the firewood so that both hands were empty. He held his arms above his head, his mouth slightly open.

Neither of them moved. In the firelight, this man looked like any other long-distance backpacker: lean, tough, and more than a little scruffy. But there was a desperation to the way he held her gaze that reminded Hannah of a rabbit caught in a snare, and she once again acknowledged the absurdity of bringing the axe. What was she going to do—cut off his head for trespassing?

"Who are you?" she asked.

He slowly lowered his hands, but not his guard. "Name's Bernard. Who are you?"

Hannah took a moment to process this. This was either the craziest coincidence in the entire universe, or she was face to face with Ray's estranged father. "I'm Hannah."

"You're… Ray's wife?"

"I am. And I guess that makes you his father."

A muscle in his jaw slackened. "Yes."

She let out a breath as the smoke changed direction, stinging her eyes.

"I'm sorry," Bernard continued, taking a step sideways in order to see her better. "I didn't mean to intrude. I came by the house earlier, but it seemed like no one was home, so I thought I'd make camp and wait until Ray came back."

Hannah blinked a couple of times as her phone went off in her back pocket. She ignored its buzzing as Bernard began collecting the branches he'd dropped and made a pile next to his tent. *Like father, like son.*

She told him gruffly, "You can't stay here. Marcus is in town and he doesn't know…"

"I wanted to see Ray," Bernard explained once he was finished arranging the fuel for his fire. He stood up, turning to her with a pleading expression. "I know I don't deserve forgiveness after what I did, but I thought maybe if I could talk to him, it would give him some closure about his mother. Is he here?"

Hannah looked him over, taking in the long, greasy hair, the threadbare sweater, and the ripped, filthy jeans that told her he'd been living in the woods for months. *This* was the man Ray had been trying to save? If she weren't so exhausted, she was sure she would've combusted with anger. Thankfully for Bernard, the fire in her belly was nothing more than a smoldering heap of guilt over the role she'd played in Ray's transformation. She clutched the axe in one hand and brushed back her hair with the other, the heat of the fire making her face uncomfortably warm.

"He's not here," she answered quietly as Bernard leaned in. "He's at the hospital."

His eyes widened. "Did something happen?"

"He was looking for you. Why he thought you deserved a second chance I'll never know, but he's good like that. Innocent. He fell off his horse and we didn't find him for three days. When we did, he was on the brink of death." Hannah held his gaze, ensuring Bernard heard the next words out of her mouth. "He lost his right leg because of you. And I just can't imagine that he's going to want to hear your excuses now, much less forgive you for what you did."

Bernard's strained expression flickered between her and the fire. "I have to see him," he whispered. His gaze boomeranged back to her, urgent and glistening with tears. "Can you take me to see him?"

"Not tonight."

"But he's my son!" Bernard exploded. As he took a step in her direction, Hannah subconsciously tightened her hold on the axe, and he froze. "Please. I don't have any other way to get there. I need to see him."

She looked him over coolly. He could have run away, but that wasn't the case. Perhaps there was still hope for this deranged mountain man after all.

She decided to tread carefully. "I'll take you to him, but first, I have to talk to Marcus. You can't camp out behind the house tonight."

"Where do you want me to go?"

"We have a bunkhouse. It's small, but it's... out of the way." Hannah gestured in its general direction. "You can spend the night there, and I'll try to explain everything to Marcus. I can't promise he's not going to kick you out when he learns you're here, but—"

"I'll take the risk."

She nodded. So it was settled: Bernard was back, and come what may, she'd done her part to try and heal the wounds of the past.

Hannah helped him break camp and extinguish his fire. Once everything was packed up, she led him down the hill toward the house, with no further conversation between them and nothing to disturb the awful silence but the rustling of their feet in the grass.

Once they arrived at the bunkhouse, she pulled the key out of her pocket and unlocked the door.

"Victor used to live here, before he moved out," she said as she reached inside to flip on the light. "We mainly use it as a guesthouse now, but as you can see, we don't have guests very often."

A thin layer of dust had built up on the dresser, but Bernard hardly noticed. The last time he'd been surrounded by four walls and a bed had been sometime in March, when he'd spent the night in a motel room in Salt Lake City. He'd been without a fixed address since January and his savings were running low. Realizing that he'd soon have no money, he'd decided to spend whatever was left on camping gear, including a tent, rain cover, and proper sleeping bag, if he didn't want to freeze to death on his way to Texas. The road had been his home ever since, and while it pleased his wanderlust to be able to pack up and relocate whenever the urge struck, being back in the presence of running water and electricity felt like being touched by the good Lord Himself.

Hannah crossed to the bathroom and turned on the light there as well, revealing a vanity with brushed nickel taps, a toilet, and a shower enclosed in frosted glass in the corner. White crepe curtains covered the room's only window, but the real privacy came from the bunkhouse's remote location, with nothing but trees in all directions.

She explained, "The hot water tank isn't very big, so I wouldn't recommend taking long showers. There are towels in the top drawer of the dresser and extra toilet paper under the sink. And if you want to watch something on TV, we have a DVD player."

Bernard lingered on the threshold, gobsmacked by the beauty of his surroundings. Hot water sounded absolutely divine. And the bed—his body ached for the comfort of a real bed, although he had to fight the urge to crawl beneath the covers before he'd washed the filth off his body. He knew he reeked: Hannah was being polite about it, but it was impossible not to notice the musky odour that clung to his skin and clothes. His hair looked like something not of this world, and within only a couple of minutes, the greasy smell took over the room.

He stepped aside as Hannah made her way back into the bedroom, eager to cut the tour short. "Firewood is outside. You can hang your sleeping bag over the railing to dry. I'll drop by tomorrow and make sure you're settled in."

"Thank you," Bernard said. "Thank you for being so kind."

Hannah nodded, feeling uneasy about letting Bernard stay. Not because they had valuables worth stealing or children worth protecting, but because there was no telling how long he'd stick around before the road called him back. Ray wouldn't be able to handle losing his leg and his father in the same week, and it would be her job to pick up the broken pieces. What it came down to was this: she didn't want to be stuck cleaning up after Bernard, in either the physical sense or the emotional one.

She slipped outside, closing the door behind her. Taking several deep breaths of the cool mountain air, she set her feet on the path back to the house, dreading the conversation she would soon be having with Marcus.

Twenty-four

Hannah was waiting by the door when Marcus arrived an hour later. At first, he didn't seem to notice her standing there, chewing on her bottom lip. He removed his sweater and hung it on one of the pegs, ran his hand through his hair, and appeared to consider something before his gaze finally drifted her way.

She asked, "How's Ray?"

"He's okay. He was kind of upset that you left, but he understood you had things to do here."

"Did you tell him I was coming back tomorrow?"

"You know I can't read your mind." Marcus headed into the kitchen. "Did you make dinner?"

"No, but I did pick up some groceries on my way home. We were getting low on a few things…"

As Marcus approached the refrigerator and pored over its contents, Hannah drew a breath and said, "There's something I need to talk to you about. Would you prefer to do this before or after you eat?"

He pulled out the egg carton and the sliced bread and set both on the counter. "We can't talk *while* I eat?"

Hannah blew out a breath. "Fine."

"Look, if this is about money, then I'll look for the insurance papers tomorrow. You may have to sell some of your farming equipment in order to pay off your medical debt. Or your horses."

"We need our equipment, and Ray would never agree to sell off his herd."

"I didn't mean your whole herd. But let's be realistic: several of your horses are retired from ranch work, but they'd still make decent trail or pleasure riding horses." Marcus placed a frying pan on the stove and turned the dial halfway. After a minute, he added a pat of butter to the pan and pulled two eggs out of the carton, then cracked them one at a time over the sizzling pool of fat. With some difficulty, he told her, "I'd understand if you decided to sell Abby."

"We'd never sell Abby. She's the lead mare. And even though you're a big, tough cowboy, I know you'd be a weepy mess if we sold her." Hannah smirked, moving to stand beside the counter as the eggs turned white around the edges.

"So I have a soft spot. Sue me." He waved the spatula at her.

She sighed. "This isn't about money. It's about why Ray went into the backcountry."

"We've already had this discussion. Russ and Micah found a cougar kill site during the cattle drive, and Ray wanted to see if the cougar was still in the area."

"Well, one of those statements is true," Hannah said quietly. Her hands had gone cold, so she tucked them under her arms before continuing. "They did find a dead calf in the backcountry, but Ray wasn't looking for the cougar. You know Lucky, the one in the isolation paddock?" As Marcus glanced out the window and nodded, Hannah said, "He got out while Ray and I were away from the ranch, so he jumped on Abby and went to track him down. As you can see, we found Lucky, but Ray also found... your dad."

"Bernard? Our deadbeat father who's been missing for twenty years?"

"Yes." She added, "Ray and I were going to wait and tell you together when he got out of the hospital, but obviously there's been a change of plans. Marc, I'm so sorry. I know this is probably the last thing you expected to hear. It's okay if you're upset. If you need to let it out—"

"Bernard is alive?"

"Yes," Hannah said again. "His hair's grown out and he looks, well, let's just say he looks like he's been down on his luck for a while, but—"

"How do you know what he looks like?"

Her throat closed up. "Because he's staying in the bunkhouse."

The eggs were starting to turn brown and thick like leather, but Marcus didn't notice. His attention was fully on Hannah, his expression both irate and uncomprehending, and the spatula he held was locked in his white-knuckled grip.

"Whose brilliant idea was that? Yours? Or Ray's?" he asked.

"Mine. Bernard was camping in the woods behind the house, and I figured if I let him stay in the bunkhouse, it would give me a chance to talk to you." As Hannah took a step toward him, Marcus retreated. "I know this is a lot to process. I wouldn't blame you for being mad at me."

"Oh, believe me, I'm not even close to mad. I'm about ten miles past it. Do you have any idea what it was like to grow up with Bernard as a father? While other kids were doing fun stuff with their dads like fishing or playing catch, we were working for him, taking orders as if we were no better than the ranch hands. You'd never hear him say 'I love you' or 'I'm proud of you' because he thought showing affection would make us weak—I believe the correct term was *pansies*. And forget about him supporting our dreams—our destinies were chosen for us before we were born, and any deviation from that path was met with ice-cold indifference. You know what our mom said right before she killed herself, Hannah? She said she'd finally found a way out of this prison. For a long time, I thought she was talking about her depression, but she wasn't. She meant her marriage."

"Marc," Hannah said softly, "I'm so sorry."

"If you were sorry, you would've left him out there. And Ray—Jesus." He shook his head furiously. "He lost his *leg* because of that selfish prick. But I should've known. Ray doesn't value his life because Bernard never taught him how. He's spent twenty years idolizing a man who couldn't care less if he lives or dies."

"That's not true! When I told him about Ray, Bernard demanded I take him to the hospital tonight. He came all this way to try and make amends. You don't think maybe he's changed?"

180

"People don't change, Hannah. You're still a planner, Ray's still an idealist, Victor's still dodging this family like his life depends on it, and I'm—"

"Still a know-it-all?" she finished acerbically. "Maybe you're right! Maybe people never change. But deep down I like to think they're capable of it. And yes, Ray lost his leg and his life will never be the same again, but if we push Bernard away now, then all of this—" Hannah spread her arms "—the rescue mission, the surgery, not to mention the avalanche of debt that's about to come crashing down on us in a few weeks, will have been in vain."

"Oh, so we're keeping him around to justify butchering my brother," Marcus scrapped out, "which, in case you've forgotten, I voted against."

"I thought we were past that," she seethed.

"Oh, we are. Ray's leg is gone. So, congratulations—you won."

Hannah bit her lip until she tasted blood. She brought her hand up to cover her mouth as she fled the room, leaving the smell of burnt eggs hanging heavy in the air and Marcus standing by himself in the kitchen.

As her footsteps faded, he braced his hands against the stove. His stomach was churning with every feeling except hunger. A million repressed memories swirled in his mind as he pictured his never-do-well father hunkered down in the rustic cabin Marcus had built with his own two hands. It was the biggest slap in the face he'd ever gotten not delivered by an ex-girlfriend. Bright-coloured spots danced in his vision and his jaw ached from clenching his teeth.

When the room started to spin, Marcus lowered his head and forced himself to take a deep breath. At least he wasn't sitting in traffic this time, but that only meant he couldn't run away from his demons—one of which had just come strolling back into his life to bedevil him again.

He couldn't fight it, the anger. The heat built inside of him until it surfaced on his face, red-hot and threatening to erupt. Back and forth he paced, silently begging for the invisible hands wrapped around his throat to let him go, but they merely tightened, cutting off oxygen until he thought he might faint.

The beast inside of him broke free, seizing control over his body. In a split second, all reason dissolved. Marcus wheeled back to the doorway, and his hands, like the eggs, became something unrecognizable. He drove his fist into the kitchen wall, leaving a ragged, dusty hole in the plaster just like the one Bernard had left in his heart.

Twenty-five

"I'm sorry I ran out on you yesterday," Hannah said. "You know how it is with anxiety. You've dealt with it yourself."

"I know. I wasn't mad, just worried." Ray ran a hand through his hair. The cut on his forehead was almost fully healed, leaving nothing but a faint pink scar above his brow. As Hannah shifted her phone to hide the mess of empty feed bags in the background, he said, "Is Marc coming today?"

"I don't know. I actually haven't seen him all morning."

Ray furrowed his brows. "Did you guys have another fight?"

"What do you think?" Hannah stood up and walked into one of the empty stalls to continue mucking out. She propped her phone against the window and dug the bedding fork deep into the layer of shavings to uncover the hardened clumps of manure.

"That's not like him. Marc and I used to argue about how to run the ranch and stuff, but that's plain, old sibling rivalry. He's never been this hotheaded, especially not with you."

Hannah tossed the excrement into the wheelbarrow. "I guess he's still mad at me."

"For what?"

"For, you know, letting them amputate your leg."

She glimpsed the screen as Ray looked down at his lap, his expression unreadable. The garbled sound of the hospital paging system rang out in the background. "Are *you* mad at me?" she asked.

"Not mad, just..." He fixed the collar of his gown and sighed. "I'm still processing it, okay? All that stuff I said yesterday... it was wrong, but it needed to come out, I guess. You know I've never been good at finding the perfect words to describe how I'm feeling."

"You don't have to explain it to me, Ray. And for the record, if there had been *any* other option, some way to keep your leg and heal you, I would've chosen it in a heartbeat." Hannah bent down and heaved another pile of wet shavings into the wheelbarrow. The work had been piling up around here, and she'd been trying to tackle as much of it as possible without Marcus's help. If he didn't make an appearance soon, she'd have no choice but to march up to the bunkhouse and offer the job to Bernard, who would probably agree to anything that brought him closer to seeing Ray again.

As if divining her thoughts, Ray asked, "How's my dad this morning?"

"I haven't been up to see him yet."

As she said this, a black Ford F-150 came tearing down the driveway. It shot past the house, gravel flying out behind its massive tires, and skidded past the barn so quickly that for a second, all Hannah could see, smell, and taste was a cloud of dust. Marcus's destination was no mystery: he was on a warpath to the bunkhouse, the events of the previous evening coming to a head in broad daylight. As he disappeared into the trees, a cold sweat broke out over Hannah's body and she dropped the bedding fork, letting it fall into the layer of shavings at her feet.

"I have to call you back," she said in a rush, grabbing her phone before darting out of the stall.

"What's going—"

Hanging up the call, Hannah followed the truck into the thicket, her breaths coming short as adrenaline flooded her veins. She'd walked this path countless times, but her feet stumbled over it now, too blind with panic to notice the tree roots that twisted treacherously beneath the deadfall. When she emerged at the edge of the clearing, she saw Marcus's truck parked a few steps from the porch and her brother-in-law pinning Bernard against the doorframe. Marcus didn't notice Hannah's arrival until Bernard looked over at her with both hands raised in surrender.

"What are you doing?" Hannah shouted.

Marcus glanced at her. "Why did you bring him here?" he bellowed. "Of all the places you could've sent him, you let him stay *here*." Turning back to Bernard, Marcus growled, "You did this, you know. You're responsible for *all* of this, so don't look at me like you didn't do anything!"

"Marcus. Let him go."

"No. I don't think he realizes how much damage he caused, so I'm going to show him."

Hannah had no idea what this entailed, and she wasn't about to ask. All she knew was that she was terrified. Ray was right: Marcus was off, and it was time to start digging beneath the surface to uncover the root of his troubling behaviour.

Bernard wrapped his hands around Marcus's wrists and stared deep into his son's eyes. "You don't want to do this. Trust me—I've been in enough fights to know they never end well."

"Marc, stop it." Hannah climbed the steps to the porch. When she reached out to touch his arm, he jerked back, causing Bernard's body to fold forward as he was released.

Refusing to hear reason, Marcus stomped down the steps and over to the driver's door. Hannah had discovered the hole in the wall when she came downstairs for coffee this morning, but Marcus was nowhere to be found. Thinking he'd gone into town for supplies to patch the hole, she'd started on the barn chores and called Ray. It was all too easy to ignore the signs of impending disaster when there was so much to take care of at home... Looking at it from this angle, she could almost sympathize with Bernard and his inability to notice Emma's declining mental health. Sometimes, there was just too much to do to worry about something that might never happen.

Until it did.

"They're not right..." Hannah heard Bernard say.

She turned to him. "What are you talking about?"

"His eyes. They weren't right." Gesturing to his own eyes, Bernard posited, "I think he's been drinking."

185

"Marc doesn't have a drinking problem." And yet, the signs were all there in glowing neon colours. After all, hadn't she had a drinking problem at one time? The impaired judgment, the desire to escape, the hankering for control... For all their disagreements, maybe she and Marcus had more in common than she realized.

As his truck circled back toward the path, Hannah took out her phone again to find several messages from Ray. Two hasty departures in less than twenty-four hours didn't exactly convey the sense that things were under control. As his wife and co-owner of the ranch, she felt she should have been able to handle whatever came her way, and yet, as she watched the taillights on Marcus's truck vanish through the trees, Hannah knew she would need some help.

She turned back to Bernard and asked, "Are you okay?"

He shrugged. "Well enough."

"I'm sorry. You being back here... it's hard for him. Hard for all of us." As Bernard avoided eye contact with her, Hannah said, "I can take you to see Ray later, if you want. But first, we need to discuss your future here on the ranch. Right now, Ray is still several weeks away from being released from the hospital. Normally, he looks after the horses and the barn chores, but since he was rescued, I've been taking care of everything by myself. And to be honest, it's too much."

"What about Marcus?"

"Marc doesn't live with us anymore. He moved to Wyoming a few months after the wedding. The point is, I know Ray would like to get to know you, and if you're open to the idea, I thought maybe you could work here. We won't be able to pay you, but you're welcome to stay in the bunkhouse. This ranch means the world to Ray, and I don't want to see it fall apart."

Bernard studied her face. He was a man of no fixed address and few possessions, but he hadn't totally forgotten how to run a farm. At the very least, tending to the livestock would allow him to build up his strength before he inevitably headed south, where the herds of Texas longhorns would put the cowboy back in him again.

"I'll consider your proposition," he said slowly. "Let me know when you're headed over to the hospital and I'll join you. I think it's time I gave my son the apology he deserves." With that, his hand reached for the door and he stepped inside to nurse his wounds in peace.

*

Hannah wasn't counting on Marcus coming back to the ranch after the fiasco at the bunkhouse that morning. There'd been no answer when Victor tried calling him, and even texts from Ray were left on read. But around 10PM, just as Hannah was preparing to give up on the book she was reading and go to bed, Marcus's truck pulled up to the house.

"So, you decided to come back after all," she said the moment she heard the front door open. The fire flickered placidly in the hearth, keeping the chill of their exchange at bay.

"I'm not sure I had a choice," he replied as he removed his jacket and boots. He walked over to the armchair and sank into its familiar comfort, just a few feet from where Hannah was curled up on the couch.

Nodding at the book on the coffee table, he asked, "Is it helping you forget about everything?"

"Not really. The house is too quiet." Hannah glimpsed his face before turning her attention back to her fingernails. "Where did you go?"

Without looking at her, Marcus said, "I went to the cemetery where our mom's buried. I haven't seen her in a while, so I thought I'd pay my respects." He rubbed his forehead. "After that, I drove over to see Jim and Laney, had dinner with them, got gas for my truck, and came home."

"We were all expecting you to go back to Wyoming."

"I considered it."

"What changed your mind?"

Marcus's deadpan expression drifted over to her. "What do you think?"

"I think we need to talk about Bernard," she said firmly, and slid her legs off the couch to perch on the edge of the cushion.

As expected, Marcus looked elsewhere. But he made no move toward the door, so Hannah proceeded.

"I know this is a lot to take in. I'm still trying to process everything, too. But, all things considered, was it really so bad seeing Bernard today?"

"Yes. For me, it was." Marcus sat forward in the armchair and hunched his shoulders. When his gaze rose to meet hers, Hannah saw that in the half-darkness of the room, his eyes were more black than blue. Shadows wavered on his face as the fire danced and dwindled.

"That man took everything from me," he said softly. "The version of Bernard that Ray's told you about is not the one who raised me. Dad loved Ray. Once Ray was old enough to start working around the horses, that was it—he became dad's little buckaroo. I was destined to inherit the ranch, but it was pretty clear early on that Ray was the one dad wanted to run it."

"And now he does," Hannah whispered.

Marcus nodded. "I was an okay rancher. I understood the business side of things, but I didn't have the magic touch when it came to breaking horses. Dad often told me I'd never make anything of myself out there in the real world, so I should consider myself lucky I was the firstborn. And you know, I think maybe he was right all along. Ray's got you and this place, Victor's got Addy and his beautiful baby girl, and I'm..."

"You were more than okay, Marcus. You kept this place running during the worst years of yours and Ray's life. You were just a kid when Bernard walked out, so how can you blame yourself for any of this?"

"That's the point. I grew up too fast." Marcus ran a hand through his hair and reclined in the chair, staring at the fire. "I hated him then, and I still hate him now. Don't let Bernard trick you into thinking he's a good guy just because he hung around to see Ray. Once he's cleared his conscience, he'll move on like he always does."

"What if he doesn't?" Hannah asked. "What if—hypothetically speaking—he stayed?"

Marcus turned his head toward her. "You did something, didn't you?"

"I—yes."

He lifted his head slightly, his eyes narrowing. "Did you tell Bernard he could stay here?"

"I did it for Ray," Hannah snapped. "He loves this ranch, but I'm afraid we're going to lose it unless we find someone to help us. And Bernard knows what he's doing. I offered for him to stay in the bunkhouse. He'll complete the barn chores and turn the horses out, and we'll keep him fed and housed. In the meantime, Ray can focus on getting better."

"Of all the people in this world you could've offered that job to, you chose our deadbeat dad? Are you really that desperate?"

"Yes! I can't do this by myself, Marcus. I'm not a rancher like you. I'm just some woman who happened to fall in love with a cowboy." Tears twinkled in her eyes. "This isn't going to work if you and I are enemies. And I can't afford to lose you too so, please, just trust me, okay?"

Marcus shook his head and stood up abruptly.

"Okay. Fine. It's your ranch now, not mine. Do whatever you feel is best." He crossed to the stairs, his shadow beating him by a head. "I'm going to bed."

Hannah watched him disappear into the darkness of the second floor before turning her focus back to the book on the coffee table. To own something was to take responsibility for its failure, and she'd never been particularly comfortable with plans not panning out. But this was real life, and if she truly loved Ray, then she'd have to take a chance on the unknown.

Twenty-six

"This is ridiculous," Ray murmured.

Terrance smiled, undaunted by his patient's lack of enthusiasm. "I know, but why don't we give it a try? It might work."

Ray's gaze dropped to the mirror Terrance held vertically between his knees, with the reflective side facing his intact left leg. Where his right knee had been, there was now only a jagged pink scar that ran horizontally from inner thigh to outer leg, its blushing pink colour a testament to its newness. There would be no getting used to this, Ray had thought when the bandages finally came off for good. He'd have to learn how to walk, work, and ride again with only one leg. The worst part was, even though he could see that his limb was gone, a small part of his brain refused to accept its absence. Thus, the phantom pains.

Terrance leaned forward slightly, catching Ray's eye. "How about if we start with something simple, like wiggling your toes?"

He indicated the mirror, and Ray set his focus on the image of his shoe moving up and down, then side to side. Terrance had been doing all kinds of exercises with him lately in hopes of preventing muscle atrophy and joint contracture. As Ray's condition had improved, they'd gone from doing exercises in bed to doing exercises in the physiotherapy room, where a plethora of seemingly random items promised to fast-track his recovery. Ray was doubtful that studying his movements in a mirror would be enough to trick his brain into thinking he hadn't lost a leg, but Terrance was relentless.

"That's five," Terrance said after Ray had been flexing and extending his ankle for a few seconds, "notice any improvement in the right leg?"

"You mean what's left of it? Not really. But I usually only get the pains at night."

"Okay, so we'll keep doing the mirror therapy until your brain stops firing out all those pain signals. Your recovery has only begun, so it's normal to have a few false starts."

"Does anyone in the medical community actually believe this works? I appreciate that you're trying to help, but how is this—" Ray nodded at the mirror "—any better than painkillers?"

"Because the pain's not in here," Terrance explained, placing a hand lightly above the scar on Ray's right leg before tapping on his own left temple. "It's all in here. You have a cell phone, right?"

"Sure, who doesn't?"

"Well, phantom limb pain is kind of like your phone when it's connected to the cloud. Just because you deleted something off your device doesn't mean it's gone completely. The cloud knows it used to exist once, just like your brain knows you were born with two legs and all their corresponding nerve endings. The reason we have so many cures and treatments nowadays is because someone decided to test a theory. Mirror therapy may still be in the experiment stage, but we're seeing results."

Ray traced the raised scar on his right leg. He'd known pain his entire life, but not like this: recently, he'd started experiencing intermittent throbbing where his right calf used to be. Some nights, the pain was so excruciating that he'd wake up in tears, tossing and turning for hours in search of relief. He should have been willing to try anything, if only to avoid subjecting Hannah to the same sleeplessness when he finally got to go home.

Terrance was crouched on the floor, but adjusted his position slightly. The sun was streaming in through the window on his right, making his light brown skin shine golden on one side. "Five more reps, then we'll call it a day. Deal?"

As Ray grudgingly consented to another set of ankle rotations, the door across the room opened and Hannah entered. She watched in a blend of curiosity and confusion as Terrance counted to five, then pulled the mirror away to rest it against the nearby wall. Ray turned his wheelchair so he wouldn't have to see his own reflection, a smile breaking over his face as Hannah walked toward him.

"What are you guys doing?" she asked, switching her gaze from her husband to the physiotherapist. "I thought you were supposed to be exercising."

"I am. I'm exercising my mind," Ray added, drawling in that way he always did when he was beyond exasperated.

She shook her head and addressed Terrance. "Care to explain?"

"Sure. I'm using a mirror to try and trick Ray's brain into thinking his right leg still exists, with the goal of reducing his PLP."

"PLP?"

"Phantom limb pain," Ray contributed. "I never thought I could feel something that doesn't exist, but here we are."

Hannah tried to keep the worry off her face. Google had become her best friend in recent weeks, but all the research in the world couldn't change the fact that she wasn't a doctor or a physiotherapist: the only comfort she could offer Ray was her presence during his darkest hour, and given the demons they faced, she feared love alone wouldn't be enough.

"The wheelchair is good for now, but I'd like to start adding weight bearing exercises to the mix. We'll start seeing more progress once he gets fitted for his temporary prosthesis sometime next week," Terrance explained.

"Next week?" Hannah repeated. "That seems pretty soon. It's only been about four weeks since his surgery."

"Everyone's timeline is different. Ray still has a long road ahead of him, but Dr. Johansson is really pleased with how quickly the leg is healing."

She glanced at Ray, who had wheeled himself over to the mirror and left Hannah and Terrance to their conversation in the background.

"I don't know if we can get the house ready before Ray comes home," Hannah confided, recalling how much work it had taken to get

Fitzgerald Farms ready for Laney's return after her stroke. "How long will it take for him to get used to the artificial leg?"

"Most people need a solid year and lots of physical therapy. In Ray's case, because of how active he was before the accident, it might take longer to recondition his muscles. Balance, coordination, gait—all those things need to be relearned."

Hannah nodded stiffly. Balance and coordination—the two most important requirements for riding a horse. "But the prosthesis will help, right?"

"If Ray learns to trust it, then yes."

Now Terrance was talking about trust. None of this made any sense to her.

"You said a year," Hannah said. Terrance nodded. "But that's, like, to get back into peak physical condition, right? It's just that we live on a ranch, and fall's one of our busiest seasons. I know Ray's eager to get back to work—can you tailor the exercises so that he can at least muck out stalls and ride his horse?"

A shadow seemed to pass over Terrance's face. He gazed at her sympathetically, glanced back at his patient, and told Hannah in a low voice, "If you're asking for my professional opinion, I don't think Ray's going to be able to go back to work in the fall. I think next spring is really the most realistic timeline here, if you want him to have a smooth recovery."

"We can't…" Hannah began to say. It was futile to explain precisely why she felt like she was going to be sick.

The physiotherapist added, "Ray's going to need a lot of support. I'm not telling you it'll be easy, but if you pull together as a family, I do believe he can get back to where he was before." His grin widened. "Anyway, I should be getting to my next appointment."

As soon as the door closed behind him, Hannah made her way over to Ray. He was parked directly in front of the mirror, his elbows resting on the wheelchair's armrests as he stared at his reflection in silence. Looking at him in profile, Hannah could see that his focus wasn't really on his face, but on a point about halfway down the glass. A muscle in his jaw tensed as she rested a hand on his shoulder.

"Look at me," Ray whispered. "I'm…"

"You're still Ray. That hasn't changed."

"Yes, it has." He held his own gaze for a few seconds longer, then broke away with a sudden yank of his right wheel. "I'm ready to go back to my room now."

*

Ray had been sleeping on and off throughout the day, thanks to a headache he couldn't seem to shake. Hannah had been trying to read by the light of the hallway, but her mind kept wandering to her job, Bernard, and the unpaid bills multiplying like rabbits. After several failed attempts to get through a single page, she closed the paperback and tucked it into her bag. Glancing over at the bed, she vaguely made out the contours of Ray's face, his skin glowing faintly by the light of the various machines crowded around him.

"Are you still attracted to me?" he asked.

Hannah turned back to the bed, surprised by the raspy timbre of Ray's voice and even more so by the question. His eyes were cracked open and there was a dreamy quality to his gaze, like he hadn't quite surfaced from sleep.

Nevertheless, she replied, "Of course I'm attracted to you. I've been attracted to you since the day we met."

One side of his mouth turned up in a smile. Hannah rose and moved closer to the bed, reaching over the rail to slip her fingers into his hand.

"Just checking," he whispered.

"Is that what you're worried about—that I'm going to stop loving you because of your scars?"

"I don't know. I don't know how you can stand to look at me." Ray's gaze flickered down to his lap. Even with the lights off and the blinds closed, it was hotter than a sauna in his room, but he only pulled the blanket up higher to cover the parts of him he no longer recognized.

Hannah dragged over the chair so she could sit beside him.

"You're still the most handsome man I know," she told him. "Not that looks really matter to me."

Ray boosted himself up, desperate to relieve some of the discomfort in his tailbone. He waited a few moments before asking, "Any word from Marcus?"

Hannah shook her head woefully.

"I guess I should have expected that," Ray said. "I shouldn't have tried to be a hero. I was trying to save my dad, and I ended up losing my brother."

"Marcus is overreacting. You didn't do anything wrong."

"But I did hurt him. By bringing Bernard here, I took everything Marc did for me, and everything he gave up, and threw it back in his face." He turned slightly in her direction. At least talking about Marcus would give him something to focus on instead of his pain.

"This one time, when Marc was sixteen and I was eleven, we ran out of food. I mean, there was *nothing* to eat. Marc was working as a busboy at this local restaurant to try and make some extra money so we could get through the winter. Meanwhile, I was just making trouble."

"Like always," Hannah laughed.

Ray's smile evened out. "Marc asked his boss for an advance on his next paycheck so we could get some groceries, but his boss said no. It was the middle of winter, and there was just enough gas in the truck to drive over to the church and back. So, that's what we did.

"There were lots of times when we didn't have enough to eat, but I remember this night so clearly: driving down that long, dark road with the windows all frosted up, and neither of us talking. The church gave us a small bag of food. It wasn't much, but it got us through the next two days. Then Marc got paid and bought the rest of what we needed.

"The funny thing is," Ray said as his smile returned, "I don't remember being scared. Now that I'm older, I think about money all the time—where it's coming from, where it's going. I worry constantly about not having enough, but back then, even when I knew we were flat broke, I felt like everything was going to be okay, as long as my big brother was there to take care of us."

He let his words fade into the air, the memories fading with them.

Hannah asked, "Why didn't he just ask Jim and Laney for help?"

"He was too proud," Ray answered plainly. "A few days earlier, Marc had gotten into this screaming match with Jim over his decision to drop out of school. Can you imagine if he'd shown up on their doorstep and admitted we were starving?"

"He should've swallowed his pride—for you."

"Well, he didn't. My point is, Marcus will never forgive our dad for leaving us out in the cold like that. I was stupid to think I could put these two in a room together and expect them to get along."

"You're not stupid, Ray. You're kind and brave and you believe in people's potential. That's why I don't care about how you look. I care about who you are."

Hannah had just leaned over to kiss him when Dr. Johansson appeared in the doorway, stealing Ray's focus.

"I hope I'm not interrupting anything," the doctor said, his eyes crinkling as he smiled.

"Just a much-needed pep talk from my wife," Ray answered back. "Are you here to tell me I can go home?"

"That depends. How's the list going?"

Ray's eyes roved over the dimly-illuminated room and landed on the whiteboard next to his bed, where Dr. Johansson had compiled a list of increasingly difficult tasks designed to test Ray's mobility and independence. So far, he'd succeeded in basic self-care activities like brushing his teeth and transferring in and out of the shower. He could dress himself and walk to the bathroom for a cup of water. But he still couldn't do a full lap around the floor without growing weary, or complete ten squats in a row while holding an exercise ball in front of his body.

"I'm convinced you keep adding stuff to it while I'm sleeping," Ray said.

"That's life. Just when you think something is done, something else comes up."

"When do you think Ray will be able to come home?" Hannah asked.

"Realistically, I think he should be able to do everything on that list by the end of the summer. I know that's not soon enough, but that leg needs time to get stronger." Dr. Johansson used his pen to point to Ray's missing limb.

"The only way I'm going to get stronger is if I get back to work. No offense, doctor, but I don't know how much longer I can stay in this bed without going crazy," Ray protested.

"Recovery takes time. I'm going to talk to Terrance about changing up your exercise routine so you can get out of here faster, but in the meantime, I recommend you try and get as much rest as possible."

Ray set his jaw as the doctor left the room. He didn't want rest—he wanted fresh air and the comfort of his own bed. Hannah squeezed his hand, bringing his attention back to her.

"It's okay. It's only a few more weeks, right?" she said.

"Easy for you to say. You get to leave and go home."

"You think it's easy being at home without you? All I want is for you to get better so we can continue working toward our future."

His eyes softened. "I want that too. More than anything." Looking over at the whiteboard, he asked, "Could you add one more thing to that list for me?"

Hannah picked up the dry erase pen and uncapped it, waiting for further instructions.

Ray said, "Write 'Apologize to Marc.' You can put it at the bottom."

After she'd finished writing, Hannah set the pen back on the tray and sat down next to his bed. "Just what the doctor ordered: a little heart-to-heart."

"He deserves it. Maybe it won't change anything, but he needs to know that I know how much he sacrificed for me. In case—"

"We're not even going to go there," Hannah said firmly. "You're getting better. You're learning to use your prosthesis. And Dr. Johansson said you'll be out of here by the end of the summer—no more infection, no more mirror therapy, no more bland hospital food. Just you, me, and the ranch. That's what awaits us at the end of this road."

Ray smiled. "You were always so good at seeing the positives. It's your gift." He picked up his phone. "I should probably try and get at least one thing crossed off that list today."

Hannah nodded and reached for her bag, then slipped out into the hall to give Ray and his brother some privacy.

Twenty-seven

Marcus had been sixteen years old when he realized he couldn't do it all. For years, he'd struggled to fill the hole his parents had left, often receiving no thanks from his brothers in return. Of course, he couldn't really blame Ray for that—he'd been too young to understand what was going on. And Victor, the quiet middle child, had been too busy trying to help Adrianna get away from Jason. So, when he'd decided to take a job as a busboy, Marcus knew exactly what he'd have to give up in order to keep his family together. His education. His future. His freedom. Even now, seventeen years after formally withdrawing from school, Marcus was learning that he was only as good as his family name—and as the firstborn, he carried that burden more than anyone else.

When Hannah found him the following day, he was sitting on one of the chairs in the kitchen. Old grocery store flyers covered the floor, and a tub of spackle sat open by his feet. She leaned in the doorway and watched as he attempted to cover up the hole in the wall, laying a thick glob of the compound onto the vertical surface and scraping away the excess.

After a while, Hannah asked, "Is this your way of apologizing?"

"And what am I apologizing for, exactly?"

"Defacing our property. Attacking Bernard."

"If that's how you want to look at it." He smoothed more spackle onto the wall to create an island of white in a sea of yellow.

Hannah relaxed her shoulders. "Thanks for doing this. I wouldn't have known where to begin."

"It's not the first time I've filled holes in this place—literally or figuratively," Marcus explained. "I just cut the hole to size, measured out a piece of drywall, popped it in there, and filled in the cracks with the spackle. Once it dries, I'll sand it and paint over the patch. You won't even notice anything's different."

"That easy, eh?"

He smirked. "Like I said—lots of experience."

Hannah crossed to the counter and filled a mug with coffee. "So, I guess Ray called you yesterday," she said, scanning the yard for Bernard. She spotted him in the paddock, unrolling a large, round bale of hay that would keep the horses fed for days.

Marcus hesitated before answering, "He did. We had a nice conversation."

She turned away from the window. "He does appreciate you. We all do. And who knows? Maybe having Bernard around won't be so bad. At least he's making himself useful, right?"

Hannah brought the mug to her lips and took a sip, watching Marcus over the rim. Being too optimistic hadn't seemed like such a bad thing when her life had imploded in high school, but here, she ran the risk of invalidating Marcus's feelings about his childhood if she spent too much time fraternizing with the enemy.

After a moment, he put the lid on the spackle and tossed the putty knife back into the toolbox. He bent down, displacing some of the dust he'd created as he gathered up the flyers. His eyes flicked toward her. "I should've asked if you wanted to keep any of these before I started my little project."

"That's okay. I have a flyer app on my phone."

"Of course you do."

"The doctor said Ray should be able to go home by the end of the summer. I know that's still several weeks away, but I thought it might be nice if we hosted some kind of get-together for members of the community. A lot of them haven't seen Ray since before he went missing."

"If it makes your little planner heart happy, I say do it." Marcus rose from the chair, holding a ball of crinkled paper in each hand.

Hannah searched his face. "You don't think we should?"

"At the risk of reigniting the old debate over which of us knows Ray better, I think a party of any size is going to be overwhelming for him. Why not give Ray a few weeks to settle in first?"

"Because I'm worried that if we wait, things will get busy—kids go back to school in the fall, and a lot of our neighbours are ranchers too, meaning they're tied to the same breeding and selling schedule. I just don't want people to think we're not grateful for their help." To emphasize her point, Hannah indicated the part of the wall Marcus had punched. It wasn't as obvious as the hole, but the chemical odour of the spackle was hard to ignore.

He glanced back at his work, then met her gaze with a nod. "Okay. Throw a party then." Marcus stepped around her and walked into the mudroom to dispose of the flyers.

Hannah couldn't help but feel disappointed in his lack of enthusiasm. Once he'd had some time to process Bernard's return, perhaps Marcus would be open to the idea of helping plan the event—but there were still several weeks of rehab and medical appointments between now and then. Hannah pushed Ray's homecoming to the back of her mind and turned her focus to more immediate concerns.

As Marcus cleaned up his work area, Hannah prepared herself breakfast and sat eating it at the table, where she could keep an eye on their tenant. Most days, Bernard avoided coming to the house, so Hannah had made it a habit to bring him food and water three times a day. *Like a prisoner,* she thought now, although Bernard wasn't being held against his will any more than she was. With the eldest brother still occupied, Hannah quickly made a second egg sandwich, pulled a bottle of water out of the fridge, and took both down to the barn, just in time to see Bernard walking back from the manure pile pushing an empty wheelbarrow.

She smiled. "I'll bet you've worked up an appetite this morning."

Bernard eyed the sandwich and water. "Is that for me?"

Hannah extended both toward him, saying, "I saw you put out more hay."

201

Nodding, Bernard took a seat on the ground outside the barn door and pried the lid off the container that held the sandwich. Hannah glanced back at the house before crouching next to him, not wanting Bernard to feel like she was looking down on him during a moment of vulnerability.

"I know they're on pasture during the summer," he began after biting off a noticeably large piece. He chewed a couple of times before he continued. "But you've got hay that's going moldy. That bale in the field's still good, so I rolled it out."

Hannah looked between him and the horses in the paddock. "How many bad bales do we have?"

"Counted six, so far."

"Ray was worried about that this past spring. We had an issue with our hay supplier. What about the square bales?"

"They're still good." Bernard bit off another mouthful of fried egg and bread, chewed it, and added, "I never kept round bales here. Not sure why Ray's got it in his head that he needs them, especially during the summer."

"He says they're more cost effective."

"Maybe for the farmer to make, but not for you to keep, if they just end up going to waste."

Hannah didn't have the heart to debate him right now: the ranch had always been Ray's domain, and even though he'd made some questionable business decisions in the past, she always trusted he had his reasons.

When she came out of her thoughts, she noticed Bernard looking toward the house. Marcus had loaded the bed of his truck with a couple of black garbage bags and a box of recycling, but chose not to collect the trash at the barn, despite the fact that Hannah could see the bin in the storage room overflowing with empty feed bags, excess baling twine, and other evidence of their daily operation.

Bernard broke the silence by saying, "I keep wanting to go over there and talk to him, but I'm worried he'll tear off my head if I try." As Marcus climbed behind the wheel to drive the trash out to the road, he asked Hannah, "What's he like?"

Hotheaded, stubborn, bossy. Those adjectives may have had their place on bad days, but the truth was, Hannah had never known Marcus to be anything less than a devoted big brother and a humble friend. So she told Bernard:

"He's responsible, smart, caring. Sometimes he thinks he knows everything, and other times he actually does. And he's great at taking care of Ray."

"He always wanted a baby brother. I'm glad I could give him that, at least."

Marcus may have wanted a baby brother, but he needed a father. Hannah kept this thought to herself as she stood up and brushed the dust off her jeans. She didn't know Bernard that well yet: at this point, she was a conduit delivering free food and updates about Ray, and he was an extra set of hands keeping the place running. Who knew if Bernard would still be here by the time Ray was well enough to come home?

"I should head over to the hospital," Hannah said. "You can leave the container on the porch and I'll pick it up when I get home tonight." She began walking back to the house, only for Bernard's voice to ring out behind her.

"I'd like to see him again," he blurted. "Maybe not today, but soon. There's still a lot that needs to be said."

"I'm sure you'll have plenty of opportunities to say everything you need to say." She held his gaze, letting the unspoken half of her thought linger in the hot, dry air.

"Will you give Ray my best?" Bernard asked, his blue eyes wide and unsettled.

"Of course." With that, Hannah turned and continued toward the house, wondering if she was ever going to see that sandwich container again.

"I hate you." Ray's face contorted, sweat running down through his sideburns until the golden hairs turned dark.

Terrance laughed. "You'll thank me later. That's nine, by the way."

Ray closed his eyes. He was stuck in a squatting position, holding the pale grey exercise ball between his hands, and his muscles were burning from the tops of his shoulders all the way down to his backside. He was pretty sure he didn't have it in him to do another rep, even with Terrance's childlike expression fixed annoyingly on his.

Hannah had been hovering in the background, but came forward as Ray started feeling like he might be sick.

"How much longer are you going to make him keep doing this?" she asked.

"If he can do one more rep, I'll stop torturing him for the day," Terrance promised. "He's made incredible progress in only a couple of weeks, but I don't want him to overdo it."

Ray sank his fingers into the ball. *Just one more*, he told himself. Then he could take a shower, go back to his room, and take off his prosthesis for the remainder of the day. His new routine.

He concentrated on using the rest of his strength to push his body to its full height, keeping his feet spread slightly apart to help maintain his balance. As soon as he was upright again, a feeling of relief filled Ray from head to toe. Terrance grinned and reached out to accept the exercise ball from Ray's hands, then turned away to place it back in the corner of the room with all the other equipment.

The dizziness hit out of nowhere, and before Ray knew it, Terrance was urging him back down to the mat. Ray sat on the floor watching the formerly stationary objects float around his field of view, and wondered how he was going to manage the rigors of running a ranch, even with Hannah and Bernard's help.

Hannah sat down on the floor beside him. "Did you eat breakfast this morning?"

"A little." Ray rested his elbows on his knees. "I don't get it. I never used to get dizzy doing anything."

"Your body's been through a major trauma. It's going to take some time for everything to heal." She gazed at his prosthesis, the grey pylon so jarringly narrow compared to the calf of his left leg. "How does it feel walking around on your new leg?"

"Kind of weird. I think it controls me more than I control it."

"It just takes time," Terrance assured him. "A few months before I met you, I had a client who was a double-amputee—lost both legs in a bad motorcycle crash. He worked his tail off in physio, and within a year he was back to running full-marathons."

"I think you need to work on your motivational stories," Ray told him, leaning back on his hands. His shirt was damp with sweat, and as it cooled, it made the air conditioned room feel like a giant ice box. "Really? A year? That guy must've been a one-in-a-million case."

"He was pretty extraordinary," Terrance agreed, getting the room ready for the next patient.

Ray looked at Hannah, who smiled. "What?" he asked.

"You're one-in-a-million too. You survived three days in the Colorado wilderness with nothing but the clothes on your back. Not many people can say they've experienced that."

"I made a stupid decision. The woods were my punishment."

Turning to Ray's physiotherapist, Hannah asked, "Terrance, when do you think Ray can expect to go home?"

"If he keeps exercising like he has been lately, I wouldn't be surprised if he was discharged within a couple of weeks."

Ray's eyes widened. "A couple of weeks? Dr. Johansson said by the end of the summer—that's a month from now."

"If you want to hang out here for another month, that's up to you." Terrance laughed and crossed the floor to where the couple was sitting. Placing his hands on his hips, he asked his patient, "Do you want to get out of here sooner?"

"Of course I do. What a stupid question."

"Well, then," Terrance said, undaunted by his client's recurrent bouts of self-doubt, "the first, and most important step, is to get off the floor. After that, anything's possible."

Twenty-eight

Hannah hadn't been prepared for how stressful it would be trying to plan a party, even though she'd managed just fine organizing the reception for their wedding. Of course, the circumstances were different this time around: she was expecting roughly the same number of guests, but these were people who, like her, had been caught up in the media storm surrounding Ray's disappearance. This fact was sure to put a damper on the revelry, but it was too late to worry about that now, after the invitations had been sent out.

"I don't know how Laney does it," Hannah admitted to Therese, who'd dropped by to check on Lucky. "All I want is for everyone to have a chance to see Ray, but Marcus is worried it'll be too much for him, too soon. And honestly, maybe he's right."

"Look, I grew up in this community. The people here don't care about every little detail being perfect. What they care about is knowing Ray's okay. So, fire up the barbecue, put out some chips, and everyone will have a great time."

Marcus strolled into the barn in that moment, a preoccupied look on his face. His attention shifted from the vet to his sister-in-law before he continued to one of the stalls, where he'd promised to fix the loose bolt on the door.

"Have you heard from Ray recently?" he asked as he set down his toolbox and got to work.

"About an hour ago. He's itching to get out of the hospital. Meanwhile, I'm on the verge of a mental breakdown," Hannah said.

"Ah, good—he'll be coming out right as you're going in." Marcus jiggled the bolt. "I overheard you talking about the party. Therese is right—you really can't go wrong with some food and fresh air."

"That's easy for you to say, given how close you are to Laney and how many of her parties you've attended."

Marcus sneered. "It's not rocket science. Don't stress on it so much. The more you stress out, the more Ray stresses out, and that's the last thing either of you need right now."

Hannah switched her focus back to Therese. "You're coming, right?"

"Are you kidding? I haven't seen Ray since that wormy guy dropped Lucky off and made a run for it." She patted the gelding's neck as he twisted his head around to nuzzle her pockets. "I'm bringing mini cinnamon sugar donuts."

"That's an oddly specific contribution, but I'm all for it," Marcus said. At last, satisfied with the position of the bolt, he tightened the screws.

"Great. Everyone loves donuts," Hannah said.

"And burgers. I can handle those." Marcus turned to Hannah. "If you make a list of what you need, I can go into town later."

Her shoulders sank. So, he was on board after all, despite their ongoing Cold War over Bernard's lodging. "Thank you. That would be incredibly helpful."

He nodded once, then gathered up his tools and headed off to his next task, ducking under Lucky's crosstie on his way out of the barn.

Therese was nearly finished with her work too, and in a hurry to get to her next appointment. At least, that's what she would've said if Hannah had asked. But Hannah didn't say a word, and the longer they stood around, the more difficult it became to ignore the awkward silence. Although Therese had been legitimately busy this summer, she hadn't been so heavily booked that she couldn't have made it out to the hospital to see Ray. And now she was going to get her first look at him post-amputation in front of half the ranching community. It was stupid, but a part of her still pictured him as a rangy teenager and not a grown man who'd been through more than most people could ever imagine.

"Ray's looking forward to seeing you," Hannah said. "He thinks you're an amazing vet—and a great friend."

Therese stuffed down her guilt. This was *Ray*, one of her closest friends since high school. "I'm sure everyone is looking forward to seeing him, too." She hastily repacked her bag. "I'd better get going."

"Right. And Lucky…?"

"He seems fine to me."

Hannah nodded, not quite reassured by the vet's response. But she had a million other things to worry about right now, so 'just fine' would have to do.

As Therese got back into her Jeep and pulled away, Hannah unhooked Lucky's crossties and led him across the yard to the isolation paddock. The gelding plodded through the gate and into his enclosure, going straight for a patch of dark green grass in the middle of it. He was obviously content here, despite his prolonged separation from Dolores and having minimal contact with the main herd. Maybe certain creatures were designed to thrive in a state of isolation, but Hannah didn't count herself as one of them. In fact, she'd never been good at being alone, which inevitably led to her seeking out comfort wherever she could find it—in a partner, or a party, or more often than not, in a bottle of wine. With Ray in the hospital, she'd tried her best to steer clear of old habits by focusing on the running of the ranch. And when the craving for alcohol struck, as it usually did in the silence of the empty farmhouse, Hannah had been working to replace that destructive habit with something more productive—like journaling, for instance. Anything to avoid being sucked into the vortex of negative self-talk that had become her one true and constant companion.

The last thing Ray needed right now, besides more stress, was to come home and discover his wife had turned into a full-blown alcoholic. *That won't be me*, Hannah promised herself. Ray had faced his demons down in that ravine, and now it was time for her to do the same.

Hannah left Lucky to his grazing and headed for the house to write a shopping list for Marcus.

*

Ray's stomach was churning when Hannah steered into the driveway a few days later. It had been three months since he'd set foot on his own land, and despite regular updates from his family, he wasn't entirely sure what to expect at the end of the road. Ray stared out the passenger window, seeing his reflection clearly in the glass. He looked different— more tanned, and yet somehow paler than a ghost. The cheap, disposable razors the hospital provided had only succeeded in adding to the number of scars on his face, so he'd given up on shaving and let his beard grow out. A thick fringe of golden hair covered his cheeks and chin, and Hannah had become obsessed with stroking it at every opportunity.

She glanced at him and smiled.

"What?" Ray asked.

"I'm not used to seeing you with a beard. It's sexy."

"Don't get used to it. I'm shaving this thing off once and for all tonight." Ray petted the side of his face. As the house came into view, he panned his gaze over the multitude of cars and said, "I didn't think there'd be so many people."

Neither had she, but now that they were here, Hannah was determined to make the most of it. The house was too small for a gathering of this size, but the yard had an abundance of space, and Jim and Laney had been kind enough to lend them all the chairs and tables they needed.

Hannah parked the truck in front of the house and turned off the engine. A string of lights was wrapped around the porch railing, suggesting that the partygoers expected the festivities to carry on until well after dark. As they sat taking in the sights, Hannah could smell the barbecue smoke and assumed Marcus was somewhere out back, supplying their guests with a steady stream of grilled meat and friendly banter. As for Bernard, he was hiding out in the bunkhouse, no doubt waiting for Hannah to deliver whatever scraps remained after the merriment died down.

Concern darkened Ray's features. He'd been expecting a casual get-together with a few of their closest friends and neighbours, but clearly his godmother had not gotten the memo. Or, worse, she had.

"So, did you invite half the town, or did Laney?" he asked, turning to Hannah.

"I only invited a few people, but word got out and, well, this happened." She sat back in the driver's seat. "I know it's probably overwhelming to come home to this, but everyone wanted to see you. When they heard you were missing, this town came together in the most incredible way to try and find you. We all love you, Ray, and we just want you to be okay."

He nodded, suddenly numb. After everything he'd been through, surviving an afternoon of small talk and picnic food should've been a breeze, and yet he was a bundle of nerves. Then Hannah reached for his hand.

"We'll do this together, okay?" she said.

Ray smiled and opened the passenger door. He hadn't tried walking on gravel with his prosthesis: the first few steps felt precarious, but he kept his balance, thanks to Hannah holding onto his arm. They entered the house through the front door to find the kitchen table had been converted into a cornucopia of food: plastic trays of cut vegetables and fresh fruit, several containers of dip, bags of tortilla chips, jars of salsa and homemade queso, bowls of pretzels, plates covered in cold cuts and cheese cubes, and of course, the mini cinnamon sugar donuts Therese had promised. Guests were invited to quench their thirst with cans of pop, bottles of water, or by dipping into the beer cooler on the back porch, where Marcus had set up a burger station complete with frozen patties, sesame seed buns, and all the condiments a hungry partygoer could desire.

As Hannah and Ray appeared, he tossed four more patties onto the grill and pulled the corresponding number of paper plates from the plastic sleeve on the table, keeping the one-man assembly line in proper working order between snatches of conversation about the fall cattle drive and life in Wyoming.

"I hope you're hungry," Hannah whispered to Ray.

It was a good thing she hadn't bet money on Ray's appetite, because he had none. The backyard was teeming with people, seated in clusters in the shade of the house or soaking up a few rays of late-summer sun. Had all these people really participated in the search party? Ray found it hard to believe, but questioning their loyalty seemed rude. The ranching community was his family, and although he was closer to some members than others, he was determined to show respect to everyone equally.

"Nah, I don't do that kind of thing anymore," Marcus was saying, apparently not noticing that the guest of honour had arrived. "Abby and I tore up the rodeo circuit for years. It wouldn't be fair for us to keep hogging the spotlight."

Russ's attention shifted to the porch, and a grin split his face. "Look who's here!"

Marcus turned, saw Ray standing behind him, and set down the spatula. He wrapped his arms around Ray in a quick, bone-crushing hug.

"Good to see you, little brother," Marcus whispered. He pulled back slightly to take Ray in, looking him over from head to toe before his mouth flexed into a smirk. "When did you hit puberty?" Marcus chided, lightly slapping Ray's cheek.

Ray swatted his hand away and forced himself to smile. "Shouldn't you be at work?"

"I am at work." Marcus swept an arm over the table before picking up the spatula and resuming his previous task. "You want one burger, or two?"

"Just one." Ray surveyed his guests again as Hannah disappeared into the house to fetch more beer for the cooler.

Russ pulled up an empty chair and added it to the circle of friends chatting in the grass. "Come grab a seat over here, buddy," he told Ray. "Marc was just telling us about his rodeo days."

"I'll bet he was very modest about it," Ray replied. Marcus stuck a plate containing an undressed burger into his hands and shot him an exasperated look.

"Didn't you used to ride broncs?" another neighbour asked as Ray squirted mustard onto the bun and spooned a dollop of relish onto the patty.

Ray said, "Bulls. Or a bull, at least. Longest four seconds of my life." He joined the group and took a bite of his burger, the juice exploding on his tongue. Those nights at the fairgrounds, watching Marcus break records in tie-down roping, might as well have been from some other life. They were both young and stupid back then, but eventually Marcus had grown up, while Ray continued to tempt fate at every turn.

There were several conversations occurring simultaneously, and Ray was trying to follow as many of them as he could. Russ's wife, Tori, had tagged along too, and insisted on giving him a light peck on both cheeks in a way that he found strangely endearing.

"We're so happy to have you back," she said, "Russ hardly slept at all."

"I'm still not sleeping great," he admitted, toying with the last morsel of burger on his plate. After a bit of hesitation, he asked, "So, you, uh, got a new leg, then?"

Ray nodded. No sense hiding it, he figured as he lifted the right leg of his jeans. A couple of his friends leaned in to get a better look at the prosthesis before Ray covered it up again.

"It looks good," Russ said awkwardly. "Sturdy."

Yeah, sturdy. The complete opposite of Ray's emotions right now.

"Must've been a rough couple of nights down there," Darrel put in. Curiosity sparked in his gaze. "Did you see anything spooky in the woods?"

Ray humored him by saying, "Other than the ghosts, not really." Chuckles reverberated in the air around him. "But I think something might've been stalking me."

At this, Marcus looked up from his grilling. "Stalking you?"

"What, like, a cougar?" Darrel asked.

"I don't know," Ray admitted. "It was the first night, a few hours after I fell. I heard something walking around in the underbrush, but when I shone my flashlight on it, it stopped moving."

"Damn." Russ paled, remembering the calf corpse they'd discovered during the cattle drive. "You got lucky, then. I mean, not *lucky*. You still lost your leg. But at least it wasn't your life."

"What are we talking about?" Therese's voice rang out over Ray's shoulder.

"Werewolves," Darrel supplied. "Why don't you pull up a chair, doc?"

"I think I will."

The group expanded to accommodate Therese's arrival. As she squeezed in between Russ and Ray, Hannah and Marcus carried on a muted conversation in the background. Something in their expressions stirred Ray's suspicion, causing him to miss the second half of Therese's story.

"Your dad's practically retired anyway. Which is good, since it means a speedier recovery," Tori pointed out.

"Oh, I know. That's what I told him."

"Did he get a referral for a cardiologist?" Russ wondered.

"No, but I've been on his case about following up with his doctor," Therese answered, her expression growing more determined as the conversation went on. "I said, 'Dad, this might be a one off, or it might be a sign of a more serious problem. And if it *is* a serious problem, we want to nip it in the bud—'"

"What happened to your dad?" Ray cut in abruptly.

Therese's gaze flashed on him in surprise.

"Oh, right—I forgot to tell you. Dad had a syncopal episode back in July, but he's okay now."

Therese's hand reached out and settled on his right knee before she realized what she was doing. She had only meant for it to be a friendly gesture, but as soon as her fingers felt the socket of Ray's prosthesis through his jeans, regret swept through her. She withdrew, her face flushing bright pink, and vacated her chair before crossing the lawn and trotting up the steps into the house.

Darrel twisted back to the group. "What's her deal?"

"Not sure. You okay, buddy?" Russ asked, looking past Therese's empty seat at Ray.

Ray wasn't okay: those few seconds Therese had spent staring directly into his eyes had revealed not only pity, but a hint of revulsion too. How could that be, coming from his former lab partner—a girl who had willingly dissected a baby pig with nothing on her hands but a flimsy pair of latex gloves?

Shock, disappointment, anger—all three of these emotions conspired to beat the tiny shred of Ray's appetite senseless.

The conversation resumed, but Ray had lost interest in what everyone was saying. He excused himself, then stood and carried his plate inside, where he set it on the kitchen table before trailing Therese down the porch steps.

"Hey." Ray furrowed his brows as she faced him. "You're leaving?"

Therese fumbled for a response, her green eyes searching him up and down.

"I just remembered—I have to check on a client's heifer," she told him, striking what she hoped was a casual pose as she leaned on the open driver's door.

"Now? But I just got here. I was kind of hoping we could catch up a bit."

"Right. Well, you know how it is with veterinary emergencies."

Ray wasn't buying this excuse. Sure, emergencies happened, but it wasn't like Therese was the only qualified large animal vet in Aspen.

As she was about to duck into her car, he said, "You were the only one who didn't visit me in the hospital. Everyone else did—Jim, Laney, Russ, Darrel, even Micah, for crying out loud. But not you." Ray studied her coldly. "What's going on, Therese?"

"Nothing is going on! Like I said, between work and dad's health, I haven't had much free time… Look, I've got to go. I'm sorry."

Her apology meant nothing to Ray, who watched helplessly as her Jeep vanished down the driveway. Coming home had been hard enough, especially since everyone else's lives had remained more or less unchanged. And now he was witnessing the beginning of the end of a twelve-year friendship with someone he'd cherished like a sister, and all because he'd lost his leg. So much for having someone to lean on.

Ray staggered into the house and crossed the living room to the stairs, all the emotions of the day culminating in a dull ache that spread through his chest and throat. He walked into his bedroom at the end of the hall and sank onto the edge of the bed. The mattress creaked, rather than crinkled, under his weight, but Ray was too tangled up in his anxieties to take comfort in knowing he was finally back home where he belonged.

Hannah made her way down the hall toward their bedroom. The door was cracked open, and inside she saw Ray hunched over his lap. He raised his head as she came into view and eased the door shut behind her, cutting the volume of the party by about fifty percent.

Embarrassment swept over Ray's features.

"I know I shouldn't have left like that," he said, turning his attention back to his hands. His voice shrank to a whisper. "I know you're just trying to make me feel better, but I don't want any of this."

Hannah dropped her gaze to the floor. "I heard you talking to Therese, just now."

Ray screwed his eyes shut. Hannah moved to sit beside him, the party long forgotten.

"I fucked everything up by going out there and looking for my dad," he whispered.

"No, you didn't." Hannah stroked his arm.

"Yes, I did. Therese can't even look at me now, Marc had to come home to help take care of the ranch, and I'm partially disabled. And the worst part is, I don't even know if my dad's going to stick around." Ray inhaled a ragged breath. "I don't need, or want, a party. All I want is you, my bed, and a chance to catch my breath. That's it. I don't want ramps or wheelchairs or people looking at me like I'm different. I *know* I'm different. The whole way home all I could think was, how the hell am I supposed to do this?" He turned to her suddenly, his eyes dark and brimming with tears. "You're not saying it, but I know you're angry with me. And Marc—"

"We're not angry with you, Ray. We're just trying to grapple with this new reality." Hannah sighed. "Marcus punched a hole in the wall. I told him about Bernard staying in the bunkhouse, and he didn't take it well. Sometimes I think I changed your lives for the worse by coming here."

"You think I would've been better off without you? You were the only thing that kept me going down in that ravine. When I was alone and scared, you were right there with me the entire time." His expression evened out. "As for Marcus, he's either going to accept Bernard or he won't, but either way, I'm still..." He placed a hand on his right leg, where his thigh tapered inward to fit snugly into the prosthesis's socket. Plastic and aluminum had replaced muscle and bone, and although his mobility had improved considerably with Terrance's help, some things simply couldn't be synthesized.

Placing her hand over his, Hannah curled her fingers into the empty spaces.

"You're still mine, and you always will be." She stood up and crossed to the door. "I better go tell everyone it's time to go home. I'm sure they'll understand."

As Hannah slipped out of the room, Ray reclined on the bed to stare at the ceiling. Finally, he was in his own bed, in his own house. He spread his arms flat on the lumpy old quilt and closed his eyes, breathing in the piney scent of the room and the lingering traces of Hannah's perfume. It felt so good to be home. And so overwhelming.

Tomorrow, or maybe the next day, he'd have to go back to his old life in a totally new way. He hadn't ridden a horse since Jack had thrown him off... Fear flooded through his veins, making his stomach clench. He'd have to start slow, of course, and build up his strength by working around the ranch, but there was no way to avoid getting back in the saddle. Not unless he wanted to give up being a cowboy for good.

Now if only there was some way to stop feeling like half the man he was before the accident.

There was a knock at the door. As it opened, Ray lifted his head to find Marcus leaning into the room, his expression inscrutable.

"Whatever you're about to say, save it," Ray grumbled. His head dropped back to the pillow. "I get it—it's bad form to walk out on your own party."

"Actually, I was going to say I told everyone to go home. You need your rest."

"And they were agreeable to that?"

"Everyone except Micah. But he'll get over it."

Marcus retreated, pulling the door closed behind him. Ray furrowed his brows at the window, picturing his guests heading out to their cars after the shortest get-together this town had ever seen. But Marcus, as usual, was right: Ray had been home for less than an hour, and already he could feel the exhaustion taking control of his body. In only three months, he'd gone from being the kind of person who worked all day to one who could barely fight off the urge to nap. The worst part was, he didn't *want* to fight it—his mind felt empty and grey, like the raw canvas his mother used to stretch over wooden frames and mount on easels in her studio. There was just one giant, blank space where all the colour in his life used to be. He couldn't even imagine what the future held, so instead, he closed his eyes and let the darkness consume his thoughts.

Twenty-nine

"I just don't know how to help him. I've tried everything—talking, giving him space, sending him links to online therapists. Nothing makes a difference. He's completely shut down, and it's scaring me," Hannah admitted.

"Maybe that's the problem," Adrianna replied. "Maybe you're overdoing it." She glanced at Emily, sitting in her high chair and eating dry cereal from a spill-proof plate. The bubbly one-year-old made what sounded like an earnest attempt at saying *mama*, prompting her mother to smile encouragingly.

Eventually, Adrianna turned back to Hannah and said, "Trauma is complex. What Ray went through isn't going to have an easy solution. After the incident with Doug, it took me months to feel comfortable enough to open up and talk to someone. Even though the attack wasn't my fault, I felt like it was my responsibility to carry the burden alone."

"I know. I mean, I spent four years studying psychology. You'd think I would know what to do to help him get out of this rut." Hannah leaned back and folded her arms. Her mind simply wouldn't rest until it devised a solution to Ray's listlessness, and the lack of answers was driving her crazy.

Contrary to Marcus's predictions, Bernard had not disappeared at the first sign of trouble. The day after he'd shown up at the ranch, Hannah had taken him to the hospital to see Ray. Their initial conversation had been brief, and Bernard had left the room looking like a broken man. Afterwards, Ray had revealed the details of their exchange, which included allowing his father to take over the horse training side of the business.

"Just until I get back on my feet," Ray had insisted, trying to ignore the irony of his words. Despite her doubts about his plan, Hannah had opted to trust the process. With the future of the ranch in peril, they needed help wherever they could find it: Micah had agreed to oversee the fall cattle drive, and Russ was amenable to managing their supply of hay and feed. All hope of salvaging their business hinged on the client horses, which would generate enough money to get them through the tough months ahead. If Bernard was willing to chip in, who was Hannah to tell him he couldn't?

Adrianna glanced over her shoulder as Victor entered the kitchen. He dropped the handful of mail on the counter and sorted it quickly, looking over at his wife and sister-in-law as silence swelled between them. "I hope I'm not interrupting," he said.

"We're trying to figure out how to help Ray," Adrianna explained as Emily flung a half-chewed Cheerio over the edge of her table.

Hannah added, "Bernard is going to be staying with us until October. In the meantime, I need to make sure my husband doesn't starve himself."

"Ma-ma," Emily babbled, making a grab for Adrianna as she picked up the fallen Cheerio.

"Can you say 'da-da'?" Victor asked as he came around the island and scooped his daughter into his arms. "Let's say it together: *da-da*."

"Ma-ma," Emily cooed.

Victor met Hannah's gaze. "Why October?"

"Because that's when the cows go to market. Micah's going to be in charge of the cattle drive, and Bernard agreed to tag along. Riding drag, of course."

"I'm sure that'll go over well, considering Micah was at mom's funeral." Victor sighed. "You said Ray's starving himself? Have you told him to call his doctor?"

"I've told him everything I can think of. I even installed that Virtual Shrink app on his phone so he could talk to someone without, you know, *actually* talking to someone, but he deleted it. I'm at my wit's end here."

Adrianna frowned, a pensive look taking over her face. "Maybe he just needs something to look forward to. I don't mean going back to work. Believe me, that was the *last* place I wanted to be after the Doug situation." She waved her hand.

"What did you have in mind?"

"Well, Victor and I have been talking a bit. Since Laney's moving to Alpine Terrance at the end of September, we thought it might be nice to throw a going away party for her at Fitzgerald Farms. Ray always looks forward to those, right?"

"I don't know—he wasn't exactly thrilled about the party Marcus and I threw for him last week. I'm just not sure how excited he's going to be about saying goodbye to what is essentially his second home and his second mother." Hannah leaned forward, planted her elbows on the table, and cradled her head in her hands.

"I'm sorry," she said delicately. "I shouldn't have shot it down like that. I'm just so desperate to help him, you know? More than anything, I want my husband back."

Hannah tried to swallow the ache in her throat. She'd been strong during the search, and stronger still during Ray's three-month hospital stay, but the tears hadn't gone away simply because she'd ignored them. She pressed the heels of her palms against her eyes, but tears were already spilling over, making her lashes clump together.

"I'm sorry," Hannah said again as Adrianna rose from her chair, a box of tissues accompanying her as she relocated to Hannah's side.

"Why are you sorry? You went through a traumatic experience too. Crying is a healthy way to let that stress out."

"I know. But I can't do it at home."

"Why not?"

"Because anytime I start crying, Ray wants to take care of me. And if he can't even take care of himself, I'm just going to make him feel worse."

"So, let him," Victor said.

"What?"

"Let him take care of you. Ray might not think getting out of bed is worth the trouble for himself, but he might do it for you. Worth a try, right?"

Hannah tore a tissue out of the box and dabbed the underside of her nose and the corners of her eyes. "I wish this hadn't happened. I wish things would go back to how they were before."

A thoughtful silence crept into the conversation. Victor carried Emily over to the living room window to admire the starlings that had invaded the front lawn, and Adrianna considered what "going back" entailed in the context of her own life. She'd gone back to bad men too many times to count, and now that she was free from their torment, the only direction she wanted to move was forward: to Emily's first day of school, her first Girl Scout meeting, her first sleepover, her first driving lesson, her first job... The day she'd become a mother, Adrianna had lost any and all desire to go back to who she'd been before. But for Hannah, whose future was filled with unknowns, the past was a bottomless well of comfort, offering bucket after bucket of fond memories.

"Okay, how about this: instead of a goodbye party for Fitzgerald Farms, we host a dinner party here?" Adrianna suggested. "Nothing fancy, just four adults and a baby sharing a meal together. You and Ray can stay as long as you want, and you don't have to bring anything."

"That would be nice," Hannah replied. "I know Ray loves seeing Emily. I'll run the idea past him and see what he says."

*

Ray could smell himself. He knew his personal hygiene had suffered since returning home, but he hadn't thought it was that bad until Hannah walked in that morning, cracked the window, and left without saying a word. He didn't even bother to get up and shut it when the room became too cold. Instead, he simply drew the comforter around himself and nestled deeper into the warmth of his bed. At least when he was under the covers, he didn't have to look at what was left of his leg.

During the day, Ray drifted in and out of sleep; at night, he stared at the ceiling or the wheelchair across the room, trying to piece together a new identity from the remains of his old life. What was real, and what was possible, had never seemed so distant from one another. Three generations of ranchers had come before him, and he couldn't help but feel like he'd let them all down by turning into this… a slovenly, unkempt pile of regret. At least when they put old horses out to pasture, the animals retained some of their usefulness by protecting the herd and helping to care for the foals. But Ray couldn't even take care of himself right now, much less Hannah or their home.

The clanking of a gate chain told him someone was about to enter the sand ring. Curious and somewhat annoyed by the sounds coming from the barnyard, Ray sat up and peered through the window. Sure enough, there was Bernard leading Calypso into the dusty enclosure. The flashy Trakehner gelding strutted alongside his handler for a few paces before whipping his head sideways, triggering a chain of events that ended with the glistening black horse arching its back and striking the top rail with both rear hooves.

Bernard stood in the centre of the ring, watching Calypso's theatrics. The mountain man was as calm as the eye of a storm, and Ray was mesmerized by his easy, quiet movements. Just like when he was a kid and believed his father was a magician in a cowboy hat. He'd begged Bernard to teach him everything, to divulge every trick of the trade and nugget of age-old wisdom, and yet his curiosity had never been satisfied. Of course, it only made sense to allow Bernard to take over working with the client horses, but a part of Ray was envious of the fact that he was the observer in this situation and not the participant. If Bernard could see him working with Calypso—or any of their horses, for that matter—would he think Ray was just as good, if not better, than him?

It was almost enough to make Ray want to get out of bed.

Hannah's car pulled up. She cut the engine and got out, then walked down to the round pen to exchange a few words with Bernard. A few minutes later, she left Ray's father to his work and made her way up to the house. Ray continued to monitor Bernard's progress as her footsteps creaked up the stairs and carried her into the room, fresh air rushing past her face as she opened the door.

She looked Ray over and stepped toward the bed as he sat up to lean against the wall.

"Where did you go?" he asked as she sat down on the edge of the mattress.

"I went to see Victor and Addy," Hannah replied, tucking her hands between her knees. "They're worried about you, too. We talked about ways we can help you get out of this situation."

"I'm coping as best I can. No need for an intervention," Ray bristled.

"You need to take a bath, and you need to shave. You know I'm right about this." When Ray looked away in embarrassment, Hannah added, "If you're agreeable to it, Addy invited us over for dinner on Saturday. Nothing fancy, but I think it would be nice if you wore something with buttons. The longer you stay in this bed, the harder it'll be for you to get back to living a normal life."

"I hate to break it to you, but I don't think our lives are ever going back to normal." Ray crossed his arms. He knew he was being petulant, but just the thought of owning up to his behaviour was enough to rankle his insides.

"So, that's it? You're throwing in the towel?"

"Why not? Look at me, Hannah." Ray reached for the covers and threw them back to expose the stump of his right leg. He slapped his thigh a couple of times, making the skin jiggle. "This is disgusting. I can barely stand to look at it."

"It's not disgusting."

"Well, I'm disgusted."

Getting to her feet, Hannah retrieved the wheelchair from the corner of the room. Ray eyed it disdainfully as she positioned it parallel to the bed and put the brakes on the wheels before straightening to look at him again. "Come on, cowboy. It's time to get up."

The entire time she was filling the bath, Hannah didn't speak. When she was moving the shower chair out of the way, she was quiet, and when she slipped out of the room to retrieve an armful of fresh towels from the closet, she was quieter still. Ray sat in his wheelchair watching her, captivated by the efficiency of her movements and saddened by their lack of communication. He wanted to take her into the protection of his arms right then and there and tell her he was sorry, so truly sorry, to have put her through this. But maybe she already knew that.

Eventually, Hannah turned off the tap. Ray reached over the edge of the tub and dipped his fingers into the water.

"Is it too hot?" she asked.

He shook his head and summoned a smile she didn't return. "No. It's perfect."

The mirror didn't steam up, but Ray felt the heat in the room clinging to everything. He stared at his clothes on the floor as Hannah sat on a small footstool behind him, circling his back with a loofah. Her bare hands skated across his wet skin as she moved to the opposite shoulder, her movements as determined as they were absentminded. It felt nice to be touched this way, Ray thought. To be touched by her, period.

He drew a breath in. "Do you remember when we used to shower together?"

Hannah paused in her scrubbing. "Of course." She resumed in a counter-clockwise fashion, sluicing the lather from his back with a trickle of water.

"Do you miss it?"

She sat back. Ray turned around, but her eyes weren't on him at all. He faced the faucet again, and soon she picked up the showerhead to wash off the soap.

"Sorry," he whispered.

"For what?"

"For putting you through this." Ray shook his head. He hadn't taken a bath since he was a small child, and he wasn't used to letting other people do things for him. "I know you said you'd always take care of me, but I never meant for you to do this. I should've been thinking about you when I went to go find my dad. You're the most important person in my life, and I let you down."

Hannah picked up the bottle of shampoo. Squeezing a glob of the satiny blue substance into the palm of her hand, she massaged it into Ray's hair, saying, "There are lots of important people in your life."

"I let them down, too."

"No one's saying that."

"Just because they're not saying it doesn't mean it isn't true. I know I've always been kind of impulsive, but what I did this time I'll never be able to undo. It wouldn't be so bad if it was just me who had to live with the consequences, but it's not. It's you and Marc and my dad... I ruined this family, Hannah."

"You didn't ruin anything. Things are different now, but we'll figure everything out like we always do." She smiled at his hair, engulfed in the foam her fingers had created. He smelled better already, and more importantly, he was talking. "Is this helping?"

"A bit."

"Good. Close your eyes." Ray screwed his eyes shut as Hannah once again picked up the showerhead and cleansed the shampoo from his hair. As the foamy rivulets ran into the water, she wondered if he would enjoy bathing her as much as she enjoyed bathing him—if he'd take pleasure in relearning every curve of muscle and ridge of bone, his skin separated from hers by the fragrant oils of her favourite body wash. In marriage, intimacy was often elusive... but when they found it, Hannah was always amazed by how the simplest acts could express the deepest form of their love, unbound by the script of expectation.

She'd moved on to washing his chest. As the loofah moved toward Ray's sternum, he reached up and wrapped the fingers of his right hand around her forearm, his skin like a hot branding iron against hers. He smiled.

"I can take it from here," he told her.

Hannah smiled and relinquished the mesh scrubber to him, then rose from the stool to lay out the towels. The larger ones she placed within his reach next to the tub. The smaller one she spread over his wheelchair to cover the back and seat before laying out the razor and shaving cream next to the sink. As long as Ray agreed to be an active participant in his own recovery, she was happy to help in any way she could.

He yanked up on the drain stopper. Ray then pulled himself onto the edge of the tub and wrapped one of the towels around his body, shivering as the chill of the room settled on his wet skin.

"That didn't take you long," Hannah remarked.

"Terrance made me lift a lot of weights. He said I'd become flabby and weak if I didn't exercise my upper body, too."

"Those were his exact words?"

He nodded. "Call me crazy, but I'm actually going to miss that guy." Ray sized up the distance to his wheelchair, then, reaching for the armrest, swung down into the seat from his perch on the edge of the tub. He smiled and removed the brakes before rolling over to the sink.

"You don't have to hang around, if you have things to do," Ray said. "I'll be heading outside once I'm done here."

"Okay. Just call me if you need anything." Hannah squeezed his shoulder and turned to leave. For the first time in days, she had hope that everything would work out. Maybe not all at once, and maybe not even soon, but she'd seen enough of the old Ray just now to believe he was still in there, and he was trying to get back to her as quickly as possible.

It wasn't clear where Hannah had gone. Her car was still parked beside his truck when Ray stepped out onto the porch and leaned on the railing, pausing to take in the view. It was a cool, clear autumn day and the mountains were visible for miles. Like the trees, he could name every one of them, and as he rattled off the peaks in his head, Ray felt something settling inside of him. The rest of his life was in a state of transition, and yet home hadn't changed at all except for one tiny detail currently standing in the middle of the sand ring.

Ray set his feet on that course, trying not to think about the act of walking as his boots kicked up small clouds of dust. Terrance had promised that one day this would feel natural. It certainly felt better than the wheelchair, but Ray wasn't sure he'd ever fully come to terms with the loss of his leg.

Bernard still had Calypso on the line and was turning circles with the gelding, leading with one hand while driving with the other. The former dressage horse trotted expressively around him, trained and all too willing to put on a show. Like humans, horses had their own personalities and quirks, but Ray had barely scratched the surface of Calypso's bucking problem when he discovered Bernard's campsite.

The black horse lowered his head as if to buck. A soft flick of the rope in Bernard's hand kept him moving forward, thus quelling the impulse.

"So, you decided to get out of bed, did you?" he said to his son.

Leaning on the gate, Ray smirked. "I didn't have a choice." He scanned the yard. "Where's Hannah?"

"She's up at the bunkhouse. Not that I asked her to do this, but I believe she was bringing me more towels." Bernard pulled the lunge line taut, bringing Calypso to a halt. He switched the line to his other hand, and the routine resumed in a clockwise fashion.

Ray cocked a brow. "I didn't realize we were operating a hotel now."

"You married a good woman. I would've been perfectly content to keep living in my tent, but she insisted I stay at the bunkhouse. It makes a difference, you know."

"You mean, indoor plumbing?"

"I mean having someone who cares. You're one of the lucky ones. I was lucky too once, and I squandered it—every last bit."

Well, there was a conversation Ray didn't want to have right now. Pushing away from the round pen, he turned and headed for the barn. The shift in position brought his prosthesis to the forefront of his thoughts again, but he continued to put one foot in front of the other until he was safely inside the wooden structure. The stalls had been mucked out first thing that morning, leaving the air smelling faintly of pine shavings. He strolled down the wide aisle, glimpsing each empty stall and finding a pile of fresh hay in the corner. The water buckets had all been scrubbed clean and refilled, the cobwebs banished from the beams overhead, and the lead ropes hung neatly on the hooks placed at regular intervals along the aisle. Even the never-ending list of tasks on the chalkboard had been rubbed out sometime in the last three months, proving to Ray that while this was technically his ranch, his presence wasn't a necessary part of its daily operation. Bernard had the place running like a well-oiled machine, doing everything from turning the horses out in the morning to curing them of unwanted behaviour.

Ray paced back and forth in the storage room. Anger seeped through his gut until everything from his face to the tips of his fingers were warm. He'd only intended to talk to Bernard about why he'd left—he hadn't been offering him a job, much less a place at their dinner table. As far as Ray was concerned, he was still the head of this ranch, and yet Hannah had had to drag him out of bed less than an hour ago. Everything he did these days left him feeling weak and useless.

He wasn't a cowboy anymore. Hell, he wasn't even sure if he was still a rancher. Just the thought of getting on a horse again made him want to puke.

Ray grabbed the first saddle he saw and, with a strength he didn't know he had, lifted it off its stand and threw it across the aisle. It crashed into the nearest stall with a spectacular bang, and from somewhere outside came a startled whinny, followed by Bernard yelling "Whoa!"

The desk in the corner of the room was covered in everything from strips of leather to old breeding records. Ray swept its contents onto the floor, sending several papers flying through the air like snow. He kicked over a stack of empty buckets, upended a plastic tub filled with beet pulp, and tore the calendar off the wall. By the time Bernard came rushing in, nothing was where it should have been and Ray was standing in the middle of the chaos, his breaths coming short and his head spinning from lack of oxygen.

He shot his father a caustic look. "Why the hell couldn't you have just gone to Texas?" Ray bellowed. "Why did you have to come here and ruin everything?"

Bernard absorbed the mess in a blend of sadness and disbelief. He turned back to his youngest son and whispered, "I wanted to see you again. To apologize."

"I don't need your apologies. I don't need *you*." Ray surveyed the disaster, but his vision was blurry with tears. A frigid sweat drenched his body and his legs were quivering so badly he could barely remain upright.

Bernard motioned for him to take a seat on the bench. At first, Ray refused, knowing that once he sat down, a conversation about his mother would inevitably follow. But his leg was killing him—clearly it hadn't been designed to withstand a rage-fueled remodel of their storage room. He eased himself down onto the wooden bench and put his head back against the wall, closing his eyes so he wouldn't have to witness the pain in Bernard's gaze.

"Is that what you think?" Bernard began as he sat down on Ray's left. "I didn't come here to ruin your life, or your brothers' lives. Believe me, Ray. If I could go back in time and fix all of this, I'd do it in a heartbeat."

Ray kept his eyes closed. Bernard continued.

"I know we haven't had much chance to talk. But I want you to know that I'm here. If there's anything you want to get off your chest—"

"Why didn't you just go to Texas? You could've been there by now, and I wouldn't be sitting here with a leg made out of metal and plastic."

Bernard nodded slowly. "I know."

"But you came here," Ray pressed, "why?"

"Because… I guess I hoped you might forgive me. I spent all those years wandering, searching for something I never found. But my conscience wouldn't rest until I made peace with you and your brothers."

"So, you came back just so you could leave us again," Ray deadpanned. "You know, I used to think you were the worst father in the world. Now, I *know* you're the worst father in the world. At least I can take comfort in knowing I'll be a better dad to my kids than you ever were to me."

"You will. I guarantee it." Bernard's expression sobered. "Hannah told me you have a daughter back in Canada."

Ray glanced at him, his face not quite registering surprise at Bernard's words. "She's not my daughter anymore. Hannah felt we were too young to be parents, so we gave her away to a couple in Toronto."

"Bullshit. I haven't seen you in twenty years, and you're still my son."

Ray scoffed. "Technicalities."

"What do you want me to say, Ray? I am sorry. I screwed up. After your mother died, I should have stayed and raised you, but I didn't. I was a coward. And I know I can't change what happened in the past, but I'll be damned if I don't try and make things right now."

As the barnyard grew quiet again, Ray recalled his first meeting with Terrance a few short hours after the surgery to amputate his leg. Ray had still been in a drugged-up stupor when the physiotherapist began articulating his limbs, abducting and adducting the remains of his right leg so that Ray's hip wouldn't succumb to irreversible immobility. When Ray had questioned the need to start exercises so soon, Terrance had said it was easier to prevent damage than to repair it. Unfortunately, Bernard had not heeded this wisdom when he'd made the decision to walk out on his family.

"I miss her," Ray whispered, referring to his mother.

"I miss her too." Bernard's expression grew thoughtful. "Your mother was the love of my life. She saved me when I didn't even know I needed saving. And when I lost her... when I lost her..."

Ray studied his dad's eyes, seeing Marcus in their sapphire depths. Growing up, he had never seen Bernard cry. He'd only seen him yell, bark orders, and withhold the affection that would've kept their family alive. And, he'd seen him work with countless horses the way an artist worked with clay, moulding them into reliable partners and sturdy companions. But tears welled freely in Bernard's gaze now, revealing the

231

very thing Ray was afraid of: that all these years, he might've been wrong about his father.

"When I lost Emma," Bernard continued with considerable self-control, "I knew I had to change something. Somewhere along the way, we forgot how to communicate. Or how to trust. At one point, she thought I was having an affair."

"Were you?"

"No. I'd never dream of it. But I was in the habit of staying out late, you see. I'd drive around at night just to look at the stars and the way the moon reflected off the blacktop. I could never explain to her why I needed to do this. I was never good at picking the right words…"

Ray's skin prickled. "Maybe I'm misremembering, but you and mom seemed to fight more than you talked."

"That was really only toward the end. You were so young, I'm surprised you noticed."

"Not that young. I remember how she used to hide in the bathroom a few times a week and cry her eyes out. It scared me," Ray admitted. He looked down at his nails; he wasn't used to seeing them so clean. "She'd go through these phases. One day she'd be singing while she ironed, the next she'd be lying in bed cradling a bottle of whiskey. And on the singing days she was like the first flower that blooms in the spring—I'd look at her and I'd feel hopeful."

Bernard prompted, "And on the whiskey days?"

Ray couldn't get the words out. They were stuck in his throat like the sharp edges of the popcorn kernels he'd accidentally swallow on the nights Jim and Laney babysat him and his brothers, and no amount of coughing could dislodge the little buggers. But as father and son sat in silence, everything Ray had been forcing himself not to feel crawled forward into the light.

"On the whiskey days," Ray confessed, closing his eyes as if this were his greatest sin, "I wished she would go away."

Bernard didn't react with the anger Ray had been prepared for. Instead, he nodded and let the wave of silence break over them. "You didn't cause any of this. I want you to know that."

"I do, but it doesn't change anything. She's still gone."

"But not because of you. She loved you, Marcus, and Victor with every bit of herself she could find. And when I look at you, I see her—I see her in your softness and your smile, so open and warm. She named Marcus after her older brother, Marcus Westley. When he died, your mother was devastated—and when your brother, Marc, was a child, he brought Emma so much joy. They'd make up these silly games during the day. Marcus was clever—he always knew how to win."

"That's because he makes the rules," Ray stated. "What about Victor?"

"He brought your mother peace. Kept Marcus company during the day. Helped me around the ranch. And when you were born, he watched over you. Not as much as Marcus did, but Victor had a way of knowing when you needed something. An intuition."

So that was it, Ray thought: the story of his family. They'd all played their roles perfectly, and yet the ending had still been tragic.

"Did you ever remarry?" Ray asked after a long pause.

"I went out with a few women. God said 'It is not good that man should be alone.' He was right. But as for marriage..." Bernard shook his head. "I wasn't made for it. I figured if I couldn't make it work with your mother, there was no use trying again."

When a crack formed in a ship's hull, it didn't sink immediately. It took on water bit by bit, until the pressure outside became too great for the walls to withstand. After twenty years, Ray had finally reached his bursting point. The tears poured out of him in a warm, salty flood as he leaned his head against Bernard's shoulder and cried for the mother he hardly knew, the one who'd taught him the names of the trees and the mountain peaks. In this moment, he was a scared, lost little boy trapped in the body of a grown man.

Bernard took his chances and wrapped both arms around Ray. "You're my son, and I love you." After a moment, he asked, "What's a cowboy's golden rule?"

Ray recited it flatly, "If you fall down, you have to get back up."

Bernard nodded. "Every damn time."

Ray pulled himself up, dusted off the back of his jeans, and walked over to the barn door. Far off in the distance, a series of chutes and gates facilitated the cattle herd's movement and ensured the safety of anyone responsible for managing it. Once they were rounded up in a few weeks, they'd spend their final days in a designated holding pen before going to slaughter, and in the spring, the cycle would begin anew with a fresh crop of calves. This was how it had been for generations, and Ray had never questioned the tactics that kept a roof over their heads until now.

Bernard smoothed a hand over his beard and sidled up next to Ray. His eyes went to the isolation paddock as he asked, "What's your plan for the grey gelding?"

Ray followed his gaze. "Not sure. He was dropped off here one day and I haven't heard from the owner since."

"What's wrong with him? Maybe I can help."

"He has a habit of jumping the fence. Really, the only way to correct that behaviour is to make what's inside the fence more appealing than whatever's outside of it."

Bernard furrowed his brows.

"What?" Ray asked.

"Nothing."

Ray observed him for a moment, trying to decipher the older man's expression. "Don't take this the wrong way, but I'm not sure training something to stay in one place is your area of expertise."

A tiny smile wrinkled Bernard's mouth. "You're probably right. You always said what was on your mind, even if it got you into trouble." He met Ray's gaze, surprising him again with his physical likeness to Marcus. "I saw your sign out front when I first arrived. Equine rehabilitation wasn't exactly the direction your great grandfather was thinking it would go when he built this place, but it seems you've found a way to make it work."

"Laney got me into the business. She's retired now, but the demand for her skills is steady. Lots of people out there buy horses without knowing what it takes to care for them, and they end up being abandoned. I buy these horses at auctions, start them under saddle, and sell them to other cowboys as ranch stock." Ray went on, "I know my being away has negatively impacted the business. It was hard enough running this place when I had both legs, and now I don't know if I have it in me to turn things around."

"Why not? Seems you got a pretty solid foundation built already."

"I haven't ridden a horse since Jack threw me off. Even just watching you work with Calypso made me edgy. I've never been scared around a horse before. Never had reason to, until now."

Bernard's eyes bounced from his son to the round pen, where Calypso was wandering circles in search of an exit. Bernard had left the lunge line in a heap on the ground when he heard the commotion in the barn, and the chain for the gate swung idly in the intermittently cool breeze.

He stepped forward, indicating for Ray to follow him. "Come with me."

Ray complied reluctantly. As Bernard bent down to pick up the line, Calypso looked over his shoulder at Ray, one shiny, brown eye trained on him like a laser. Ray lingered near the open gate, watching as Bernard proceeded to the centre of the sand ring and adjusted his cowboy hat to block the sun.

"Do you remember the first time I brought you in here?" Bernard asked.

Ray shrugged, trying to act like his heart wasn't clobbering the inside of his ribs. "Not really."

"You were three years old. Your mother didn't want you anywhere near the sand ring, but I told her you had to learn to do things before you got a chance to be afraid of them. I brought your brothers in here when they were around the same age for some old-fashioned cowboy initiation."

"You mean desensitization training, but for people."

"Exactly." He glimpsed Calypso in the background, but the spirited gelding seemed more interested in trying to reach the blades of grass outside his enclosure than kicking Ray's head off.

Still, he wasn't taking any chances. "I don't know if this is the best idea, with my leg and all."

"And what's going to happen in a year from now if you haven't faced this fear? You won't be able to ride, and you won't be able to manage the herd. I've had my share of bad falls, and it never crossed my mind to do anything other than get back on."

"Well, I'm glad you're immune to fear, but I'd like to still be mobile by the time I'm thirty," Ray snapped.

"I never said I was immune to fear. Hell, fear is all I've known for the past twenty years. And I'd very much like to prevent you from going down the same path." Bernard relented. "Ray, please let me help you." He waved a hand, beckoning his son to step into the open-air classroom with him for a refresher on what it meant to "cowboy up."

Ray slipped through the gate and closed it behind him before joining Bernard at the centre of the pen. No doubt Calypso sensed Ray's apprehension and, not understanding the source of that fear, could only respond by orbiting nervously around the pair, ready to fight or flee at the first sign of danger. Ray tracked his movements with a wary eye.

Bernard said, "Turn around."

"What?"

His father took hold of his arm and turned him one hundred and eighty degrees so that he was facing the gate again. Bernard then placed his hands on Ray's shoulders, reaching up this time instead of down.

Memories flashed crystal clear in Ray's mind. There he was at three, still little enough to believe people were good and fathers stayed. A much younger version of Bernard stood directly behind him, his hands on his shoulders and his voice as deep as a river when he spoke.

"Your muscles are tense," Bernard had said.

"No, they're not." The lunge line, all thirty feet of it, had felt like a lead snake in Ray's arms.

"A horse always knows when you're nervous or unsure. When you feel yourself starting to get scared, take a deep breath and tell yourself 'I'm safe.'"

"I'm safe," Ray had repeated.

"You forgot to breathe."

Ray had taken a deep breath, impatient and eager to get to the part where they saddled their horses and went for a ride in the mountains. As he'd let it out again, his shoulders had dropped, the muscles on either side of his neck suddenly slack.

He'd turned to Bernard expectantly. "Now what?"

His dad had smiled. "Now, you're ready to talk to the horse."

"Breathe," Bernard said now, softly.

As Ray exhaled, his shoulders sank under Bernard's hands.

"Are your eyes closed?" Bernard asked.

"Yes."

"Where is he?"

Ray focused his senses, listening for the small noises most people wouldn't have noticed, but that to him were impossible to ignore. "About ten feet to my left." He felt something rough being placed in his right hand: the lunge line, dusty and frayed from years of service.

Ray opened his eyes. As a sense of calm fell over the ring, Calypso walked up to him and pressed his whiskered muzzle against Ray's shoulder. He fastened the line to the gelding's halter and used the untethered end of it to re-establish a cushion of space around himself, with Calypso circling the ring at a brisk trot. From this vantage point, it wasn't difficult to see why he'd excelled in the dressage world, with his high-stepping gait and fluid grace. The bucking had been a symptom of a larger issue, namely the amount of pressure he was under to perform flawlessly in the showring. Once unseating his rider had become a habit, he'd been labeled a "problem horse" and sent to Ray's ranch for rehabilitation. So far, his progress had been minimal, but with Bernard's assistance, Ray saw no reason why Calypso couldn't go home within a couple of weeks.

Bernard had stepped out of the ring, but stuck close in case he needed to intervene. As he watched his son work his magic with Calypso, Hannah came to stand beside him, placing her elbows on the fence rails as a tender smile surfaced on her face.

"People say Ray has a gift," she said. "It's not hard to see why."

"He sure seems to be in his element out here." As Calypso changed directions, Bernard said, "Ray's lucky to have you. I hope you know that."

"What I do know is this is just the beginning. When we got married, I knew this life wasn't going to be all glitter and rhinestones. In fact, it's been mostly blood and guts, but when I watch Ray working with a horse, I feel those butterflies all over again." Hannah blushed faintly. "Do you know what happened to the storage room? It's… kind of a mess."

Bernard shrugged. "Messes can be cleaned up. In fact, I'll get started on that right now."

As he headed up to the barn, Hannah faced the sand ring once more to find Ray stroking Calypso's neck. When he spotted her out of the corner of his eye, he led the horse over to the gate, then leaned on the metal bars inches from where she stood.

"Seems like you're making progress," she said.

He smiled. "Something like that. I was thinking I might pay Dolores a visit tomorrow."

"Do you want me to drive you over?"

"That might be a good idea, at least until I get more comfortable with using my new leg."

Hannah nodded and brushed some hair out of her eyes. "I'll see you up at the house, okay?"

"Okay."

When she was halfway up the driveway, he unlatched the gate to exit the pen. The saddle he'd thrown earlier had been placed in its rightful spot among the other tack and accessories, and Bernard was leafing through the loose pages he'd scooped up off the floor, trying to restore order in the tiny, cluttered room.

"You can leave those on the desk," Ray told him as he walked by. "I'll sort through everything later."

"Do you spend a lot of time down here?"

"Not as much time as I spend in the sand ring." Ray shut the stall door behind Calypso and walked over to the storage room to lean in the doorway. "You didn't have to do that, you know."

"Do what?"

"Cover for me. Hannah knows I made the mess. I should be the one to clean it up."

Bernard shuffled another stack of papers and set them off to the side. "I'm happy to do it. This room brings back a lot of memories for me."

"In that case, go nuts." Ray lifted his black cowboy hat off the wall and pressed it onto his head. "I'll be outside if you need me."

His father nodded. They were still a long way off from spending Christmas together, but this was a start. He settled into the quiet work with newfound hope, and for the first time in years, the ranch started to feel like a place he could call home.

Thirty

It wasn't the road trip Hannah had hoped to take, but she was happy to be going anywhere as long as it got Ray out of the house. She drove while he gave directions, and by the time they pulled into the driveway at Dolores's place, it felt like their marriage was slowly getting back to normal.

She parked the truck in the patch of gravel off the porch and killed the engine. Silence came rushing back into the forest as if they'd entered a giant, green vacuum. In the passenger seat, Ray was staring straight ahead, his right hand absently massaging his thigh as he pondered the best way to explain the delay in Lucky's progress without making Dolores feel culpable for the loss of one of his limbs. Not that he imagined she'd need much of an explanation, if she was still in the habit of interpreting auras.

"So, I guess we just go knock on the front door?" Hannah asked, glancing over at the house. "It's cute. I like the picture frame windows."

"I doubt she's even at the house, but we can try."

She slanted him a sympathetic smile. "Is your leg bothering you?"

"Not my leg, per se. I'm just not ready to hear some big spiel about forgiveness, or whatever the lesson of the day is."

Rather than press for an explanation, Hannah released the seatbelt and dug her purse out of the backseat. "You don't need to tell her everything. We're just here to give her an update about Lucky. If she asks us to stay, we'll say we have errands to run."

It was a simple plan; Hannah always had an abundance of those. Ray thought about how he should've listened to that gut feeling the first time he'd met Dolores, although at the time he couldn't put a finger on what had made him apprehensive. Maybe just the fact that she lived alone in the woods was reason enough for his viscera to send up red flags. It hardly mattered now, but the truth was that her horse had changed his life, and Dolores had unwittingly played a key role in that metamorphosis.

Hannah said, "We really should go talk to her. I doubt she'll be upset about the fact that Lucky's still not ready to go home, but she deserves to at least know why."

"You're right. Let's go." Ray unlatched the door and pushed it open, inviting a crisp breeze to wash over him as he stepped outside.

The couple made their way up to the front door, the carpet of pine needles and dry twigs crackling under their feet. Hannah knocked as Ray gazed around at the trees, trying not to think about his time in the woods: the strange noises, the eerie shadows, and worst of all, the feeling that something had been watching him from a distance. No one had mentioned seeing a cougar since he'd gotten out of the hospital, but he was nearly certain he hadn't been alone on that ledge—just lucky enough to have fallen several feet out of the big cat's reach.

Eventually, a woman with close-cropped white hair and a rose-pink turtleneck sweater came to the door. She flicked her eyes between the couple, asking, "Can I help you?"

"Hi. I'm Hannah, and this is my husband, Ray. We're here to see Dolores."

"What's this concerning?"

Ray spoke up, "I specialize in equine rehabilitation. I've been working with her horse, Lucky. We just wanted to drop by and give her an update about his progress."

The woman crossed her arms, her voice taking on an edge that matched the chill in the wind. "And when did you last talk to her?"

"I was here in April," Ray replied as he glanced over at Hannah, "unfortunately, we've been dealing with some unexpected changes around our ranch, but if it's not too much trouble, we'd really like to see Dolores and let her know what's going on."

"And reassure her of Lucky's wellbeing," Hannah put in.

Her words hung in the air. Suspicion lingered on both sides of the threshold, until finally the woman sighed and her shoulders dropped, heavy with defeat.

"I'm very sorry to tell you this, but my mother, Dolores, passed away," she informed her visitors. "She hadn't been well for several weeks, so it wasn't entirely a surprise. Not to us, anyway."

"When did this happen?" Ray asked, his shock apparent.

"In July. We had a small service, just me and my siblings and a few of mom's closest friends. Of course, now the real fun begins—divvying up the inheritance." The woman gestured to the house, a smile tinged with dread lifting one corner of her mouth. She soon extended her hand to Ray and said, "I'm Shannon Cooper, by the way. I know, it's a funny thing—I went from Hooper to Cooper. But what can you do?"

"I'm Ray Fisher. We have a spread just outside of Aspen and about four hundred head of Black Angus."

"Ah, okay. I thought you looked a little familiar." Shannon stepped aside. "Please, come in. Sorry about the mess. Mom was a big collector, as you can see. She kept the place more or less organized, but it's been tough going through it all."

Hannah entered the house first, with Ray following closely. The musty smell that filled the air had gotten into everything: sofa cushions, window drapes, paperback books, and the handmade dresses on the dolls keeping an eye on the place from the safety of their toy pram. With every step the group took, the old wooden floorboards sent up a symphony of displeasure. Hannah tried to tread lightly as Shannon led them through the living room and down a narrow hall to the kitchen, where the light of day provided ample illumination. A simple wooden table, carved from maple, occupied the majority of the floorspace, leaving just enough space around the room's perimeter for the mint-green cabinets, vinyl counters, and a retro Frigidaire that resembled a decaying tooth.

"Have a seat. Unfortunately, all I can offer you is Coke. I think mom's got some glasses hidden somewhere around here," Shannon said, then laughed. "What am I saying? She's got a thousand glasses, I'm sure."

She began opening each of the cupboards until she stumbled upon a trove of drinkware. She placed a pair of crystal tumblers in front of Hannah and Ray before dipping into the fridge for two red cans of pop. After serving her guests, Shannon pulled out a chair at the table and sat down across from the couple, her demeanour decidedly more benevolent than it had been only minutes before.

"So, how is my mother's horse?" she began, looking at Ray.

"He's doing well. Hasn't jumped the fence, anyway." He emptied the can into the glass, hoping this conversation wouldn't include any talk of auras or horse-whispering. "She said he would often get out and go into the woods, but since arriving at our ranch, he's been the perfect guest: quiet, respectful, and happy to eat whatever we feed him."

Shannon chuckled, "I'll bet he's fattened up nicely. Mom loved to spoil him—more than she ever did any of us or the grandkids." She waved off her late mother's inconsistent displays of generosity and admitted, "I never really got into the whole horse thing. Mom just adored them. We always had horses growing up, mostly because my dad used to train them for police work."

"Were you close to your father?" Ray asked.

"Oh, of course. It drove mom crazy, the schemes he and I would cook up." Shannon shook her head in fond recollection before her face adopted a more serious expression. "I didn't realize this until I was much older, but he loved his horses more than he loved his wife and kids. And it's not like we could really fault him for being an animal lover. That was the thing *he* liked to collect—mom had funny-looking Christmas ornaments, and dad had whatever poor creature he could scoop up from the ditch on his way home. They made it work, somehow."

Ray nodded uneasily. "I guess it takes all kinds."

"For sure. Now, you said you specialize in equine... something."

"Rehabilitation. We have our cows, and they provide the bulk of our income every year, but on the side, I work with horses that have developed vices or bad behaviour, or that have been abused or neglected.

Not that Lucky was either of those things. He's more like…" Ray turned to Hannah, searching for the tail-end of his thought.

"I think what Ray's trying to say is that Lucky is a really special horse. He and Dolores were bonded in a way we don't often see, even in high-level competition." Hannah changed the subject, much to Ray's relief. "So, I guess you're planning to sell this place? It's so beautiful, I don't think you'll have any problems finding a buyer."

"No, I don't think so either. It's finding the right one that worries me." Shannon sighed. "But before we can sell anything, I have to try and cut down on all this clutter. I've been coming up a couple times a week and working my way through the rooms, but the stuff is just endless. I'm almost tempted to sell the place as-is and let the new owners do the dumpster diving."

"Correct me if I'm wrong, but I believe you have a brother—Curtis? Maybe you could ask him for help," Ray suggested.

Shannon's laugh rang out, and she lightly rapped the table with her fingers. "Oh, my brother won't do anything unless there's something in it for him. When did you meet Curtis?"

"When he came to drop off Lucky."

"Huh. That's strange. I wonder what deal he made with mom…"

Ray continued, "There was an incident where Lucky got loose and cut his leg, but our vet said there was no long-term damage to the tissue or his mobility. In fact, you can't even see the scar." *Unlike mine*, he thought involuntarily. "If you're planning on selling the place, I can try to arrange a buyer for the horse. Unless Dolores already had some kind of plan in place to rehome him after she passed."

"She might've, but I don't honestly know. But I think that if she asked to meet with you in person, she might've wanted you to keep him. Mom was like that: she had to really know someone before she decided to let them into her life."

"Keep him? I appreciate the sentiment, but I don't think that's what Dolores had in mind. I mean, Lucky's got a great personality and the right bones to be a ranch horse, but…"

But this was all wrong—Ray didn't want Lucky, period. The amount of catastrophe that had precipitated just from keeping the horse on his property was immeasurable. There had to be another solution.

Shannon gave him a look that made his insides freeze up. "Did she mention your aura?"

Oh, God, here we go. "Briefly."

"That's what I thought. Look, I loved my mother, but she wasn't exactly the kind of person you point to when someone needs an example of sanity. She had her good days and her good qualities, but she believed in things that can't be proven, and reading people's auras was one of them. For the record, mine was red—because I was such a troublemaker, apparently."

"She said mine was a rare colour. She didn't specify which one." But they were getting off-track here. Ray spread his hands on the table, saying, "Is there anyone in your family that has room for a horse? He's used to being outside, so a stable isn't necessary."

"I can ask, but I think I know what most of my siblings will say. Our mother lived alone in the woods in a house filled with flea-market treasures. That horse *was* her family. The last link she had to our dad. It's crazy, but I truly think that giving Lucky to you and Hannah was her dying wish. I'd like to see it carried out, if I can."

This was not the direction Ray had anticipated the conversation going at all, and he could think of no greater insult to Dolores's memory than to turn her gift down. He'd say yes for now, but he wouldn't get attached to the grey gelding. In fact, he wouldn't do anything beyond keeping him fed and watered. With any luck (no pun intended), a more suitable buyer would come along before the horse's presence wreaked further havoc on their lives.

"I see. Well, we certainly have the space," Ray told her. "If you ever change your mind, though, you're welcome to have him back."

"Terrific. I'm glad I was able to take care of one thing, at least."

"Ray and I should really be going. But thank you for your hospitality," Hannah said with a smile. "And we're sorry for your loss."

"My pleasure. You can leave everything on the table for now and I'll clean it up later." Shannon stood up, making the chair scrape across the floor behind her. "I'll walk you out."

They said their goodbyes on the porch. It was a short walk to the truck, and when they were safely back inside, Ray felt his confusion turn to anger.

"This can't be right," Hannah said. "You barely know Dolores. Why would she want you to keep Lucky?"

"I guess if she knew all her kids would say no, it made sense to pick someone else," Ray replied.

"Yeah, but why you?"

"She must've known I had a ranch. Maybe she figured I had the extra space. Problem is, when I take on a client horse, I do it with the assumption that I'm going to get paid for my time. That money then pays for the horse's feed and board. Only in this case, I'm not getting paid."

"How about we just go home and work out a plan over dinner? I know you have a lot of mixed feelings about keeping Lucky, but maybe this won't be so bad."

Hannah started up the engine, deciding to save her search for the silver lining until Ray had a clear head and a full stomach. They made a brief stop in town to pick up the ingredients for that night's dinner, and by the time they pulled up to the house, dusk had fallen along with the temperature outside.

Hannah moved to Ray's side as he gazed out over his family's multi-generational legacy. Lucky had spent three months living apart from the rest of the herd, but had developed a habit of standing by the fence and watching the other horses graze and socialize freely. Hannah wrapped her hand around Ray's arm as the grey gelding turned away from the fence and rooted through his hay pile.

After a moment, she said, "You know, ever since Lucky arrived, he hasn't tried to jump out once. It's odd, don't you think?"

Ray nodded soberly. "The only time he actually escaped was the day I forgot to secure the gate. He's not the reason I found my dad or lost my leg—I am." He covered Hannah's hand with his own and waited for her to meet his gaze. "I've been angry for a long time. At first, I was blaming everything on Bernard leaving. And when I woke up in the hospital and saw part of my leg was gone, I directed that anger at you and Marcus. But now I can see you were only doing what had to be done. I owe you my life, Hannah."

A smile teased her lips. "You will always be my cowboy, no matter what happens." She flicked her gaze back to the newest member of their herd. "He is beautiful. Maybe you should try riding him."

"I don't know. It still feels too soon."

"Then you take it slow… one step at a time." Hannah used her free hand to turn his face toward her, then rose up on the balls of her feet to kiss his cheek. As she untangled herself from his arms, she suggested, "I was thinking we should have a picnic on Sunday. We can go to the lookout."

"Isn't it a bit cold for a picnic?"

"Not if we bring blankets. Besides, since when do you complain about the cold?"

Ray smirked. "It's not me I'm worried about."

"Well, that's silly. You married a Canadian, remember?" Hannah smiled and headed to the house to start preparing dinner. "I'll pack us a nice lunch. You can ride Lucky, and I'll take Blaze."

Everything about this plan struck Ray as the opposite of well thought out, but he had to admit—it sounded like fun. His life had been rather lacking in entertainment lately, and if it wasn't his phantom limb pain keeping him awake at night, then it was something related to money. He didn't want that to be his future: fighting to keep his head above water while he waited for the next wave. He had a ranch to run and a family to raise, and he was determined to do both of those things just as well as someone with a normal number of limbs.

Ray hadn't been planning to visit Bernard when he found himself on the path to the bunkhouse. Most of the trees had dropped their leaves, which covered the ground in a thick layer of golden spades that rustled and whispered under Ray's boots. He emerged from the woods to find the lights on at the bunkhouse and Bernard hauling an armful of wood down to the fire pit.

"You're lighting a fire?" Ray asked.

Bernard set down the pieces of birch and maple and dusted off his hands.

"It's a bit chilly tonight," he said, "but it's supposed to be clear. The stars should be nice and visible." Bernard glanced at Ray in between arranging the logs. "How did your visit go?"

"Dolores is dead. Hannah and I met her daughter and she told us that Dolores had been planning on giving Lucky away."

"To whom?"

Ray hesitated. "Me, apparently."

"Huh. So, I suppose you're keeping him then."

"I don't know. Part of me wants to see if he makes a half-decent ranch horse, but another part of me doesn't want him around as a reminder of what happened in the woods."

Bernard chuckled. "Guess my days here are numbered too."

"That's not what I meant."

"I don't expect you to play host to me forever. If you want me out, just say the word."

"I don't want you out. I mean, I never expected you to stick around this long, but I'm not upset about it." Ray added, "It's because of you that we still have the ranch. You stepped up when I couldn't. I know Hannah appreciated it."

"And I don't regret it. You've turned into a fine cowboy—one that would've made your grandfather proud."

The conversation was getting too personal, too quickly. Ray changed the subject before Bernard could descend into full-fledged self-deprecation. "By the way, Hannah and I aren't going to be here tomorrow night—we're going over to Victor and Addy's for dinner."

"Can I come?"

"What?"

"To Victor and Addy's. I'd like to join you." Bernard hunched his shoulders. "I'd like to meet my granddaughter. I was hoping Victor might bring her over sometime, but I'm sure he's probably busy."

Ray hesitated. "It's not really my call, but I'll talk to him."

Bernard's expression lifted. "I'll wear something nice," he promised.

Ray nodded, bristled by his father's audacity. "Hannah and I will see you at the house around six," he told him, and turned to leave without another word.

Thirty-one

When Sunday morning came, Hannah woke up to a layer of frost on the ground. By 10AM, most of it had melted, and while the air retained its autumnal chill, she was confident that a couple of blankets and a thermos of coffee would keep them warm enough to enjoy each other's company. She packed a couple of roast beef sandwiches, some fresh fruits, and the last batch of Laney's homemade chocolate chip cookies into an insulated lunch bag, then retrieved a pair of gloves and a scarf from the laundry room and headed out to the barn to find Ray.

"Do you think they'd let me see her again?" she overhead Bernard ask.

Ray replied, "I don't know. You'd have to ask Victor. She's his kid."

His father nodded, somber but determined. "I don't have a phone."

"Do you have anything that identifies you as a member of society? A social security number, a driver's license…?"

"I've got all that. Just don't know how easy it'd be for me to pick up where I left off."

Ray sighed and lowered the stirrup into position on Lucky's left side. He was used to rehabilitating horses that hadn't been ridden in a while, but human beings were exponentially more complicated. The system simply wasn't designed to accommodate the whims of barely-civilized mountain men.

"I'll do whatever it takes," Bernard promised, "I might need your help though. Someone to help me navigate the ins and outs of getting back on my feet."

"Your job was supposed to be helping *me*," Ray reminded him as he attached the breastplate to Lucky's saddle and cinch.

"I know."

Ray shook his head and moved to Lucky's opposite side. He didn't notice Hannah standing in the doorway until he turned to grab the bridle off one of the nearby stalls.

"I couldn't help but overhear," she said as she walked in and set the lunch bag on the bench. Turning to Bernard, she told him, "You're welcome to stay here as long as you need. I don't know how easy it'll be to get an apartment in Aspen, given your work history."

"And let's not forget that we're not paying him," Ray added tartly.

"I know this seems like an impossible situation," Bernard put in, "but I think this year has shown us we can handle impossible situations."

Hannah nodded, but it was clear Ray was in no mood for a motivational pep talk.

As a final point, he said, "I need time to think about all this. You hanging around here wasn't exactly in our five year plan."

Bernard raised his hands, then picked up the bedding fork and disappeared into one of the stalls, the discussion plainly over.

Hannah emerged from the storage room with a pair of blankets draped over her arm. She handed the leather saddle bag to Ray, who slung it over Lucky's back.

"Blaze is saddled and hitched out front," he told her.

"I saw that. Do you want to carry the blankets or the food and coffee?"

He reached for the blankets and stuffed one into each bag. Halfway down the aisle, Bernard was humming what sounded like some old work song. In Ray's mind, the man was a disgrace to hardworking Americans: not only had he bucked his duties as a parent, but he'd turned his back on every possible resource that might've helped him avoid falling into poverty. To be asking for favours now, when he knew his adult children were financially stable and raising families of their own, showed what a parasite he truly was.

With the saddle bags secure, Ray collected Lucky's reins, reached for his cowboy hat, and pressed it down onto his head. He led the grey gelding out into the front yard, where Hannah had just finished packing their lunch into the bags affixed to Blaze's saddle. She slipped on her gloves and turned to her husband, sizing up his mount with a look of caution.

"I'm assuming you lunged him this morning," she said.

"I did. We were in the sand ring for almost an hour."

"No issues?"

Ray shook his head. "He's not a young horse, so I'm sure he's been ridden before. But that's not what I'm worried about."

The fear was back, and this time, it felt like a spring under pressure. Ray walked Lucky a short distance down the path before doubling back on his tracks, hoping the tight feeling in his chest wouldn't suddenly cause him to lose his nerve. It seemed totally irrational to be afraid of something he'd been doing his whole life. Then again, maybe he was finally realizing that being a cowboy didn't mean he was invincible.

Hannah had already climbed onto Blaze's back and was waiting patiently for Ray to join her.

"It's okay—we're just going for a quiet trail ride," she assured him. "I'm sure everything will be fine."

"I'd love to know where you find all this confidence," Ray replied.

She smiled. "That's easy: I know you. You never let anything keep you down."

Well, she might've been right about that much, although Ray didn't feel like his most formidable self at the moment. He took up the reins in his left hand and placed his foot in the stirrup, then pulled himself up onto Lucky's back before he could talk himself out of going anywhere. Bernard's rendition of a song neither of them recognized carried on in the background as they rode away from the ranch.

*

It wasn't long before the only sound to be heard was the soft percussion of the horses' hooves on the trail and the wind blowing through the trees overhead. As Ray rode beside her, Hannah kept glancing over at Lucky to gauge his reaction to being out in the woods. The gelding was remarkably calm, his ears alert but not tense. Ray seemed to have settled down too, and his expression was a mask of deep contemplation.

After a few minutes, he said, "I don't know what I'm going to do about Bernard. Or if I should do anything."

"You know, even if he somehow manages to turn his life around and get his own place away from here, he's probably still going to want to be a part of your life."

"He had his chance to be a part of my life, and look what happened."

"So, why not just send him packing, if that's how you really feel?"

Ray sealed his lips tightly. The only reason he hadn't kicked Bernard to the curb yet was because he wasn't sure he could run the ranch in his current state, and a responsibility-dodging dad with a spotty work history seemed like better help than none.

"What does our five year plan look like, anyway?" Hannah asked.

"It looks like you and me running the ranch together, building up a nice little nest egg. Maybe a kid or two."

"You're thinking about it then."

"For a long time, I was trying not to think about it at all. But, yeah, I guess I am thinking about it. If you're still on board."

The lookout appeared before them. The grass had turned brown in several spots, but the sky above it was a perfect, crystal blue. A stand of pine trees offered some protection against the elements, as well as a place to tie the horses.

As he approached the trees, Ray reached back into one of the saddlebags and pulled out a red and black tartan blanket.

"You want to get us set up?" he said as he handed it to Hannah.

She swung down off Blaze's back and took the blanket from his hand. Passing Blaze's reins to Ray, she walked toward the sunny meadow, found a spot that was relatively dry and flat, and spread the blanket on the ground, leaving Ray to hitch the horses and bring over their refreshments.

"Are you starting to feel like this was a good idea?" Hannah asked.

He passed her the thermos and a warm smile. "I never said it was a bad idea, did I?" He held up the second blanket. "Where do you want me to put this?"

"Just off to the side. In case we get cold."

"You mean, in case *you* get cold."

Ray lowered himself onto the blanket and stretched out his legs. Hannah began unpacking the contents of the lunch bag, laying each item down between them as Ray once again lapsed into a thoughtful silence.

As she added the cookies to the pile, Hannah ventured, "You must have had a very uncomfortable sleep in that ravine."

"That's putting it mildly. I froze my ass off down there." He sat up and picked up the cookies, wrapped in reusable wax paper sporting a floral print. "Laney's?"

"Of course. Anything less would have ruined the occasion."

He smiled sadly and set the cookies down, then turned his attention over to one of the sandwiches.

"Bernard was right about one thing though," Hannah said as he took a bite. "It's been a crazy year, but we survived it. And I know you probably don't want to think about work right now, but perhaps we should consider using what happened as a way to reach more people."

"I don't know if I'm ready to embrace the whole one-legged cowboy gimmick yet. Remember how, after Cameron died, everyone saw you as his poor little girlfriend? Not exactly the most flattering light to be cast in."

"It wasn't, but it also taught me that tragedy can be a good way to start a conversation. Because if I hadn't opened up to Bexley and told her what happened in Canada, we might have never gone to the movies, you and I wouldn't have bumped into each other, and she wouldn't have finagled your number out of Michelle."

"Yeah, Michelle," Ray said with false wistfulness. "Such a nice girl—not like the crazy chick I ended up marrying."

Hannah slapped his arm as he laughed. "You mean the crazy chick who got less than six hours of sleep in three days because she was so worried she'd never see you again?"

"I'm sorry I put you through all of that," Ray said. He lay flat on his back, watching the only cloud in the sky drift out of view behind the trees. "You know what the weirdest part about being in the ravine was? The fact that I got to slow down and really notice my surroundings. At times I would just sit there and listen to the birds or smell the pine trees, and it helped me forget about the pain… I've been running so fast for so long that I don't even know how to be okay with not running anymore. Every step means something now."

"Maybe that's a good thing. No one knows how much time they have, Ray, or what tomorrow will bring. We just have to do the best we can while we're still here."

Ray propped himself up on one elbow, leaning over her with a wry smile. "So much for our five year plan."

"Oh, we're sticking to the plan, cowboy. And you know what? Just for the fun of it, I think I'll make a ten year plan, too."

Ray laughed and put a hand on her waist. As amusement continued to dance in his eyes, his voice grew serious, and Hannah was struck by a deep feeling of adoration knowing that this man—this wild, fearless mountain man—was all hers.

"I promised I'd always come home, didn't I?" he said.

Hannah smiled. "And here you are."

As Ray leaned down, Hannah slid her hand behind his head, keeping his lips locked on hers. The ranch had seen countless changes over the years and would undoubtedly see plenty more, but in this moment, the world was only as wide as their arms. And it was perfect.

Thirty-two

"Last week, I had the most amazing idea. When I tell you, you're going to wish you'd thought of it yourself."

Ray braced himself for whatever absurdities would come out of Mickey's mouth. It was no secret that The Horse God was addicted to the limelight, but sometimes he took looking for the next big thing a little too far. "We'll see. I have enough on my plate at the moment."

Mickey grinned, lighting up the corner of the coffee shop where they'd agreed to meet. "Mustangs," he said simply.

"Mustangs." Ray stared at him flatly.

"You know what I'm talking about—the wild ones. The Bureau of Land Management has been keeping an eye on a couple of herds in Colorado. And I was thinking…"

"I'm not adopting any mustangs. They're wild animals. Better to just leave them be."

"Well, according to the Bureau, those 'wild animals' are pests. But you know me: I've built a whole career on training even the most dangerous horses to be kid-friendly. And I'm telling you, Ray, if you're willing to branch out a bit, you could really do a good thing here. You'd save these animals from being needlessly destroyed, and you'd be educating the public about their versatility… I know you're just getting back on your feet after everything that happened, but this could put you firmly back on everyone's radar."

Ray drawled, "Oh, yeah, I can see the headline now: 'One-legged cowboy loses other leg trying to ride a wild horse.'"

Mickey picked up his coffee and took a sip, trying to hide his smile behind the rim. He set it back on the table and chuckled, "At least it would grab people's attention."

Ray shook his head in disbelief. "Why am I even friends with you?"

"Because you know I'm right. What you went through in those woods changed everything, just like almost losing Josh changed me. But you know, at some point you have to keep going. It's tempting to sit around and feel sorry for yourself, but they don't tell stories about people who quit." As Ray's gaze dropped to the table, Mickey lowered his voice and leaned in. "They're going to remember you, Ray. So, tell the best damn story you can."

Silence drifted over their conversation. Ray hadn't been looking for fame when he'd set out to locate Bernard's campsite, but since returning to work, it seemed like everyone had heard about his harrowing ordeal. And now, more than a year after he'd gone missing in the mountains, Ray's life was almost back to normal. The cattle were fattening up in the high country, the horse training side of his business was booming, and Laney was still bragging about his gift to her new friends at Alpine Terrace. If there was a story to be told here, it was that life on a working ranch carried on, day after day, generation after generation.

Mickey asked, "How's your dad?"

"He's all right, actually. We're still trying to track down all his documents and stuff, but he's a big help around the ranch. I guess when you leave for twenty years, there's a lot to make up for."

"Are you happy to have him back?" Mickey slurped another mouthful, his eyes brimming with expectation.

Ray studied the white, ceramic mug between his hands. "I'd be happier to have my right leg back, but Bernard is a decent consolation prize." He added, "Victor has been slowly warming up to the idea of Bernard being involved in Emily's life. It's… kind of bittersweet to see how much Bernard adores my niece when he wasn't much of a father to me."

"And your other brother—Marcus?"

"He's a long way off from any sort of reconciliation. I can't say I blame him."

Mickey nodded understandingly, and the look in his eyes told Ray he was about to be subjected to some sappy lecture about fatherhood.

Mickey seemed especially sentimental today—or maybe the lack of sleep was making Ray more irritable than usual.

"It'll take time," Mickey said. "Time for Bernard to figure out where he belongs, time for Marcus to make peace with his return. And it'll take time for you to realize that mustangs are the future of this industry."

Ray cocked a brow. "Are we back to that?"

"Yes. Think about it and let me know what you decide. When you're ready to take the leap, I'll call my buddies at the BLM and get you all set up with your next project horse."

Ray wasn't holding his breath on any of Mickey's plans working out when an attachment from Hannah popped up on his phone. He clicked on the bubble, and a picture of a small, pink face filled the screen.

Hannah wrote underneath: *He's finally asleep.*

Ray smiled and replied: *Now's your chance to take a shower. Or a nap.*

Do I have to choose just one?

He glimpsed Mickey across the table, evidently waiting for some kind of response to his proposition. Ray turned his phone face-down, but his mind was stuck on the picture of his son, every feature perfectly symmetrical. He couldn't imagine bringing something as unpredictable as a feral horse to the ranch at a time when their lives revolved around diaper changes and regular feedings, but Mickey wouldn't let up without an answer.

"Is there an expiration date on your offer?" Ray asked.

"Not yet. But you know how fleeting opportunities can be."

Ray nodded thoughtfully and looked at his phone again. "I know. That's why I'm saying no." He smiled. "I want to watch my son grow up, and I don't want to miss a single moment of it. I appreciate that you thought of me when you heard about the mustangs, but I can't take the risk that I'm going to get hurt again. Not when I have a family to support."

Ray reached for his jacket and slid out of the booth. He slipped his arms into the sleeves, then pocketed his phone and pulled some cash out of his wallet to pay for his coffee.

Mickey eyed his former cohost. "You sure about this?"

"I am."

In fact, Ray had never been more sure of anything in his life. His family came first, always, and though he didn't know quite what the road ahead looked like, he knew he wanted to be on it.

*

In a year marked by impossible decisions and extraordinary change, Hannah didn't think twice about how she was going to spend the next thirty minutes. She was on the precipice of falling asleep when she heard the front door open downstairs, and Ray's boots echoed on the hardwood floor. Bernard, as usual, was down at the barn. Most days, the mountain man kept a low profile and seemed to prefer the quiet company of the horses to all but the most crucial human interaction. Hannah couldn't say she blamed him: since giving birth to their son, Jaxon, she took every opportunity to be alone, even if it meant embracing the uncomfortable feelings of guilt for daring to be away from her baby for longer than five minutes.

Ray came up the stairs slowly, trying to keep his footsteps light on the old floorboards in case Hannah was asleep. After a brief stop in the nursery to check on their son, he continued toward the room at the end of the hall and slipped through the door. Hannah forced her eyes open a crack to see him walk toward the hamper and remove his shirt, followed by his jeans and socks.

Confused by what she was seeing, Hannah asked, "Are you taking a shower?"

"I will later. I'm exhausted."

Ray took a seat on the edge of the bed and proceeded to remove his prosthesis, stripping off the various layers that kept the device properly positioned throughout the day.

"I talked to Bernard on my way in," he said, "when he was checking the perimeter the other day, he noticed that several of the fence boards were rotted, so he's going to go out and count how many need to be replaced."

"Hopefully not too many. Lumber's not cheap."

"I know." Ray freed his residual limb from the socket and placed the device on the chair where it normally rested, close enough to the bed that he could reach it if Jaxon started to cry. Swinging his other leg into bed, he rolled onto his side and wrapped his arm around the familiar shape of Hannah's body. She pressed her back against his chest, letting the warmth of his bare skin and the firmness of his physique surround her with comfort.

He traced his fingers down the back of her arm toward her waist. But he didn't stop there. His hand continued to migrate and explore, skating over the edge of her shorts and down the slope of her thigh until he reached her knee. Then his fingers glided back toward her shoulders, got tangled in her hair, and drew a random pattern on the side of her neck, which made Hannah giggle.

"What are you doing?" she asked.

Ray replied soberly, "Making sure you're real."

"I'm as real as you are. And you're tickling me."

His hand once again settled on her waist, which was practically designed to fit the width of his fingers. "I was afraid I'd never get a chance to do this again. Sometimes I wake up in the night and I think I'm still down in the ravine."

"Well, you're not. You're here with me and our son. And nothing's going to take you away from us." Hannah meshed her fingers with his and drew his arm around her like a blanket. "How was your meeting with Mickey?"

Ray chuckled, his husky voice reverberating through her. "Mickey's got some wild ideas. I decided not to hop on the bandwagon this time." His eyes slipped closed, but he fought off sleep long enough to add, "As tempting as it is to see where this all goes, I can't take the risk that I'm going to get hurt. Not when I have you and the baby to look after."

"Good, because I don't want to do this without you."

"Me neither."

The gaps in their conversation stretched into unbroken silences as exhaustion settled over them. These days, they took nothing for granted, including each other. In the blink of an eye, Ray's entire life had been turned upside down and shaken out like an old pair of jeans, but somehow it had led him to this very moment, when everything was exactly the way it was supposed to be. *I'm safe*, he thought as his shoulders relaxed and he drifted off to sleep.

At last, he was home.

Other books by Jessica Ingold:

Fate Unwritten (Moving Mountains, book 1)
Roads Untraveled (Moving Mountains, book 2)
Words Unspoken (Moving Mountains, book 3)
Faith Unbroken (Moving Mountains, book 4)

—

The Spirit Catchers

Captured

—

The Absentees

—

Our Infinite Depths

—

Quiet: Poems about love, loss & healing

Listen: Poems for a noisy planet

www.ingramcontent.com/pod-product-compliance
Lightning Source LLC
Chambersburg PA
CBHW022055170626
46807CB00014B/331